PRAISE FOR THE NOVELS OF RUTH GLICK
WRITING AS REBECCA YORK

"Action packed . . . and filled with sexual tension . . . A gripping thriller."
—*The Best Reviews*

"A steamy paranormal . . . Danger, shape-shifters, and hot romance. The best of everything. Brava."
—*Huntress Book Reviews*

"A compulsive read."
—*Publishers Weekly*

"York delivers an exciting and suspenseful romance with paranormal themes that she gets just right. This is a howling good read."
—*Booklist*

"Mesmerizing action and passions that leap from the pages with the power of a wolf's coiled spring."
—*BookPage*

"Delightful . . . [With] two charming lead characters."
—*Midwest Book Review*

"Rebecca York delivers page-turning suspense."
—Nora Roberts

"[Her] prose is smooth, literate, and fast-moving; her love scenes are tender yet erotic; and there's always a happy ending."
—*The Washington Post Book World*

"She writes a fast-paced, satisfying thriller."
—UPI

"Clever and a great read. I can't wait to read the final book in this wonderful series."
—*ParaNormal Romance Reviews*

ETERNAL
MOON

REBECCA YORK

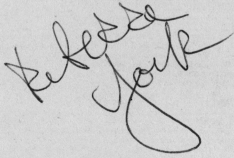

BERKLEY SENSATION, NEW YORK

THE BERKLEY PUBLISHING GROUP
Published by the Penguin Group
Penguin Group (USA) Inc.
375 Hudson Street, New York, New York 10014, USA
Penguin Group (Canada), 90 Eglinton Avenue East, Suite 700, Toronto, Ontario M4P 2Y3, Canada
(a division of Pearson Penguin Canada Inc.)
Penguin Books Ltd., 80 Strand, London WC2R 0RL, England
Penguin Group Ireland, 25 St. Stephen's Green, Dublin 2, Ireland (a division of Penguin Books Ltd.)
Penguin Group (Australia), 250 Camberwell Road, Camberwell, Victoria 3124, Australia
(a division of Pearson Australia Group Pty. Ltd.)
Penguin Books India Pvt. Ltd., 11 Community Centre, Panchsheel Park, New Delhi—110 017, India
Penguin Group (NZ), 67 Apollo Drive, Rosedale, North Shore 0632, New Zealand
(a division of Pearson New Zealand Ltd.)
Penguin Books (South Africa) (Pty.) Ltd., 24 Sturdee Avenue, Rosebank, Johannesburg 2196,
South Africa

Penguin Books Ltd., Registered Offices: 80 Strand, London WC2R 0RL, England

ETERNAL MOON

A Berkley Sensation Book / published by arrangement with the author

PRINTING HISTORY
Berkley Sensation mass-market edition / April 2009

Copyright © 2009 by Ruth Glick.
Excerpt from *Dragon Moon* by Rebecca York copyright © 2009 by Ruth Glick.
Excerpt from *Sea Lord* by Virginia Kantra copyright © 2009 by Virginia Kantra.
Cover art by Springer Design Group.

ISBN: 978-0-425-22700-8

BERKLEY® SENSATION
Berkley Sensation Books are published by The Berkley Publishing Group,
a division of Penguin Group (USA) Inc.,
375 Hudson Street, New York, New York 10014.
BERKLEY® SENSATION and the "B" design are trademarks of Penguin Group (USA) Inc.

PRINTED IN THE UNITED STATES OF AMERICA

10 9 8 7 6 5 4 3 2 1

To Norman, as always.

CHAPTER
ONE

RENATA CORDONA TOUCHED the Glock model twenty-eight concealed at the small of her back.

She might be waiting in an empty house for a man who could be a killer, but she wasn't going to end up dead—like the three women who had been murdered in the past nine months.

"Come on," she muttered, pulling out the contact page she'd printed and reading the guy's name. ". . . Mr. Lanagan. Why are you late? Are you playing mind games with me?"

Once again, she looked out a front window of the converted farmhouse, but she saw no cars coming up the long driveway.

Kurt Lanagan had phoned Star Realty a few days ago, asking to see properties with several acres of land around them. That fit the MO of the murderer, so she was masquerading as a real estate agent, with the proviso that if she actually did end up selling anything, the money would go to the company's owner, Dick Trainer.

Which was fine with her. She wasn't doing this for money. She hadn't gone into PI work for money. She could sit back and collect interest and dividend checks from her parents' estate for the rest of her life and not have to worry about supporting herself.

But from her earliest years back in Costa Rica, she'd felt like she should try to make a difference. Whatever that meant.

So here she was, in an empty house, dressed in a baby blue pantsuit and open-toed high-heeled shoes, feeling like Andromeda chained to a rock, waiting for the sea monster to come and get her. She ran a nervous hand through her long hair, then flipped it back over her shoulder, unsure why her mind had leaped to that image. But it was a dark vision—and she needed the sunlight. Stepping out the front door into the spring afternoon, she looked up at the sunshine filtering through the leaves of the oaks and poplars that someone had planted here fifty years ago.

With narrowed eyes, she checked her watch again. Where was Lanagan? Was he one of those jerks who thought only his own time was valuable? Or was he lost?

Well, he had her cell phone number if he needed directions.

Striding down the driveway, she walked toward the detached garage. When she realized she was counting the steps, she stopped herself. It didn't matter how many steps she had to take. The important point was that the garage was a little too far from the house to be convenient, and she should have checked it out—since Mr. Lanagan could be a legitimate customer.

That thought made her firm her lips. She was focusing on the murder part of this assignment and forgetting that she also had to play a convincing real estate agent, who would obviously have paid attention to the selling points of the house and surrounding property.

Let's see. She'd taken a good look at the kitchen. It had been updated—but maybe not recently enough to go with the $850K asking price.

She was almost to the garage when movement in the woods made her stop. With a jolt, she turned. Had she and the police totally misread the killer's method of stalking his victims? Was he coming on foot to isolated locations where female agents were showing houses?

All that ran through her mind before she realized it wasn't a man at all—but a dog. A Rottweiler, she guessed.

He looked large and dangerous, and her blood ran cold when she saw he wasn't alone.

Behind him, five more dogs stepped out of the underbrush. They were all about his size. One looked like a Shepherd mix. Another was a Doberman. And the remaining two appeared to have at least half pit bull genes.

What they had in common was the menacing look in their eyes.

Did they belong to someone? Or were they a feral pack? Inspecting them more closely, she saw that half of them didn't appear to be wearing collars—which wasn't reassuring.

Bent on getting out of their way, she took two quick steps to the side door of the garage—and twisted the knob. Unfortunately, it was locked, and she remembered that the key was lying on the counter in the kitchen, along with the key to the house.

Good going, Renata!

The Rottweiler, who appeared to be the leader of the pack, started barking. The others followed suit.

Then, they broke off as quickly as they'd begun.

Somehow, that abrupt silence was more threatening than the previous noise.

The leader bared its teeth and snarled at her. The others did the same.

They were maybe sixty feet away, but she could clearly hear them growling.

Instinctively, she knew they were out for blood—her blood—and she was no match for them.

Her heart thumping inside her chest, she drew her gun. She'd never shot a dog, or any other animal, in her life. And the idea of doing it now made her sick, but that might be her only chance to get out of here alive.

Would a warning shot scare them away—or send them charging toward her?

Desperately, her mind scrambled for what she remembered about canines. You weren't supposed to challenge a dangerous dog by looking him in the eye. And you weren't supposed to show fear.

Yeah, right.

Should she try to run back to the house? Or should she walk?

Without turning around, she took one step back and then another, keeping her gaze slightly to the side of the pack. Still, she saw the leader raise his head, as the growling turned to a low rumble.

She knew in that terror-filled moment that they were going to charge her.

CHAPTER
TWO

JUST BEFORE THE pack could attack, a larger dog came dashing out of the woods. As her gaze swung to him, she took in the details in a split second. The pointed ears. The long, upturned tail. The dark gray fur along his back and flanks that gradually lightened as it reached his lower body and legs.

Was he a dog—or a wolf?

Her heart still pounding, she did a fast recalculation. A wolf in the Maryland woods? Was that possible?

Well, she'd heard of coyotes returning to this area. So why not a wolf?

Whatever he was, she saw how the others reacted to him.

Moments ago they'd looked ready to tear her to pieces. They were still agitated, but in a different way. Somehow the newcomer had changed the equation, taking over the position of alpha male in the pack within seconds of his arrival.

He faced the others squarely, his chest forward, his teeth bared, his tail puffed and standing straight out, as he stepped between her and the feral animals—growling a warning.

In that moment she sensed that he had told the pack she was his property, and he would tear any dog apart who dared to go near her.

He was alone, and there were six of them, but all of the other dogs had changed their stance. Their tails and heads were down.

When the newcomer pressed forward, the others backed up.

He kept advancing, challenging all of them at once, and continuing with his calm aggression.

Then, everything changed. As if someone had flipped a switch, the former leader turned tail and ran, and the others followed his lead.

Her rescuer stood, watching them disappear into the woods. His stance was still aggressive, but she saw a slight relaxation in his posture. Probably, he was pretty sure that he'd chased them away, but he was waiting—just in case they came back. Long seconds ticked by. Then a minute. Then another. Finally, he turned and gazed at her.

She caught her breath as she took in the handsome features—his light gray facial fur contrasting with his dark nose and intelligent blue eyes, rimmed with dark margins.

She waited for frozen moments, caught by the notion that he was going to speak to her. Of course, no words came out of his mouth, only a low growl that she took to mean, "Get back in the house while the getting's good."

"Yes," she answered. Then added, "Thank you for chasing them away."

He nodded as though he understood her, then growled again, this time more sharply.

"Okay." She spun around and dashed back down the driveway, running as fast as she could in the high heels.

When she reached the front porch, she turned and looked back, expecting to see him standing where she had left him, but he had silently vanished into the woods.

Stepping to the house, she closed the front door behind her, then leaned back against the barrier, breathing hard. Her narrow escape was sinking in, and the primitive part of her brain knew those dogs would have torn her apart if the big gray wolf hadn't arrived.

Wolf. Yes, he had to be a wolf.

WEREWOLF Jacob Mashall breathed out a sigh. When he'd seen the dogs getting ready to attack Renata Cordona, his heart had stopped.

He'd faced them down. And he could have followed them. Instead, he headed in the other direction—toward a spot about a hundred yards from the house, where he found what he'd scented when he first arrived. Raw meat, dumped on the ground. Meat that had attracted the animals.

What the hell was seven pounds of chuck steak doing out here on this property? It looked like someone had deliberately put it there to lure the dogs.

He turned and stared toward the house—and stopped short. The Latin beauty he'd saved was standing at the front window staring out. Looking for the dog pack? Or looking for the wolf that had saved her?

He took a quick step back, then another, fading into the woods. It wouldn't do him any good to confront her now, not when he couldn't talk to her.

He'd met her several times over the past few months. She was a real estate agent who had come to some of the meetings of the citizens' group concerned about the funding of essential county services in the face of the economic downturn.

He'd noticed her right away. There was something about her oval face, her dark eyes with their fringe of sooty lashes, her full lips, and that marvelous long, dark hair of hers that called to him in a way he couldn't explain—except in the most basic terms of sexual attraction.

No, it was more than that. He kept fighting the uncanny feeling that he'd held her in his arms before. Mated with her before. Declared his undying love—although none of that could possibly be true, since they'd met only briefly.

The fantasy had been alarming enough to keep him from

asking her out, but as soon as he'd seen she was in trouble, he'd taken the risk of stepping between her and those dogs. Now he had to make sure she was all right.

Unaccountably restless and out for a run in wolf form, he'd passed a FOR SALE sign down at the entrance to the driveway. Not long after seeing the sign, he'd picked up the scent of the dogs. Then he'd felt the dangerous vibrations coming off of them.

If he'd had to articulate what he'd sensed, he wouldn't have been able to put it in terms a human could understand, but he could have described it to the other Marshall men, his brothers and cousins who also carried the werewolf gene.

While he could have told them how he knew about the dogs and the danger they represented, he couldn't have explained exactly what he had done to make them break off the attack on Renata. For him, it was more than a canine face-off.

In his childhood, he'd discovered he had the ability to communicate with animals in ways that his brothers and cousins did not possess. He relied on that special talent in his job, working with dogs at various pounds, shelters, and training facilities around the area. And he'd used it in the past to talk dangerous animals out of attacking—one or two at a time. But he'd never tried to dominate a pack of six dogs before.

Thank God it had worked.

Now he wanted to know who the hell had put that meat there and if it had anything to do with Renata—specifically.

But he'd left his house as a wolf, and when he changed to human form, he'd be naked.

He could run home, of course, but she might not even be here when he got back, because his house was five miles away.

As he contemplated the problem, a solution leaped into his mind. A quarter mile from here, behind a rectangular cinder block house, he'd seen a clothesline with wash flapping in the breeze. He retraced his steps, until he reached the spot, then waited for a long moment, breathing in the scents that surrounded the house.

Human sweat and motor oil. Burnt rubbish and laundry detergent.

As far as he could tell, no one was outside. Still, when he broke through the cover of the woods, he approached with caution. He was able to snag an almost dry pair of sweatpants and a tee shirt off the line. After stashing them in the woods, he went back for the muddy sneakers sitting by the back door. But as he darted in to get the shoes, a guy with a shotgun came barreling out of the house.

Jacob could have leaped forward and knocked him down. But he hated the idea of adding insult and injury to theft, since the man was only defending his property from a marauding animal, at least from his point of view.

When he saw the gun, he turned tail and ran, glad that he'd had the foresight to drop the clothing back in the trees. Still, he heard an angry shout from the man, followed by a shotgun blast behind him. Thankfully, none of the pellets hit him.

Stopping to scoop up the clothing in his mouth, he hightailed it farther into the underbrush, praying that the homeowner didn't think the laundry was worth chasing him for. Because then they *would* have a fight on their hands.

When he thought he was safe, he stopped behind a tangle of honeysuckle, breathing hard and listening for sounds of pursuit. Finally sure he wasn't being followed, he began to say the words of the ancient chant that transformed the men of his family from wolf to man—and back again. Of course, as a wolf, he couldn't speak them aloud. But he said them in his head.

Taranis, Epona, Cerridwen.

Once he'd finished the phrase, he repeated it and went on to another.

Ga. Feart. Cleas. Duais. Aithriocht. Go gcumhdai is dtreorai na deithe thu.

The men of his family had passed those words down

from father to son from generation to generation. His cousin, Ross, had told him they were Celtic in origin and had theorized that one of their ancestors had been a Druid priest who had asked the gods for special powers—and had gotten more than he had bargained for.

He'd spawned a race at odds with the rest of humankind. And he'd created werewolves who were loners, because each of them was an alpha male. Which made them the head of their own packs.

Until Ross had changed the equation. He'd figured out how to get his brothers and his cousins to work together, although there was always going to be friction among the Marshalls.

Today Jacob was alone—the way he liked it. Once he had transformed, he pulled on the stolen pants, then the shirt and started back to the house, wishing that he'd also gotten the shoes. But that wasn't going to stop him from speaking to Renata while the incident was fresh in her mind.

A flash of movement outside had Renata reaching for her Glock again. Gun in hand, she watched a man coming up the road. With a jolt of recognition, she saw that it was Jacob Marshall. She'd met him at a couple of Howard County citizens' meetings. But he'd never done more than exchange a few words with her. Now he was striding toward the house like he owned it.

When he knocked at the door, she thought about pretending that no one was home. Then the knock came again, more insistent than before, and she thought he had probably spotted her through the window. It was strange that he was showing up here—and now. After hesitating for a moment, she slipped the gun out of its holster and into the shoulder bag she was carrying.

When she opened the door and stepped outside, a look she couldn't read washed over his face.

"What?" she asked.

"Are you all right?"

"Why shouldn't I be?"

He hesitated for a moment, as though he hadn't thought through the reason he was standing here, facing her. Finally, he said, "I heard dogs barking. It sounded like someone might be in trouble."

She didn't remember a lot of noise. At any rate, it had happened almost twenty minutes ago.

"If you were worried about barking, why did it take you so long to get here?" she asked.

He looked back over his shoulder, as though the answer to the question lay in the woods.

When he spoke, it took her several moments to work her way through what he was saying.

"I . . . found some meat."

"What?"

He gestured behind him and to his right. "Over there in the woods. Someone had spread around a bunch of raw meat on the ground."

"Why?"

"To lure the dogs here, I think."

"That's crazy."

"How many were there?" he asked.

"Six."

"Who knew you were going to be here alone?"

"There's a record of it at the real estate office. And I'm meeting a client."

He glanced over his shoulder, his gaze falling on her car, which was the only one parked near the house. "I guess he must be late."

"What business is that of yours?" she asked, thinking that he had somehow put her on the defensive, and she needed to take control of the conversation. Then before he could answer that question, she noticed something quite odd.

"Where are your shoes?"

He looked down, and she could see his shoulders tense. "I was out for a run."

"Barefoot?"

"Uh-huh."

She gave him a disbelieving stare.

"YES, why are you barefoot?" a grating voice asked. The question wasn't spoken by Renata—or anyone in the vicinity. It came from a man several miles from the scene. Or to be more accurate, someone who looked like a man. But he was much more—a being with powers far beyond those of mere humans, one of which was the ability to view what was happening between Renata and Jacob Marshall without being there in person.

His name was Questabaze. At least, that was his demon name. Of course he didn't go by anything so strange-sounding in the human world. Over the centuries, he'd worn many different identities. And the one he had now was perfectly designed to allow him to fit into the society where his quarry lived.

Renata's world. Where the air didn't burn your lungs when you took a breath and your bed was a soft mattress rather than a field of sharp rocks. He had fought for the honor and the privilege of being here. Fought his brothers— and won. And he would win so much more when the great dance of power finally came to an end.

As the couple confronted each other in this isolated location, Questabaze felt a flicker of anger course through him. Too bad the dogs hadn't done their work. He'd lured them to the area with the meat, then taken control of their minds. They'd been about to maul Renata. To rip her face to shreds.

But it hadn't worked out that way. He'd waited with quivering anticipation for the attack. Instead, that other animal had come trotting out of the woods and forced the pack to back off with their tails between their legs.

Questabaze wasn't sure how the animal had done it. Not with the odds stacked against him. Or even why he'd come charging out of the woods to protect Renata.

But she'd run back to the house, safe and sound. Now she was talking to Jacob Marshall—of all people—when she shouldn't be in the condition to talk to anyone.

He'd seen their attraction for each other, and he'd decided he'd been wrong in the past. Jacob Marshall was her true mate. He had to be. They'd met—as destiny dictated. And it was up to Questabaze to make sure their relationship got totally fouled up one way or the other.

Too bad they were alone together after her narrow escape.

"Fuck!"

Such a satisfying expletive for such a basic human act. Why should it offend people when it was one of the basic pleasures of this world?

The word was one of the many variations he'd learned over the centuries. In German it was *ficken*. In Norwegian *fukka*. In Spanish *chingar*. And perhaps the current English verb had been derived from the Irish *bot*. Still, no matter where it had come from, it made such a nasty guttural sound.

He said it again. Which only lowered his stress level a couple of notches. A satisfying sound wasn't what he needed. He needed results.

Of course, there had been other men who had seemed to be candidates for the role of Renata's true consort.

He'd had to watch as each of the men met her. After they'd gotten involved with her, he'd wiped them off the face of the Earth, thinking that he'd accomplished his mission. Then, each time, he'd come to the conclusion that the relationship had been a false alarm. It was just their bad luck that they'd had to die to prove him wrong.

It was also bad luck that his end run hadn't worked just now. But even without the help of the dogs, he would win another round in the great game of power.

Always in the past, after his victory, the cycle had started over again, but he could feel the finish vibrating just out of reach.

And I will have the final triumph, he promised himself,

because it was the only outcome he could allow. He had worked too hard. Dared too much. Yet even as he made the vow, something was still nagging at him.

How had Jacob Marshall known Renata was here? Had he followed her? Or was he checking up on her?

It wasn't possible for Questabaze to observe Marshall on his own, the way he could sometimes do with Renata. She was his focus, although he couldn't watch her every minute because he had to put in time maintaining his human persona.

When the scene in his mind began to waver, he realized he had lost his concentration. With another curse, he clawed to hang on to the vision.

He was a being of great cunning and great power. But there were limits to his potency. Despite his efforts, the image snapped off, and he was left staring at a blank wall. His anger flared, making a pile of leaves outside his window smolder.

With a flick of his hand, he shot them a blast of cold.

He rarely had trouble deciding what course of action to take, but now he hesitated.

Should he get into his car and drive over there? He certainly had an excuse for appearing. Or was that exactly the wrong thing to do? Would he just make Renata suspicious?

CHAPTER
THREE

RENATA STARED EXPECTANTLY at Jacob Marshall.

"I'm toughening my feet," he said.

She made a scoffing noise. "That sounds ridiculous."

He shrugged. "What can I say? It's the truth."

She wanted to fold her arms across her chest, but that would convey a position of weakness. Instead, she kept them at her sides and her right hand within easy reach of the gun in her purse.

Switching back to his earlier claim, she said, "Show me where you found the raw meat."

He glanced over his shoulder, and she wondered if he'd been lying to her.

"I'd rather you stay inside."

"I'd rather you show me that meat."

He sighed. "Okay." Turning, he walked down the stairs from the porch and strode across the backyard where the grass was almost a foot high and full of weeds. She saw him watching the woods, and she did, too, as they stepped off the unmowed lawn into the underbrush. She could see nothing and smell nothing, but she saw him take several deep breaths, like he was using his nose to locate the meat.

After a few seconds, he tramped off into the underbrush, then he stopped short, pointing down. "There."

Coming up beside him, she stared down at a pile of beef cuts that looked like they had been purchased at a grocery store, pulled out of their packages and strewn on the ground.

"You're right," she murmured.

"Did you think I was lying?"

"I wanted to see for myself," she snapped. "I guess I should tell the cops."

"Yeah."

"Why did they go after me instead of the meat?"

"They may have thought you were going to take it away from them," Jacob answered.

A rustling in the leaves made her head snap up. With a shiver, she scanned the woods, looking to see if the dogs had come back—until she realized that the wind was shaking the tree branches.

From the corner of her eye she saw that Jacob was watching her. Without commenting, she turned and started back to the house.

"I'm meeting a client," she said, when they reached the front door. Or had she said that already? Damn, her nerves were so jangled that her short-term memory was screwed up.

Although she hoped he'd take the hint and go away, he followed her inside.

Needing some distance from him, she headed toward the French doors that opened from the dining room onto a wide deck. Outside, she dragged in a draft of fresh air, feeling like she had escaped from . . .

Well, she couldn't say exactly from what, but all at once she could breathe easier. She might have glanced over her shoulder to see if Jacob was watching her. But she was pretty sure he was still there and that he knew he was making her nervous.

To get more distance from him, she walked toward the railing about twelve feet away. She had almost reached it when the board below her right foot gave way. Too late she realized that the structure of the deck must be rotted— and her weight had been too much for the damaged wood. As she took a step back, her left foot sank through the decayed surface, and she started to go down. When she tried to scramble to safety, more wood crumbled under her.

She would have fallen through the deck, but strong arms caught her and dragged her away from disaster. A man's arms. Jacob Marshall's arms.

He held her braced against his hard body, moving rapidly backward through the door and into the dining room, as the deck continued to disintegrate.

They were both shaking as he hauled her to safety.

"Are you all right?" he asked urgently.

She stared at him, hardly able to frame an answer. He'd seen she was in trouble, and he'd come flying toward her, somehow avoiding the rotting boards.

"Are you all right?" he repeated, his hands closing over her shoulders, his voice rough and urgent.

"Yes," she managed, although that wasn't strictly true. Physically, she was fine because he had snatched her away from disaster. But, mentally, it was hard to deal with what was happening to her.

When she raised her head and gazed up at him, the expression on his face made her heart turn over. He looked as dazed as she felt, and somehow that helped her.

He still held her by the shoulders.

"Renata?" he said, his voice turning into a kind of savage growl.

He was asking a question, and this time it wasn't about her physical well-being. She knew the logical answer should have been to raise her hands and push against his broad chest.

She couldn't do it because nothing in her life had ever felt so right. It was as though the two of them had been lovers long ago—separated by time and space. Now they were back together again. She had no idea where that thought had come from, and she couldn't justify it in any normal way.

At that moment, all she knew was that she must stay with him. Her life depended on it. More than her own life. The fate of the world, which had to be some crazy illusion. This was about two people. A man and a woman. And an accident had sent them crashing into each other in some way that she didn't understand.

"Jacob." She said his name in wonder. *Jacob? Was that really his name? Or was that just the name he had now?*

Once again the strangeness of her own thoughts almost overwhelmed her.

"Renata?" The wonder she felt filled his voice, and his expression was so strange. Fierce and tender, sure and uncertain, all at the same time.

"What's happening to us?" she managed to say.

"I don't know."

"How did I lose you?" she murmured.

"You have me now." His arms folded her closer. She still couldn't make any headway with logic, but she understood one basic truth. His lips were inches from hers. Truly, she wasn't sure which of them closed the distance between his mouth and hers. Or likely it was both of them.

He lowered his head. She rose up to meet him. And the touch of his mouth on hers was like a whirlwind touching down on earth, then spinning out of control.

She heard a strangled syllable escape from her throat. Or perhaps it was from his. It didn't matter which. The important thing was the exquisite contact of his lips on hers. As he moved them urgently, feelings flooded through her. Feelings and images. And memories. He was Jacob. But he was also Michael. And Martino. Jordan. Alex. And Jalerak.

She whispered that last name aloud. It seemed so right. So real.

JACOB knew that if he didn't pull away, everything in his life would change. But it was impossible to let go of the woman in his embrace, impossible to lift his mouth away from hers.

Even as his arms slipped from her shoulders to circle her hips, his head was spinning with images that were stranger than reality. He was himself, and she was Renata. He knew that much. But he knew more. He was swept away to another time, another place. No, not just one other time and place. Many. The two of them had kissed like this before. Greedily. Urgently. A hundred years ago. Two hundred. Three hundred. A thousand. Over and over. More times than he could count.

Those buried memories surfaced and flashed through his brain. The two of them in an icebound cave. In a field full of yellow flowers. On a high cliff above a rushing river. In a brightly colored tent. And before an altar where a trio of stern goddesses looked down at them.

He had been in all those places with her. He had felt the same desperate need before. And each time something bad happened. Something that made it impossible for the two of them to stay together . . .

He shoved that part away. He didn't want to think about how it had ended. He only wanted to grab on to now. On to the need for her. The terrible urgency. The conviction that if he didn't make love to her, he would die.

He felt the heat coming off her body. And his, fusing them together with a molten urgency that he had never experienced before. It was the craving of the werewolf for his mate. He knew that, yet he understood that it was more— so much more. The two of them belonged to each other, would always belong to each other, now and through time. They were tied together in some way that he couldn't understand. Not yet.

But he understood the burning need, the fire coursing through his veins, the erection standing straight up between them like an exclamation mark.

He angled his head so that he could taste more of her, his tongue claiming her mouth as one hand slid down her body, cupping her bottom, pulling her more tightly against his cock, fueling his greed for her—and hers for him.

She made a small, needy sound and moved against him.

Her hands ranged over his back, into his hair, over his hips with the same restless urgency that he felt. There was room for only one conscious thought in his mind. He wanted her more than he had ever wanted anything in his life.

He lifted his head, looking wildly around for a bed or a rug—somewhere he could lay her down and claim her. In that moment, a sound penetrated the haze that had settled over his brain.

It was a car horn honking. Renata stiffened in his arms. Then her hand came up, pushing him away.

Her eyes blinked open, and she stared at him in confusion—the same confusion he felt.

"No," she breathed.

"We have to . . ." he said, not even sure how he planned to finish the sentence.

She yanked herself free of his arms. As she broke the contact, a measure of sanity returned to his mind.

"It must be Mr. Lanagan," she whispered.

"Who?"

"The man I came to meet. I'm supposed to show him this house."

"He won't want it with a broken deck," Jacob said, thinking how stupid that sounded, even as he heard his own words.

She lifted her hand, brushing back her long, dark hair. Then she tugged at the knit shirt she was wearing under her suit jacket. She looked like she wanted to say something. But a few seconds later, a knock sounded at the door.

Renata's gaze shot to the front hall, and he knew she must be thinking how the two of them looked—disheveled and flushed.

"*Dios mio.*"

"You almost fell through the deck," Jacob said. "Of course you're shaken up."

"Right." She gave him a grateful look. But the gratitude faded quickly.

Before she could decide what to do, they heard the door open, then footsteps come down the hall.

"Miss Cordona?" a man said.

"Yes. I'm sorry," Renata said, her voice high and strained. "There's been a little accident. I was out on the deck and it collapsed under me." She gestured toward Jacob, her hand fluttering. "And Mr. Marshall rescued me," she finished, failing to explain what they had been doing afterward.

"Yeah. Lucky I was out for a run," Jacob added.

The Lanagan guy looked from her to Jacob and back again as though he didn't quite buy the story. But Jacob kept a straight face as he inclined his head toward the French doors. "Take a look for yourself."

Renata jumped back into the conversation. "If you end up buying the house, I'm sure you'll be able to get a price concession from the owner."

Lanagan stepped to the doors and made a whistling sound, then cocked his head toward Renata. "You were out there?"

"Yes."

"You're lucky you didn't get badly hurt."

"That's the truth," she answered.

Jacob watched the interchange. He didn't want to leave because he didn't like the guy's looks. There was something off about him. Still, he made his voice hearty as he said to Renata, "Are you sure you're okay?"

"Yes, thanks," she answered. He knew it wasn't exactly true. She wasn't okay. And neither was he. Something had happened a few minutes ago. Something that went beyond passion, but neither one of them had the luxury of working their way through it with her client standing there watching them.

Pretending to leave, Jacob strode to the front door and exited the house, then began jogging down the road like that was what he'd been doing when he'd first stopped by the house.

But he didn't go very far. When he was sure he couldn't be seen from the house, he found a place where the trees and the underbrush hid him from sight. Stepping farther into the shadows, he tore off the stolen clothing and began to say the chant that would turn him from man to wolf. He did it quickly, fighting the pain of transforming three times in less than an hour, because he didn't want to leave Renata unprotected in that house with the Lanagan guy.

Once he returned to wolf form, he slipped through the woods back the way he'd come. He could see Renata through the kitchen window, gesturing as she explained the features of the appliances or something. He could see the guy, too. He still had a look on his face that Jacob didn't like, but he wasn't making any threatening moves.

When they disappeared from view, Jacob moved to another window, picking them up again in what was probably the family room.

He hadn't considered Renata's job when he'd first met her. Today he saw that it had some very risky aspects. Her profession took her to vacant houses all the time where she met with people who might or might not be on the up and up.

Now that he thought about it, he remembered that some female real estate agents had been murdered while showing property in an isolated area.

"Jesus!" And here was Renata, meeting some guy she obviously didn't know.

He tried to tell himself that if Renata Cordona wanted to put herself in danger, that was none of his business. Unfortunately, he couldn't shake the conviction that it mattered to him. Very much.

When he lost sight of her again, he shifted his position, his gaze scanning the windows as he circled the house. Only this time she didn't reappear, and a wave of panic welled up inside him. He moved closer to the building. Dangerously close. If she or the Lanagan guy looked out the window, they would spot the wolf lurking around outside. This time she might remember to call animal control, although that wasn't going to do her much good. He knew how the local system worked. If someone managed to show up tomorrow, that would be fast.

When he didn't see her, his heart started to pound. Finally, he caught a flash of movement at one of the windows and darted in that direction. When he spotted her and the guy, his relief was so profound that for a moment he felt light-headed.

Before she could look out the window and see him, he took a step back and then another.

Moving away from the house gave him a little breathing room. He'd been so preoccupied with Renata's safety that he hadn't thought much about what had happened when he'd kissed her. He'd been socked with a rush of desire so strong that he'd almost lost his head.

The savagery of his reaction was disturbing enough. The rest of it was more shocking. A barrage of images had assaulted him. It was like he'd kissed her before. Made love with her before. Many times. Over more than one lifetime. And he didn't know what it meant.

Was that what happened when a werewolf met his life mate? None of his brothers or his cousins had mentioned anything like that to him. Of course, he hadn't asked them what it was like to find your life mate, because he hadn't wanted to know. And he didn't want to know now.

It was hard to believe that Renata Cordona was the right woman for him. Maybe he was so close to the age of bonding that he was going to have a violent reaction every time he touched a woman.

Yeah, right. Like that made sense.

When the front door opened, and Renata and the man came out, Jacob decided that it was time to get the hell out of there before she spotted him.

CHAPTER
FOUR

RENATA STEPPED ONTO the front porch and stopped short, feeling her breath catch.

"Something wrong?" Kurt Lanagan moved up behind her.

"No," she managed. She'd thought she saw movement in the underbrush about twenty yards from the house. A dog-shaped shadow. Then she decided that it was just a trick of the light—and her nerves acting up after everything she'd been through over the past hour.

She took a step away from Lanagan. He was hiding something. But he hadn't made any moves that led her to believe he was going to attack her.

Clearing her throat, she asked, "How do you like the house?"

"It's got possibilities," he replied. "Tell me the listing price."

"Eight hundred and fifty thousand."

"It needs some repair work, including that deck. And the silver foil paper in the bathrooms is from the seventies."

"Yes. But I'm sure you could get the owners to lower the price, given the state of the market."

"There are only four bedrooms."

"You have a large family?

Instead of answering, he said, "I should take a look at the grounds."

"Uh . . ." She stopped, thinking about what had happened when she'd gone to look at the garage.

He gave her an inquisitive look. "You've been nervous ever since I got here. What happened, besides the deck collapsing?"

She lifted one shoulder. "A bunch of dogs came around while I was out here earlier."

His gaze sharpened. "Dogs? You mean, like a pack of wild dogs or something?"

"Not wild. Feral."

"What's the difference?"

"Wild means . . . you know . . . a different breed. Not domesticated."

"You're splitting hairs. If they're running around wild, they're wild," he snapped.

Cutting her losses, she said, "You're right. They looked dangerous."

"Then maybe this isn't the property for me," he said with a toss of his head.

"Maybe not."

He took a step down from the porch, then turned back toward her. "When you have something else you can show me, let me know."

"I'll do that," she said, wondering if it was a lie. Was he the perp she was looking for? Maybe she'd give him another chance to jump her.

That thought made her suppress a snicker, as she watched him walk to his car—a Mercedes she noticed—and climb in.

If the car was any indication, he could afford this place. But she knew that guys sometimes put on a good show with their wheels.

As soon as he drove away, her mind flashed back to the encounter with Jacob. The way he'd showed up so unexpectedly. The way he'd rushed to her rescue. The way he'd kissed her. And the way the kiss had made her feel. Hot and breathless and ready for sex.

She shivered. His touch had kindled more than sexual feelings.

She'd been flooded with a rush of strange images. Of other times and other lovers. Like memories. But they couldn't be *her* memories.

Were they from movies she had seen? Maybe that's where they had come from. The explanation felt like she was grasping at straws. But she wanted it to be true, because nothing like that had ever happened when she'd kissed another man.

Even more unsettling, he'd made her feel emotions she had shoved aside for years.

Faces crowded in on her. James. Her parents. Miguel. All of them ripped from her by death.

She shuddered. She didn't want to think about the pain in her life. But the intensity of the kiss made her remember why she'd stayed away from relationships.

She'd met James Fitzpatrick in a survey of American history class her sophomore year at the University of Maryland.

When he asked her out on a date, she knew that her parents wouldn't approve of him because he wasn't from her culture. But because she was living in an apartment in College Park, she went anyway, and after six weeks of dating him, she let him coax her into his bed.

James had been older than the typical college student. He'd come back to school after working as a waiter for a few years. And he was an excellent lover.

He taught her about a woman's pleasure. It had been good, but it wasn't like the out-of-control passion she'd just felt with Jacob Marshall.

She forced that out of her mind and was left with James again. Left with the day he didn't show up when they were supposed to meet at the student union after her Spanish literature class. At first she'd thought it was because they'd been fighting recently. Then she heard sirens blaring outside, and fear had grabbed her by the throat.

Somehow she *knew* they were coming for James. She'd rushed out to see paramedics taking him away on a stretcher.

He'd been hit by a car—the driver speeding away and leaving his victim lying broken in the street.

That was the first death that had shattered her life. Her parents and Miguel had followed.

From long practice, she thrust those memories away with an iron will and went back to the vow she'd made. Some ancient curse was following her around. Anyone she loved was going to die, and she'd promised herself she wouldn't let that happen again.

Which meant that she wasn't going to get involved with Jacob Marshall. No matter how she'd responded to him.

But she couldn't stop herself from replaying the encounter in her mind, making excuses for her behavior. The deck had given out under her feet. Jacob had rushed out to rescue her. She'd ended up in his arms, and she'd been too shook up to keep her emotions from running away from her.

Well, she was back in control now. Tomorrow she'd have to call Lou Deverel, who took care of repairs for Star Realty. Since the owners of the property had retired to Florida and put the realty company in charge, Lou would have to fix that deck before anybody showed the house again.

She reached into her purse for her cell phone, thinking she'd call Barry Prescott, her boss, and report what had happened—with the dogs and Jacob Marshall. She was carrying the primary load on this case, but Barry was a more experienced PI, and he was doing most of the background work.

Then she remembered that a discussion with him would have to wait until tomorrow morning. Five years before she'd met him, he'd lost his wife to cancer, but his daughter, Elizabeth, lived in Arlington, Virginia, and he was visiting with her overnight.

He'd made it clear that on his trips to her house every

few weeks, he didn't want to discuss business, and Renata
had always respected that request.

She was turning into her driveway when her cell phone
rang. Hoping Barry might be home early, she pulled the
instrument from her purse. Annoyance flashed through her
when she saw it was Greg Newcastle, the Howard County
detective who had been assigned to the murder case. In his
early thirties, he'd made detective less than six months
ago. With his middle-American good looks and tough-guy
chin, he could have starred in a police recruiting poster.
And she knew from working with him that he was following her progress closely.

"How did it go this afternoon?" he asked.

"What, are you checking up on me?" she snapped before she could stop herself.

"We're on the same team."

She sighed. "Sorry. I . . ."

When she hesitated, he jumped in with a question.
"Something happened?"

Reminding herself that she was planning to tell Newcastle about the afternoon anyway, she said, "I was almost
attacked by a pack of dogs."

"Jesus."

"Somebody dumped a bunch of meat out at the property where I was meeting a client."

Quickly, she filled him in on the details.

"So you don't think this has anything to do with the
murders?" he asked.

"Did you find anything like that at the other murder
scenes?" she countered.

"No. But I should check out the meat. Can you show me
where you found it?"

"Yes," she answered, thinking that she hadn't been the
one to discover the stuff. Jacob had shown her where it
was. So did she need to explain that part to Newcastle,
too?

He wanted her to drive right back to the property. Since

she wasn't willing to turn around and go back there, they made arrangements to meet at nine the next morning before she went to Barry's.

As soon as she got inside, she kicked off the high heels she'd been wearing to meet her client and sat down to massage her feet. Maybe Jacob Marshall had the right idea after all. As a kid, she'd run around without shoes, and she hated stuffing her feet into them now.

When she had the blood circulating again, she hung up her pantsuit in the closet and pulled on jeans and a tee shirt.

Then she booted up the computer. While it was going through the start-up routine, she looked up Jacob Marshall's address in the phone book.

One thing that seemed to gibe was that he lived in an isolated area of the county, a reasonable distance for him to have been running near the house she'd been showing that afternoon. At least for someone who ran on a regular basis.

That meant he was in good physical shape. Which she already knew from the feel of his body when he'd held her in his arms.

She made a disgusted sound. Did she have to keep coming back to *that*?

Pushing the personal reaction out of her mind, she logged on to the secure database that Barry subscribed to.

Apparently, Jacob was an expert in animal behavior. He worked with several local animal shelters, evaluating whether dogs were suitable for adoption. In some cases, he'd taken at-risk animals home and changed their undesirable characteristics. He also worked with organizations that trained dogs—for the blind and for the police, both in Maryland and nearby states. From his credit card records, she could see he'd been away on assignment for several weeks and had just come back—in time to show up and rescue her from the falling deck.

She poked a little more into his personal life. When she

saw he wasn't married, she felt a little zing travel along her
nerve endings before she reminded herself that she wasn't
going to go there—for a whole lot of reasons.

Telling herself that she was working, not satisfying her
own curiosity, Renata prowled through Jacob's life for a
couple of hours. Finally, glancing at the clock, she realized
she had one more task she had to take care of that evening.

With a sigh, she called Lou Deverel. After five rings,
his answering machine picked up, and she felt a little jolt
of relief.

Knowing she was only putting off an explosion, she left
him a message telling him about almost falling through
the deck. With her duty done, she hung up and walked into
the kitchen to fix dinner.

Although cooking for one was never much fun, Renata
hated fast food, so she took the time to fix some of the
dishes she'd enjoyed since she was a little girl. Peasant
food, she thought with a grin.

Back in Costa Rica her parents hadn't been all that well
off. But tourists had started shipping the furniture her father made back to the U.S., where more and more people
had wanted it. Which was why a rich backer had brought
her family north when she was ten. And why her father had
made a small fortune in his adopted country.

After peeling a plantain, she fried it in oil, then heated
some of the rice and black beans she'd made a few days
earlier. That was the food of her childhood. Comfort food.
Tonight, the meal made her think about Miguel Salazar.

They'd met at the recreation center in the Baltimore
barrio where they both did volunteer work with kids. She
knew he liked her, and even though she was cautious about
another relationship, they ended up getting into some long
talks about life back in Central America. When she invited
him to her place for a home-cooked meal, he was impressed.
That first dinner led to a lot of others—and a warm and
intimate relationship.

He joked that her cooking was the reason he was going
to marry her, but it hadn't worked out that way. They'd

planned a trip to the eastern shore of Maryland. A weekend away together, because somehow they'd started getting into little spats for no good reason. Only he was late, and he didn't answer his phone. A terrible sense of dread overtook her as she drove to his place. Somehow she knew it was all happening again.

She remembered letting herself into his Baltimore row house, calling his name, and then the tight feeling in her chest as she rushed upstairs.

He'd been sleeping in his bed, and the moment she'd put her hand on his cold face, she knew he was dead.

Even so, she called 911, then sank to her knees beside the bed, praying.

The paramedics hustled her out of the house, since they suspected Miguel had died of carbon monoxide poisoning.

She was devastated. Paralyzed. In shock. And she knew she couldn't risk that kind of pain again. So she'd kept away from men. Until her out-of-control reaction to Jacob Marshall.

She put him firmly out of her mind while she ate dinner. Then she tried to watch a program about polar bears on Animal Planet, but she couldn't stay focused on the show.

Maybe she needed to get away, but that was impossible when she was in the middle of an investigation.

A hot shower helped relax her until she walked into the bedroom and felt a wave of dread sweep over her.

Was she going to wake up in her bed? Or out in the garden? Surrounded by objects she'd collected and arranged in a mysterious pattern she didn't understand.

CHAPTER
FIVE

"NO," RENATA SAID aloud. "You are not going crazy, and you are not going to sleepwalk again. Not tonight."

Naked, she strode to the dresser, got out a long silky gown, and slipped it over her head. The sheer fabric felt wonderful against her skin.

An indulgence. She didn't allow herself many, but expensive underwear and expensive nightgowns were two of her pleasures.

After pulling back the covers and slipping into bed, she knew she had run out of delaying tactics. With a shudder, she reached for the length of rope that she'd brought up from the basement to the bedroom two days ago.

One end was already fastened around the bedpost. With shaking hands, she tied the other around her wrist, giving herself enough slack to turn over, if she wanted. The tether had kept her firmly in bed last night. She'd awakened in the morning with the rope still in place and only a small red mark where the loop circled her wrist.

It was going to work again tonight. If she tried to get out of bed, she'd jerk the line and wake herself up.

Despite the precautions, her heart was pounding as she

lay there in the dark. But she'd learned relaxation exercises to help her get to sleep, and tonight they did the trick.

In the middle of a deep breath, she escaped into her dreams. They had always been richly textured. Tonight they took her away to the land of her childhood.

THE dream was a comfort. Renata was back in San Rafael, in the central valley of Costa Rica, at the farm outside of town where her father had his little furniture factory.

It was a long, low building, full of exotic wood and hand tools, and the precious electric saw that her father and his workers used for the big cuts.

Beyond the workshop were fields where cows and horses grazed. Renata loved to bring carrots to the horses. And watch the man who milked the cows for her mother.

Her playground was the beautiful garden around their one-story house that was painted a rich brown, with orange trim. And it was surrounded by masses of bougainvillea, heliconia, and hibiscus that attracted flocks of hummingbirds and butterflies. She loved to watch the little birds and the butterflies—and the toucans flying high overhead.

As she wandered through the garden, she could smell the wonderful aroma of sawdust in the factory.

And hear Mama out on the back porch, humming a love song called "Siempre en Mi Corazón," "Always in My Heart," as she put sheets and towels into the washing machine. Renata smiled as she made her way through the garden, picking flowers and taking them to the stone bench under the mimosa tree.

When her bucket was almost full, a tiny movement on the patio made her head whip around. She saw a green iguana basking in the sun. As she came near, it opened its eyes and focused on her.

She went very still. It was just an animal, sunning itself. Yet the yellow unblinking eye she stared at on one side of the iguana's head held an intelligence that sent a shiver skittering over her skin.

She had seen animals watching her before. Maybe a coati or a giant spider or, at night, a bat. As if they had a special interest in a girl named Renata Cordona.

Pressing her hands against her sides to keep them from shaking, she faced the creature.

"What do you want?" she whispered.

She waited with her heart pounding, but the reptile didn't answer, only kept staring at her with that bright yellow eye.

She stood rooted to the spot for many heartbeats, then took a quick step back. The movement released her. Her feet pounding on the grass, she turned and ran back toward the bench, counting her steps, the numbers making her feel safe as she spoke them aloud.

It was a relief to return to the shade of the mimosa tree and the stone bench. Comforting to arrange the stones and the flowers in a pattern on the flat surface.

The pattern was important. An ancient symbol of . . .

Well, she couldn't remember exactly what. But maybe the *señoritas hermosas* would come back and tell her.

She sang as she worked, a little tune she had learned from . . . from the beautiful ladies who used to watch her and talk to her and tell her stories from the old times.

The ladies didn't come to her anymore. They were fading from her memory. The ladies and other things.

They had told her she had a vital task to perform. That the great dance of power was coming to an end, and she must not lose her chance. She struggled to remember what it was. It was from long ago, when she'd been someone else.

And it had something to do with the things she was arranging on the bench.

She put the flowers into a milk bottle Mama had given her. Then she picked up a little plastic bucket and went to gather some more of the rounded rocks along the side of the river. She wandered along the bank, picking up stones that caught her fancy. Some were speckled black and white. Some were dark with a white streak. Some were pure white. All of them felt smooth in her hands and warm from the sun.

She held them up, pretending she was showing them to the ladies.

Smiling, she brought them back and began arranging them around the bottle she was using as a vase, making them clink against the bench as she set them down.

A wolf watched Renata from the shadows of the trees. It was Jacob Marshall. He had come to her house in Ellicott City—drawn back to the woman like a thirsty animal to water. He hadn't known what he was going to see. But not this, certainly.

He'd gone still as a statue when she opened the back door of her house and stepped into the yard, barefoot and wearing a sexy white gown.

He watched the way she walked. Watched her face. And he was pretty sure that she was doing this in her sleep.

She made him think of an ancient priestess. Or a goddess. Yet at the same time, she seemed so vulnerable and unprotected.

But she had nothing to fear. He understood now that he had come here to guard her. He hadn't planned that role, but he stepped into it easily as he watched her from the shadows, afraid to move lest she see that a wolf was only fifteen yards away.

His night vision was excellent, and he could see the way the bodice of the gown cradled her full breasts with their dusky nipples. His gaze skimmed lower to the enticing triangle of dark hair at the top of her legs.

She was carrying a tray in her hands. On it was a mixing bowl and something covered by a cloth. Her arms were outstretched as though she were making an offering of the objects on the tray.

An offering? To whom?

She stood for a moment in the moonlight, then walked across the patio and set down the tray on a stone bench. He heard the bowl slosh a little, and he could tell that it was full of water.

She began walking around the yard, plucking blossoms off of pink, purple, salmon, and white azaleas and placing them carefully in the bowl.

He wanted to creep forward and bump his nose against her legs to see if she would wake up, but he stayed where he was, because if she did come awake, she would be standing next to a gray wolf.

When she finished filling the bowl with flowers, she picked up a small plastic carton from the edge of the patio and walked across the yard, down to the stream that ran along the back of the property.

He kept pace, staying in back of her, wondering what the hell she was doing.

She was asleep. But what did she *think* she was doing?

She was at the stream bank now, looking at the rounded stones that someone had piled there to reinforce the bank.

She stooped down, reaching for the stones, shifting them in her hands, putting some in the carton and discarding others.

Then she started back up the small slope. About halfway up the grass, she stepped on something that made her wince. He froze, thinking she would surely wake up. But after a moment she kept walking.

When she reached the patio, she knelt down in front of the stone bench and began murmuring softly to herself as she took stones out of the carton, arranging them on the flat surface around the bowl with the flowers.

He moved closer, trying to see what she was doing.

She was putting the stones in a circular pattern, moving them around, making some kind of intricate arrangement.

Somehow this scene seemed familiar. As though he had been here before. Watched her do this.

But that was impossible. He had never been to her house any other time. Never seen her outside in a tantalizing white gown.

He moved closer still, reacting to the woman and the setting. He was drawn to her by a powerful surge of need. Of desire that he couldn't articulate.

Drawn like a fox toward a pheasant, he crept forward, step by step.

Renata had just picked up a white stone when her body jerked. She made a small sound as she seemed to come out of her sleep state.

RENATA gasped when she looked down and saw the stone bench. She had bought it at a garden center because it reminded her of home. It was about three feet long, with an ornamental pattern at the edges and two crouching lions that served as the legs, supporting the horizontal surface. But it wasn't the structure that caught her attention now.

She was on her knees in front of it, doing the same thing she had been doing in the dream, making a pattern with flowers and rocks.

Not the tropical flowers of her long-ago home in Costa Rica.

But spring flowers from right here in Maryland. Azalea blossoms—white, purple, pink, and salmon—floating in a bowl of water that she must have brought from the house. Arranged around the bowl was a pattern of river rocks like the ones she remembered from her childhood. Only these were smaller, and she had no idea where they had come from.

As she reared back, something at the corner of her vision made her catch her breath.

The iguana. It had followed her here!

Even when she knew that was impossible, her head jerked around, and she found herself staring at the animal that had saved her from the dogs.

She would know him anywhere, and she was sure he was no dog. He was a wolf.

Why had he saved her? So he could come back and have her for himself? The wolf and Little Red Riding Hood?

Although the thought wasn't entirely rational, she wasn't capable of rational thought at the moment.

Her heart was pounding as she and the animal regarded each other for a long moment.

"What are you doing here?" she asked.

Had she expected him to speak? He stayed silent, but he raised his head slightly.

"What are you? Are you here instead of the iguana?"

Again, he only stared at her.

Then her gaze flicked downward, and she realized that she had brought more than rocks and flowers to the stone bench.

A cloth covered something on the tray, and she knew by the shape that it was her gun.

Unable to see the wolf as a friend, she whipped out her hand, reached under the cloth, and grabbed the Glock. Pointing it at the animal, she fired.

CHAPTER
SIX

BEFORE RENATA COULD pull the trigger, Jacob was already dodging to the side. But the tactic wasn't enough. The hot pain that sliced through his shoulder had him howling in shock.

Jesus Christ, not again!

He'd been shot last year when the Marshalls had mounted a massive effort to stop a homegrown terrorist group from setting off a dirty bomb in Washington, D.C.

Now he fled again, listening for sounds of pursuit.

But Renata didn't follow. Once she'd known she'd scared him off, she'd probably hightailed it into the house.

Didn't she recognize him as the animal that had saved her butt last time? Or didn't she care?

Behind him, he heard a door open. Probably, somebody had heard the shot. If Renata was lucky, they'd convince themselves that it was a car backfiring.

Jacob made it back to the tangle of underbrush where he'd left his clothing.

After stopping to catch his breath, he silently said the chant that turned him from wolf to man. Once he had transformed, he twisted his head to look at his left arm. It was bleeding, but when he cautiously probed it with his finger, he found that the bullet had torn across the skin rather than embedding itself in his flesh.

He wrapped his shirt around his arm and awkwardly tied it in place to stanch the blood. Then he flexed his muscles. As far as he could tell, the damage was minimal. Still, he shouldn't take a chance on getting an infection.

Last time he'd been shot, Ross's wife, Megan, a physician, had treated him. Then he and Ross had been working together. Now he was damned if he was going to go over there with his tail between his legs and explain that he'd been sniffing around a woman who had a gun handy.

Not on your life. Grimly, he pulled on his pants and shoes and tramped through the woods, back to his car, then drove home, wincing every time he had to make a turn.

In his bathroom, he washed off the wound, then he slopped on antiseptic, gritting his teeth at the sting.

But at least the bleeding had mostly stopped. The way the bullet had grazed him, the wound looked more like a gash than like he'd been shot. Finishing the first-aid treatment, he covered it with a sterile gauze pad and tied it on with more gauze.

Now that he didn't have to hold himself together any longer, he crawled into bed and lay in the dark, his body trembling slightly.

"Stop it," he muttered, annoyed by his own physical weakness. As a distraction he tried to focus on what he'd seen.

The image of Renata in that gown had turned him on. Still, he'd been fascinated by what she was doing with those rocks and flowers.

Which brought up the question—if he asked her about it, would she remember?

He made a snorting sound. He couldn't ask her. Because he couldn't admit that he'd been drawn to her house. Or that he'd been spying on her—as a wolf.

It flashed through his mind that she might wonder why Jacob Marshall had the same wound that the wolf had.

Then he shook his head as he realized he was getting way ahead of himself.

She wasn't going to see Jacob Marshall naked, and anyway, she couldn't be sure that she'd hit the wolf—and where.

Although logic told him he should stay away from her, he was too stubborn for that. He couldn't just walk away from a mystery. He wanted to know what kind of woman had the foresight to take a gun on a sleepwalking expedition.

He fell into a fitful sleep, and in a little while he was captured by a dream that had something to do with the pain in his arm.

He struggled to wake up, because that was his only escape from the danger all around him. But the dream held him fast in a world he knew wasn't quite real.

He was a wolf again, back in Renata's garden, standing in the moonlight. But the garden was in another place. The house was gone. As were the woods and the creek. And the edges of the scene were shrouded in mist.

In the background, he thought he saw a massive building, and he shuddered. The place was . . . bad.

He had died there.

What?

The thought was so outrageous that he flicked it away like an insect he had plucked off his fur with his teeth.

Quickly, he turned away from the edifice.

Light filtered down on him. Not from the moon, but from some source he couldn't name. It was cold, chilling him through his thick fur.

He sensed that he was in danger, yet he could see nothing, hear nothing.

He tried to use his wolf's senses to figure out who was stalking him. In the middle of a deep breath, he found he wasn't a wolf any longer. He had changed from animal to man, without being conscious of making the transformation.

The realization was like a punch in the gut. He should

be in charge of the change. Yet some outside force had gone into the cells of his body and altered their structure for him.

He tried to tell himself that it didn't matter because he was only dreaming, but he didn't believe that for a minute. Not when he was standing in this strange place—a naked man.

Another jolt hit him when he realized he wasn't alone. Far away, he heard the sound of a woman's voice. Not just any woman. Renata. She was here. Singing a song in Spanish. "Siempre en Mi Corazón." A lilting love song. Yet he knew she was in danger, too.

The need to protect her was like a burning pain inside him. On the edge of panic, he pounded forward, following the sound of her sweet voice. Iron bands tightened around his chest when he couldn't find her.

"Renata!" he called. "Renata."

She didn't answer. Maybe she didn't even know he was here. Finally, he caught sight of her, standing in front of the stone bench. Only it wasn't the same bench. It was higher, more like a narrow table. And made of marble instead of cement.

She was dressed in the same translucent gown she'd been wearing earlier, and she was doing the same thing— arranging flowers and stones on the horizontal surface the way she had done in the garden. But he saw other things, too. A small dagger that looked like it was made of ivory. A little statue of a woman carved out of light green jade. Two tiny glass bottles with ornate stoppers.

As though she finally realized he was watching her, she went very still. Moving slowly, she put down a pure white stone next to one of the bottles and turned to look at him.

His breath caught as he stared at her. The light came from behind her now, and he could see through the gown as though it weren't there at all.

He saw her beautiful breasts with their tightened nipples. The indentation of her waist. The womanly curve of her hips. The tantalizing dark triangle between her legs.

Her glorious hair flowed down her back in a dark cascade, and her full lips parted in invitation.

He was naked and there was no way to hide his desire for her. It stood out in front of him like a signboard pointing toward her.

He watched her take in his aroused body, and he was glad that he was in good physical shape, that his physique was a worthy match for this goddess.

The word stopped him. He had used it before, but it seemed to take on a more potent meaning. She had the bearing of a divine being. More than a woman.

And he—among all the men on Earth—was the man she had chosen as her mate. They had met by chance. He had come to the sea to dive for pearls, and when he had climbed naked out of the water, she had been standing there, making an offering to the winds and waves.

He shook his head, wondering why he had conjured up that story.

When she called his name, he recognized it. But he wasn't sure it was "Jacob." Maybe it was a name he remembered from long ago—when they had first met.

While he was trying to work his way through that, she held out her hand, and his only choice was to stride forward with confidence.

"I knew you would come," she murmured.

"Yes."

He took charge, then, because he didn't want to feel at a disadvantage with her.

He longed to have her as naked as he was, and he might have ripped the gown off her body. But he didn't want to start their lovemaking with violence.

When he bent down, grabbed the hem, and pulled the garment over her head, she nodded her approval.

As he reached for her, she came into his arms, and they both gasped at the contact of skin against skin.

They had shared a passionate kiss after he had rescued her from the crumbling deck. That seemed like a thousand years ago, and at the same time, it fueled his need for her.

In that moment, he knew he had to taste her again or go mad. With a low sound, he gathered her close, bringing his mouth down to hers.

She was the only thing in the universe that mattered. The only thing that anchored him to reality. If this was reality.

His lips moved urgently, the contact threatening to swamp his senses.

From some unwanted place, a wayward image flashed into his mind, the two of them hurling insults at each other. Each of them intent on inflicting damage.

Confusion stabbed through him, and he knew Renata sensed the change in him.

She moved her mouth so that she spoke against his lips. "What is it, *mi corazón*?"

"Nothing."

He didn't know where the disturbing image of conflict had come from, and he pushed it away. It didn't matter. What mattered was making love with Renata—here and now.

He gazed down at her, smiling reassuringly. Lowering his head, he kissed her softly as his fingers stroked over her face, then her neck and collarbones, savoring the contact.

There was no need to hurry. He knew from the look in her eyes that she was his. Now and forever.

Her hands moved over his back, his shoulders, his hips, pulling his cock more tightly against her.

Then one hand slid to his arm, and she went still. "You're hurt."

"It's nothing."

She drew back, examining the wound. "Who did this to you?"

He swallowed. "You."

"No!"

"It's all right. You didn't know."

"Know what?"

Because he couldn't tell her the truth, he lowered his

mouth to hers again, kissing her with savage urgency, glo-
rying in her response.

She was his. And they both knew it, deep in their souls.

He slid his hands down her arms, circling her wrists
with thumbs and fingers, and his heart leaped in his chest
when he pressed against her flesh and felt her pounding
pulse.

Raising his head, he looked around. He didn't want to
drag her down to the ground. He wanted this first time
with her to be . . . civilized.

The first time?

Yes. The first. For Jacob and Renata.

As the thought of making her his own gathered in his
mind, he found that he was staring over her shoulder at a
beautiful wide bed.

She caught the satisfied expression on his face.

"What?"

"Magic," he said in a thick voice, turning her around so
that her back was pressed to his front.

The magic of dreams.

Her breath caught as she saw the bed. And caught again
as he lifted his hands to cup her full breasts, then stroked
his fingers over the hardened tips.

"Oh!"

He could barely breathe now. Barely keep his body from
trembling.

While he could still stand, he led her to the bed.

They fell together on the silken sheets, horizontal at last.

He grinned at her, and she grinned back. But they both
sobered as he rolled her to her back, his body half covering
hers as he pressed his swollen cock against her thigh.

He wanted to kiss her everywhere. He started with her
breasts. Brushing his lips against the tops, then raising up
so he could move downward, holding the orbs in his hands
as he buried his face between them, breathing in her intoxicating scent while he turned his face one way and then the
other so that he could lick each nipple, then suck one tight
bud into his mouth.

The taste of her made his head spin. New and yet familiar. Exotic and yet the substance of his life.

Her hands came up to cup the back of his head, holding him to her as she combed her fingers through his hair.

He was dizzy with the sensations heating him from the inside out. Yet he wanted more. Craved more.

Seeking the greatest treasure of all, he slid his hand lower, into her hidden folds.

She was plump and slick for him. Ready for sex. Ready for him.

When he dipped two fingers inside her and withdrew, her hips surged upward, begging for more.

"Not just your fingers," she cried out. "I need your cock inside me. Now."

He parted her legs with his knee and claimed her with one powerful thrust.

He heard her catch her breath, and his gaze shot to her face. "Did I hurt you?"

"No. Never."

For a long moment he held himself still, staring down at her in wonder. He was inside her. It was real. And physical. Even when doubt still lurked in some tiny corner of his mind.

But the urgency was greater than the doubt. He began to move inside her, fighting the pressure to let go because he must bring her the same satisfaction that called to him.

She clung to his shoulders, and his hand moved between them, stroking and pressing as he urged her toward completion.

She spoke his name again. Not Jacob. Jalerak. And that sound on her lips made his head swim.

"You know. You always know how to do it for me," she whispered.

Yes, he knew. And the knowledge surged inside him as he felt her tighten around him, heard her cry out in wonder as he took her over the edge.

Her whole body shook as she came, the pleasure capturing him as well and propelling him into a blinding climax as the joy of finding her again surged through him.

QUESTABAZE watched in growing horror. It was all going wrong. And he had to stop it.

Jacob Marshall was making love to her. In a dream. Yet it might as well have been reality because it was real for the two of them.

"No!" he shouted. "No." And his voice was like a curse, ringing in the dream world, ringing in the still air and transmitting itself to the lovers.

He felt Renata's body jerk. Heard pain well up in her throat—and Jacob's as he turned their joy to agony.

Questabaze made a sound of satisfaction. He knew that he had won a temporary victory.

But he also knew he was only putting out a brush fire. There was something about Jacob Marshall that he didn't understand. The man was more than he appeared to be.

And Questabaze had better find out what it was because he *would not* lose this battle. He came from a world where the weak served the strong. Where you could be snuffed out of existence in a moment if you made the wrong move. Where the only security came from power. He had learned that lesson well. And he was prepared to do whatever it took to keep the power he had won over the centuries.

FROM one heartbeat to the next, a blast of pain grabbed Jacob by the throat, choked off his breath. Twisted like knives in his gut.

Panic seized him, and when he looked down at Renata, he saw the same panic and pain mirrored on her face.

"What have you done?" he shouted.

"No . . . thing," she answered, in a shaky voice, even as he felt her hands pushing against his shoulders, pushing him away, severing the intimate connection between them, because that was the only way to end the horror that consumed them.

He rolled away from her, gasping, his vision blurred, his head pounding as though a thunderstorm were raging inside his skull, the forks of lightning digging into the soft tissue of his brain.

He clawed at his head, trying to stop the agony. But he couldn't reach inside.

Her eyes were wide. "You did this."

"No."

"You."

He tried again to deny it, but he knew she wasn't listening to him. Then a circle of flames sprang up around them, enclosing the bed. And when it did, the pain stopped.

He didn't know where the fire had come from. Before he could ask Renata, the scene snapped off.

He was Jacob Marshall. Nobody else. Back in his own bed. Back in the world he knew. He lay panting in the darkness, his body drenched in sweat, the sheets tangled around his legs, and his lungs burning as he fought to drag in air.

The dream flashed back to him. The pain and the fire.

A warning that he should stay away from Renata Cordona.

Only, he didn't think he could follow his own advice.

CHAPTER
SEVEN

RENATA AWOKE WITH a headache at six thirty and vague feelings of uneasiness. She'd dreamed . . .

Well, she couldn't remember what, exactly. Her memories were hazy. She had the sense of something good. Maybe. But the ending had been bad.

Stretching, she moved her left arm and froze. She'd tied herself to the bedpost, and when her head whipped to the left, she saw the rope was still dangling from the post—but her wrist was no longer attached.

As she focused on the cord, the earlier part of the night came zinging back to her. She'd been out in the garden arranging flowers and rocks on the stone bench.

Apparently, she'd carefully untied her wrist before getting out of bed. Add that to the list of things she could do in her sleep.

With a little start, she recalled the next part.

"*Dios mio,*" she muttered as her gaze jerked to the dresser, where she'd put her gun. It stared back at her.

She'd fired at the wolf, then staggered upstairs, slammed the gun onto the wooden surface, and fallen back into bed. In the morning light, she longed to add the wolf to the category of "dream." But honesty made her admit that she'd woken up before she saw him and had gotten him mixed up with the iguana from the dream.

He'd been real. Well, at least she thought he was real. She winced. She'd fired in the moonlight and seen him jump as he dashed away.

But he'd kept running. So maybe he wasn't badly injured. Or maybe she'd find his body outside.

She clenched her teeth, then silently asked herself another question.

What was he doing at her house? Was he prowling around the neighborhood—happening to meet up with her for the second time in twelve hours?

Or had he come looking for her? And how would he know where to find her?

She had no answer for any of the questions, and she almost pulled on her robe and rushed outside to see if there was blood on the ground. But she stopped herself.

Part of her wanted to confirm that she'd hit him, and part of her cringed at the very idea.

Deliberately staying inside, she walked down the hall to her home office and booted up her computer. When it was ready, she Googled "Howard County, Maryland" and "wolf" but couldn't find anything. And she wasn't going to try her strange story on anyone in the county government. Particularly since she didn't want to end up explaining why she'd fired a gun in a residential neighborhood. Luckily, she'd aimed toward the woods, and so far nobody had come knocking at her door, demanding to know what had happened.

Should she lock up her gun when she was home? And should she talk to her boss, Barry Prescott, about it?

Was that a business question or a personal one?

Maybe both.

She sighed. At first, she'd vowed to stick to their cases with him, but he was such a sympathetic listener that she'd started opening up about her life. He knew about her parents dying. And about James and Miguel. And he'd told her about how the death of his wife had devastated him.

They'd shared the sadness that they rarely talked about, and that had brought her closer to him. She'd felt like she could confide in him—and he'd given her good advice.

But lately she'd been keeping secrets, and she wondered if he sensed it.

With a sigh, she checked her mail and was relieved to find a message from Barry saying that he was expecting her that morning.

Good. At least something was working out the way it was supposed to.

That thought lasted until she got up from the computer and remembered the rest of the dream.

The part about Jacob Marshall.

Dios! That part.

She had pushed it to the back of her mind, and suddenly, it had leaped out at her—as effectively as the wolf.

In her dream, the man had sauntered into her garden like he owned it. No, not her garden. She'd been standing in front of an altar, in some place outside time and space.

And he had come there to make love to her.

Every detail of that encounter came crashing back on her in one tremendous wave of sensation, and she staggered on the rug and sat down heavily in the desk chair to keep from falling over.

Jacob Marshall had made love to her, and it had been so real that she could still remember the feel of him, the taste, his wonderful cock inside her.

And something else. She'd called him by another name. What was it? She couldn't remember now. But with the name had come memories of other times they had met and made love. Many times.

The same memories had assaulted her earlier, too. When he'd kissed her—after the deck collapsed.

So was that another sign that she was going mad? Like the sleepwalking? And the strange ceremonies in the garden?

And the pain and the fire at the end of the dream. After the explosive climax.

She shook her head violently. No!

She was fine. Or she *would* be fine.

She clenched her fists, breathing hard while she fought off her fear. As she strode to the bathroom, she counted her steps, the numbers soothing her. She took a bottle of over-the-counter pain pills from the medicine cabinet. She'd read about the side effects of all of the products on the market. So she had a whole array of little bottles, and when she needed something, she switched them around.

After washing down the pill, she dressed quickly in jeans and a tee shirt, then went downstairs to fix breakfast, before she ended up with an upset stomach along with the headache.

First she used her one-cup pot to brew herself some of the imported Costa Rican coffee that made her feel closer to home.

While she sipped the coffee, she got rice and beans out of the refrigerator. At breakfast, Mama had often mixed them with eggs. So she took the time to scramble an egg and stir it in.

She'd heated the rice and beans in the microwave. A very modern appliance. She loved modern conveniences, but she knew that her soul was old. And her mind often turned to ancient systems of belief that had been handed down through the centuries. She'd studied many subjects that modern thinkers might dismiss as bunk. Like astrology. And numerology. And tarot cards.

Could she use some of that knowledge to find out more about Jacob Marshall?

She didn't know his birthday, so she couldn't look up his horoscope, and she had always thought it was a mistake to do a tarot card reading for someone who wasn't in the room with her. But there was another method she could try. She knew his name—and a name could be a powerful symbol of the man.

Many ancient peoples believed that the name of a thing

was its essence. Sometimes, in order to kill or injure an enemy they would write his name on a piece of pottery or wax tablet, along with a death curse—then bury the object.

Did Jacob have a secret name that only a few relatives knew? Probably not, because few people still believed that knowing a person's real name gave you power over him.

And of course, she wasn't going to curse him.

She went back to her office and got out a numerology book. It had two different alphabet tables. One was modern. The other was based on the Hebrew alphabet with some additions from the Greek to fill in missing letters like "J." That was the one she liked best because of its ancient roots.

Back in the kitchen, she pushed her breakfast out of the way and used the Hebrew table to assign numbers to each letter of Jacob's name. They added up to thirty-six. Taking the next step, she added the three and the six together and got nine—his basic number.

In another section of the book, she looked up the characteristics of people with that number. The first line of the description made her laugh out loud. Apparently, Jacob Marshall was supposed to have high mental and spiritual achievements. He was also supposed to be romantic, passionate, creative, and charming.

Other attributes leaped out at her. Strong-willed, determined, a person eager to improve the world, a maverick.

And the book noted that President Kennedy and President Lincoln had both been nines.

She could do worse, she thought, then hauled herself up short. What was she thinking? She hadn't dug up this information because she was planning to have a relationship with Jacob Marshall. She just wanted some clues to his personality.

She went back to the descriptions—this time reading the "warning" sections and found that he fell in and out of love easily. Well, that wasn't a good sign!

Again, she wondered why she cared. Then another thought struck her.

Was all this stuff with his name a subconscious bid to prove to herself that he really was Jacob Marshall—and not some guy she'd met a thousand years ago?

Closing the book with a snap, she looked down at the mostly uneaten meal on the table.

Or was she just fooling around in here to avoid going outside?

After carrying the dishes to the sink, she walked onto the patio. As soon as she stepped into the open air, she went very still, looking in all directions, half expecting to see the wolf watching from the woods down by the creek.

Deliberately, she flicked her gaze to the garden bench. The flowers and the stones lay where she had left them.

She stopped to look down at the arrangement, squinting as she studied it.

She'd been hoping to dissociate herself from whatever she was doing in her sleep. Now she tried to think about what her nighttime activity might mean.

She'd read a lot about symbols—in ancient cultures and in mythology. Take stones, for example. There was a wealth of religious meaning and superstition surrounding them.

You could go all the way back to the massive stones arranged in a pattern at Stonehenge. And beyond.

Rocks were symbols of permanence. In ancient times, they had even been called the bones of the earth. And because they lasted through time, they were a representation of life force.

There was a Greek legend of a flood, much like the story of Noah in the Bible. Only in the Greek story, the human couple who survived threw stones over their shoulder to create a new human race.

But there were darker uses for stones, too. Like the ancient Hebrew practice of stoning a condemned person to death. Andromeda had been bound to a stone, awaiting the sea monster. And in Fiji, sacrificial victims had their skulls crushed with stones.

She shuddered, struggling to banish that image. It was much better to see stones as symbols of eternal life.

That's why they were used as grave markers.

She had all that information at her fingertips. That and more. But she wasn't sure what good it did her. Just the way she wasn't sure how working out Jacob's name in numerology terms helped her.

She pushed Jacob out of her mind and went back to the arrangement on the bench.

If stones symbolized permanence, flowers were just the opposite. They budded, bloomed, and died, all in a short period of time—condensing the cycle of birth, life, and death into each blossom.

Of course, they could also be erotic symbols. She grinned as she thought of the way the artist, Georgia O'Keeffe, had depicted flowers. Close up and in detail—in ways that suggested female genitals.

That would have shocked the Victorians, who had come up with much more innocent meanings for various flowers.

Red roses and tulips were a declaration of love. Blue violets symbolized faithfulness. White lilies denoted sweetness.

She studied the azalea blossoms lying on the bench.

In Victorian terms, they stood for first love. And temperance.

She made a dismissive sound. Certainly, neither of those had anything to do with Jacob Marshall.

Had she picked azaleas because they meant something specific? Or because they were easy to find at this time of year?

Probably the latter.

After one last look at the cement bench, she strode farther into the yard, where the grass was sparse under the trees. In the dirt, she thought she could identify the spot where the wolf had been standing. There were faint depressions in the lawn, then marks where he'd turned and run.

Which brought up another interesting observation. Now that she remembered the scene, it seemed like the wolf had known she had picked up a gun and pointed it at him.

Just as she'd started to fire, he'd fled.

Could an animal understand guns? Maybe, if someone had shot at him before. But the sequence of events still seemed strange.

She walked a little farther. In some places, she saw his tracks, and at the edge of the stream, they were very clear in the soft mud.

He'd kept to this side of the stream, so she followed his trail along the backyards, until she lost it in a tangle of underbrush.

Searching around, she saw something that made her go stock-still.

A man's naked footprint.

As Renata stared at it, her mind went back to the day before—to Jacob Marshall. He'd been barefoot yesterday, and he'd appeared at the vacant house right after the wolf had chased away the dogs.

Then a detail from the erotic dream with him zinged into her mind. In their encounter, Jacob had been naked. And he'd had a wound on his arm. He'd told her she'd done it to him.

She blinked, trying to work her way through that.

If she'd shot the wolf, then she'd also shot Jacob. At least that was what the dream seemed to say.

So what did that mean? That the wolf belonged to him? And he'd been with the animal yesterday. And last night?

She stared at the footprint, her head spinning. She knew she was jumping to conclusions. No way could she assume that Jacob Marshall had made this print.

A wild scheme leaped into her head. She'd go to his house and poke around. If he was toughening his feet, he was probably walking outside a lot. Maybe she could get a cast of his footprint and compare it to this one.

She sighed.

And how would she explain what she was doing if he caught her snooping around?

Searching the ground a little more, she saw that the barefoot man had put on running shoes.

Weird.

She followed the running shoe tracks, where they finally came out on the street and disappeared onto the sidewalk.

Dead end.

She was a block from home when she glanced at her watch and realized that she didn't have much time before she had to meet Detective Newcastle out at the property she'd been showing yesterday.

So she hurried home, brushed her hair, and put on a little makeup, hating herself for feeling like she had to fix herself up for Newcastle. On the other hand, she'd learned that she could use her femininity as an advantage in dealing with him.

Ten minutes later, she was in her car—and still wondering how much she was going to say to the detective.

FROM near the end of the block, Jacob watched Renata pull out of her driveway. As she headed down the street, he stayed well back, because the last thing he wanted her to know was that he was following her.

He'd come here early this morning, and he'd seen her go into the backyard and follow the path that the wolf had taken the night before. The wolf and the man. Because after that tangle of brambles, the wolf tracks had changed to human tracks.

Damn!

What was Renata going to make of *that*? Or had he left tracks? He didn't know because after she'd shot him, he'd been focused on getting out of there.

He pulled his attention back to Renata. The woman might have been sleepwalking the night before. This morning she was functioning like a private investigator.

After about ten minutes, he knew he could stop guessing about her destination. She was going back to the house where she'd been showing the day before. When he saw an unmarked cop car turn into the driveway ahead of her, he figured she'd reported the incident with the dogs and was meeting the law out here.

Had she also mentioned meeting Jacob Marshall when she'd talked to the cops? He'd like to know.

Driving past the entrance to the property, he turned around. He longed to go in as a wolf and listen to her conversation with the cop, but he wasn't going to chance getting shot again. Instead, he waited on a side road where he could watch the driveway—and think about the night before. About the vivid dream where he'd made love to Renata.

It had been glorious, until the blinding pain at the end.

Had she had the same dream?

No, that was a crazy thought. People didn't share dreams. Or did a werewolf share dreams with his life mate?

Jacob's hands clenched around the steering wheel, as he tried to drive the life mate notion from his mind.

CHAPTER
EIGHT

RENATA PULLED TO a stop in front of the house. New-castle was right behind her.

He got out of his car and marched over, like he was a patrol officer who had pulled her over for a traffic stop. His blond hair was military short. And he had on those aviator sunglasses that cops liked, so she couldn't see his eyes. Perfect.

One thing she could say for him: he was neat and trim, in a tweed sports jacket, blue button-down shirt, and charcoal slacks. Would he develop a belly in a few years, or would he keep up his schedule at the gym?

Breaking the pattern of the encounter, she climbed out and turned to face him.

"How you doin'?" he asked.

"Fine," she answered, hoping the concealer she'd swiped under her eyes hid the dark circles.

"So you had some trouble out here yesterday," he said.

"Some."

"Show me where you saw the dogs."

She led him toward the garage. "I was here."

"And the dogs were where?"

"Over here," she said, feeling her chest tighten.

She walked to the spot where she thought they had been standing and saw tracks in the dirt.

"And another dog chased them off?" he said.

"Yes."

He gave her a considering look. "Lucky for you. Can you tell me what happened—exactly?"

She swallowed. "I was kind of scared, so I wasn't paying a lot of attention. First the pack of dogs appeared. Then the other canine."

"Did they have collars?"

She considered that. "A couple of them might have." As she answered, she was thinking about the wolf. She was sure he didn't have a collar. Should she tell Newcastle she thought it was a wolf—not a dog?

Maybe she'd keep that to herself.

"Let me show you where I found the meat," she said instead.

"How did you find it?"

She should have considered the answer. Making another snap decision, she said, "I just stumbled on it."

Without further comment, she started off into the weeds toward the spot where Jacob had showed her the cuts of beef.

When she got to the location, she stopped short.

"What?"

She gestured toward the ground. "It was here."

"Are you sure?"

"Yes."

She squatted down, moved the tall grass around, and found a place where a clot of blood had stuck to a couple of blades. Pulling them out of the ground, she held them toward him. "See."

He took the grass and turned it in the light.

"The dogs could have come back in the night and eaten it. Or some other animals."

She nodded and stood again, looking at the grass. "If they came back, wouldn't the grass be more messed up?"

"Probably."

She and Newcastle stood regarding each other.

"You should have met me back here yesterday," he said.

"I didn't think I needed to."

"Now the meat's gone." Changing the subject abruptly, he said, "So no real progress on the case."

"You mean from your end?" she challenged.

"Yeah. And yours, too, it looks like."

"We'll keep in touch," she said. "You let me know if you have any leads."

"You like putting yourself in danger?"

She shrugged. "It's my job." Glancing at her watch, she added. "I have an appointment. And I also have a call to make."

"I can take a hint."

They both walked back to their cars, and Newcastle drove away.

He'd said they were both on the same side. Sometimes she felt like he was rooting for her to be the killer's next victim.

Maybe to prove that the vacant property didn't give her the creeps, Renata sat in her car for a few minutes, although she did lock her doors.

Just as she was about to leave, a car came roaring up the driveway, and she reached for the gun in her bag.

WHEN Renata saw the face of the man in the car, she pulled her hand back out of her purse.

Too bad she hadn't left right away. She'd set herself up for a confrontation with Lou Deverel, the guy with the Star Realty maintenance contract. He came across as a jerk, but he was crafty. He liked to work behind the scenes, stabbing you in the back when he was presenting something very different to your face.

Still, it looked like he wasn't going to bother being nice this morning.

As soon as he stopped his car, he jumped out and

barreled toward her, his shoulders tense. Dressed in jeans, a blue tee shirt with a picture of a beaver on the front, and work boots, he was a giant of a man, with prematurely gray hair that he couldn't keep under control. His blue eyes were shooting sparks as he approached her. She climbed out of her own car and raised her head, meeting his gaze.

"You're here," he said. "I didn't expect you to have the guts to come back."

"What's that supposed to mean?"

Instead of showing any concern about what had happened to her the day before, he demanded, "What did you do to the deck?"

Resisting the urge to ball her hands into fists and wedge them on her hips, she said, "Nothing."

"It was okay until you arrived."

"How do you know? When was the last time you were here?"

His face darkened. "I don't make a regular tour of the properties."

"Well, all I did was walk out onto it. And it gave way under me. Maybe there's recent termite damage. This place has been vacant for months."

He ignored the comment and asked, "Were you authorized to go out onto the deck?"

Hijo de puta, she thought. Son of a bitch. But she didn't say it out loud. He was the kind of guy who wasn't going to admit his own mistakes—who was going to pin the blame on somebody else if he could manage it.

"What do you mean, authorized?" she asked in a deliberately calm voice. "I was doing my job, showing the house. The deck was part of the property. Of course I walked out onto it."

He kept his gaze fixed on her. "Are you saying a customer was with you when the deck collapsed?"

"No. He wasn't there yet."

"Then what were you doing out there?"

"Oh, come on. I was looking around the property so I'd be familiar with it when he arrived."

She no longer had the key, so she couldn't take him through the house. "You can come around and look at it."

He stayed where he was. "If you're at fault, it's coming out of your commissions."

"Nice try. But this isn't on me," she answered, unable to keep from matching his angry manner. "The structure of a deck is supposed to be sound."

He glared at her.

Dick Trainer had warned her about Deverel, and she'd already had a run-in with him after a client had tossed her a curveball and brought five kids along to a house she was showing him. While she'd been touring the upstairs with the father, the kids had run wild, smeared mud on the living room walls, and broken the door of a kitchen cabinet.

She'd been inexperienced in real estate protocol. As soon as she'd realized what was happening, she should have told the client that he needed to come back without the kids.

Deverel had been furious, and he'd made such a stink that she'd ended up paying part of the repair costs.

This time she knew that the homeowner was responsible. "Don't get angry with me," she said, punching out the words. "I didn't do anything besides step on a structure that should have been fine. You can do the repair work and send the bill to the homeowners."

"What if they don't want to pay?"

"Get authorization first. Or work it out with Dick," she said. Then, very deliberately, she got back into her car. As she drove away, she could feel Deverel's malevolent gaze on her, and she couldn't help wondering if he'd had something to do with the deck collapsing.

But why?

Did he know she was working undercover, and he wanted to get her off the job? But how would he have found out, since she knew Dick wouldn't have told him. Or would he?

She made a face, annoyed she was so off balance that she was suspecting everyone in sight.

She needed to get a grip on herself, and going to see Barry would help. He always had a grounding effect on her.

JACOB leaned forward over the steering wheel. The cop had left. But a few minutes ago, another car had barreled up the driveway.

The other guy was apparently still there, and Renata was coming back—alone.

Jacob breathed out a small sigh and wished he could see her expression.

Since he was too far away for that, all he could do was wait until she'd gotten a little head start before pulling out and following her. While they were on the country road, he had to stay well back. As soon as they hit Route 40, he was able to fit himself into traffic and follow along behind her, putting a couple of cars between them so she wouldn't spot him.

This time she headed straight down the highway and kept going toward the west side of Baltimore.

The area along the highway was run-down. Older shopping centers were populated by liquor stores, fast-food restaurants, and dollar emporiums.

But on the side streets, in a suburb called Catonsville, the atmosphere improved. He followed her onto a street where the businesses gave way to single-family homes, although some of the houses had been converted into offices.

He passed a dentist, a chiropractor, and a dog grooming service.

Renata pulled into the driveway of a two-story brick house. As he drove past, he saw the sign hanging on the light post and blinked.

It read: BARRY PRESCOTT, PRIVATE DETECTIVE.

Jesus.

So why did she need a private detective? Had she contacted the guy recently? Or was he a client of hers?

He kept driving to a nearby recreation area.

Pulling into a parking space, he looked around. An old couple were sitting on a bench. And two teenagers looked like they were trying to swallow each other's tongues in one of the picnic areas. At least he didn't see any dogs.

He got out of his car and walked rapidly down a path, thinking that a wolf could get closer to Barry Prescott's place than a man.

Of course, changing in broad daylight in an exposed location was risky. But that was his only chance to find out what Renata was up to.

Trying not to look suspicious, he disappeared into the woods, downhill toward a ravine.

As he plunged farther into the trees, he didn't stop to question why he was being so reckless. Finally, he came to an outcropping of rock and decided it was going to have to do.

RENATA picked up the mug of hot water she'd heated in the microwave and walked to the shelf where Barry kept his stock of imported teas.

She was conscious of him behind of her, watching. Sometimes he did that and waited for her to say whatever was on her mind. She knew it was a PI technique—one she'd used herself on many occasions.

Glad of the excuse to keep her back to him, she selected a Yorkshire Gold tea bag and slid it into the mug, then stirred. When the brew had turned golden brown, she took out the bag and carefully dropped it into the trash can. Then she put in a spoonful of buckwheat honey and some of the half-and-half that was always in the refrigerator.

When she turned, he smiled at her encouragingly but still said nothing.

Maybe she'd tell him about the wolf. But she wasn't going to talk about her sleepwalking. That was more than she could handle.

* * *

AFTER changing to wolf form, Jacob skirted the edge of the park and found that a stream valley led back toward the PI's house.

Through a sliding glass door, he saw Renata and a man in a wood-paneled office. The guy was behind a desk, his profile to the door, and Renata was sitting in a leather armchair facing him.

Jacob had to assume he was the PI, Prescott. So what was Renata's business with him?

Slipping from tree to tree, Jacob moved closer.

The guy looked to be in his late fifties or early sixties, with salt-and-pepper hair and weathered skin. He was wearing a burgundy V-neck sweater over a blue button-down shirt. All he needed was a pipe to complete the picture. Instead, he picked up a mug from the desk and sipped.

Renata also had a mug of something. Which was good, because getting the stuff had probably slowed down the conversation.

"How was your visit with Elizabeth?" she asked.

"She's fine. She fixed me an oven stuffer roaster." He made an appreciative sound, but kept his gaze steady. "But you're not here to talk about my daughter."

"Well, I was hoping your visit went well."

"It did." He took a sip from his mug. "But you seem troubled."

Under his steady gaze, she shifted in her seat. "Those dogs unnerved me."

"The way you described the incident, they'd do it to anyone." He set down his mug. "Do you have any ideas about how they got there?"

Jacob's hearing was excellent, and he had no trouble following the conversation.

Renata shook her head. "Maybe it wasn't directed at me—specifically. Maybe someone wants that house to stay on the market."

"Why?" he asked.

She shrugged. "I'd have to dig into the background of the sellers and maybe their neighbors. What if someone has a beef with them, pardon the pun? Or maybe a developer is after the property and wants to lower the price before he buys."

"Those are possibilities," the detective observed.

They were both silent for several moments. Renata looked uncomfortable. Prescott stayed relaxed, waiting for her to say something else.

Finally, like a therapist, not a PI, he asked, "Is there anything else you want to tell me?"

Jacob watched her lean forward, her face earnest. And her words jolted him.

"I don't want to screw up this assignment," she said.

What assignment?

"You won't."

"It's hard for me to play real estate agent," she said. "I keep thinking about the undercover job, not what a real estate agent would be saying to the clients."

Jacob crept closer.

"Don't beat yourself up," Prescott said.

"But what if another woman gets murdered? It will be my fault."

The detective shook his head. "Of course not. You can't know where the guy will strike. All you can do is show properties where the situation fits the pattern."

"We don't even know if it was someone the women were showing the house to using a false name. Or someone who had access to the records at the real estate office. Or someone who followed the women there."

"At least now, everybody who has an appointment has to show a picture ID."

"Which could still be faked," she argued. "A killer wouldn't give his real name."

"Everybody in the company will be thankful when you nail the bastard."

"Will I?"

"You're well trained. You know what you're doing. If anybody can catch this guy—it's you."

As he listened, Jacob had been doing a fast reassessment

of his previous assumptions. Renata was working for the detective. Which explained why she'd gone outside armed, even when she was sleepwalking.

But back to her assignment. It sounded like she was trying to lure the perp into the open by acting as bait.

A wave of fear and anger caught him by surprise, choking off his breath.

Renata was putting herself in danger. He wanted to protect her, and at the same time, he wanted to strangle her for doing something so rash.

He started forward, not even sure what he was planning to do.

Just as Jacob stepped onto the patio, the man talking to Renata climbed out of his chair and started toward the window.

Jacob turned and ran around the corner of the house, wondering if the guy had spotted him, or if he'd gotten away.

He thought he heard the door open, but he kept running, taking a chance on dashing between the houses and down the street.

Halfway along the block, he saw a woman leaning over a baby carriage. Damn.

To avoid crashing into her, he ducked between the next set of houses and found his way blocked by a picket fence. His only choice was to gather himself for a mighty leap. He managed to jump over the barrier, and landed in a yard where a miniature poodle started barking its head off, announcing the presence of the interloper.

Grimly, he kept going, dashing to the end of the property, over another fence, and into the woods.

RENATA followed Barry onto the patio.

Her chest tightened as she watched the rigid set of his shoulder.

"What did you see?" she asked as she looked around, searching for movement in the underbrush.

Barry made a frustrated sound. "I'm not sure."

"Do you think someone tailed me here?" she asked.

He glanced toward the doors again. "I don't think it was a person out there."

She felt a stab of alarm. "A dog? A wolf?"

"I don't know," he answered, then gave her a sharp look. "A wolf? Where did you get that idea?"

CHAPTER
NINE

RENATA HEAVED IN a sigh and let it out. Although she'd tried to avoid the subject, she'd trapped herself. "The big dog that chased the other ones away looked like a wolf."

"Maybe it was a German shepherd," he suggested.

"Maybe." Barry hadn't seen the animal, so there was no point in arguing with him about it.

They went back inside and she resumed her seat, then continued, "It could have been a deer out there. There are a lot of them around, and your house backs onto the woods."

Barry nodded.

They sat in silence for several moments, and she felt herself swallow hard.

He looked at her with concern. "What are you not telling me?"

"You know me pretty well."

"Yeah. You're like my daughter. You keep stuff to yourself when you should open up."

"It's hard for me to confide in people."

"I know. But it's better if you get it off your chest."

She shrugged, suddenly thinking about all her secrets.

Would Barry fire her if he knew she was in the habit of counting her steps as a kind of ritual protective measure?

And then there was the sleepwalking, a more recent development. She tried not to think about last night's dream, when she'd made wild, passionate love with Jacob Marshall. She certainly didn't want to open herself up to such a personal discussion. She'd never talked about her sex life with Barry and she wasn't going to start now.

Her sex life! It had just been a dream. But it had seemed so potent. Probably because there weren't any real lovers in her life. And that's how she wanted it.

"What are you thinking about?" Barry asked.

She felt a flush spread across her cheeks. Fighting to come up with an answer, she said, "A guy named Jacob Marshall showed up right after the dog attack. He had a story about why he was in the area. But I had the feeling he wasn't telling the truth."

Barry looked thoughtful. "Jacob Marshall, doesn't he work with dogs?"

"Yes."

"Could he have gotten the dogs to attack you?"

She felt a shiver go over her skin. "I don't know."

"Maybe we should get some more background on him. One thing I've thought is that he's living above his income."

"You've done some checking up on him?"

Barry shrugged. "I did background on all of the men who came to those meetings on Howard County services."

Although Renata nodded, she didn't want to put the whole focus on Jacob Marshall. Maybe he really had shown up innocently.

"He wasn't the only one connected with the incident," she said.

"Who else?"

"The client I was meeting was named Kurt Lanagan." Reaching into her purse, she brought out a copy of the sheet he'd filled out at the real estate office. "I guess you should start off by verifying that that's really his name."

"Yeah." Barry read through the information. "He's looking for high-end properties."

"That's what he says. But he found a lot of things wrong with the house. Besides the deck, I mean." She shifted in her chair. "Did you check Lou Deverel's background?"

"The maintenance man, right?"

"Yes."

Barry pulled out a folder and flipped it open. "He has a record for domestic violence."

"Oh, does he?"

"You don't like him."

"That's right. He's given me a hard time more than once, and he likes to assert his authority over women."

"That doesn't make him the killer."

"But it certainly puts him on the suspect list, and if you think about it, he's got access to the properties. He's even got a legitimate reason to be there. So what if we're going in the wrong direction? What if the perp isn't a client but someone who works for Star Realty—or someone who has access to the Star Realty schedule of appointments?"

"You could be on to something," Barry allowed. "I'll dig into Dick Trainer's background, too."

"But he hired us."

"That could just be a smoke screen."

JACOB pushed through the change and quickly pulled on his clothes, then slapped his right fist into his left palm. He'd lost his head and gotten too close to the house, and Prescott had spotted him.

Or maybe not.

He gave a bark of a laugh. Even if the detective had seen something. It was a wolf or a big dog—not a man.

But however that part shook out, Jacob had gotten to the point where he needed some advice, and if he had some questions about a private detective, he knew where to go for answers: his cousin Ross, who was also in the PI business.

His relationship with Ross was a little rocky. He didn't really like the way his cousin had stepped in and started calling the shots in the family.

But Jacob was going to use the connection, because it was convenient.

Returning to his car, he fished the cell phone out of the glove compartment and called Ross.

His cousin answered on the second ring.

"Hello?"

"This is Jacob," he said, sure that Ross already knew that from his caller ID before answering.

"Nice to hear from you."

"Likewise." Getting right to the point, he said, "I need to ask you some questions about a PI named Barry Prescott."

"How did you get tangled up with him?"

"Renata Cordona is working for him. It turns out they're investigating some murders of women real estate agents in the Howard County area. She's on point. Apparently, he's sitting back and letting a woman put herself in danger while he does the paperwork."

His assertion was followed by several moments of silence.

Ross cleared his throat. "Who is Renata Cordona?"

The hesitation and the question made Jacob realize he'd launched into an explanation without thinking through the implications.

Hastily, he backed up. "I met her at a Howard County citizens' meeting called to discuss funding for essential services. I thought she was a real estate agent, but she's really a private detective working for Prescott."

"Uh-huh."

He had the feeling he was digging himself into a hole. And he was as deep as he wanted to go. At least he hadn't started talking about meeting her in a dream, for God's sake.

"Prescott's got a daughter named Elizabeth," he blurted. "So is she married? Divorced?"

Mercifully, Ross didn't ask why that was relevant.

"I'll see what I can find out."

"Appreciate it," Jacob said, then got off the phone quickly.

His hands were cold and clammy. He'd given more away than he intended, and he was angry with himself. Angry that he'd let Ross know that he was interested in Renata and angry that he cared what his cousin thought.

If she was his life mate, then the whole clan was going to know about it soon enough, because he'd stake his claim on her.

That stopped him short. Was he really letting his thinking drift in the direction of "life mate"?

Yeah, he was.

He pictured the pleasure on his mother's face when she found out he was settling down. She wanted all her boys happily mated. And she wanted to mitigate her own sadness. Her infant daughters had all died because only males could survive the werewolf chromosome. But Ross's wife Megan had changed that equation. And now Jacob's mom was looking forward to granddaughters as well as grandsons.

His father was another matter. He was from the older generation of Marshall werewolves and set in his ways. He wanted things to stay the way they had always been. He'd be smug when he found out Jacob had met his mate. He could just hear him saying, "Now you'll find out how much it costs and how much work it is to raise a family."

Damn him.

The old man was a lawyer, of all things. He'd been a decent father, compared to Ross's dad who was a garage mechanic and a thief. He'd had enough money to feed and clothe his family—and pay for a college education for his sons. But Jacob wasn't looking forward to the "I told you so" look on his face when he heard another one of his cubs had mated.

Still, if Renata was his life mate, he was stuck with it. Even when he didn't trust her.

He wasn't even sure where the mistrust came from. Of

course she'd lied about being a real estate agent. But keeping her assignment secret was part of her job. So was setting herself up as a target for a serial killer.

That thought made his insides suddenly feel like they'd been bathed in acid.

He had to protect her, and maybe the way to do that was to solve the case for her.

Were the women who'd been killed all working for the same company? Or what?

He drove home and put her name into one of the computer databases where you could look up personal information.

He found that she owned a house in Catonsville but was also renting the house in Howard County.

Which meant that she wasn't very good at covering her tracks. Of course, maybe she didn't have to be, since the killer wouldn't suspect she worked for anyone besides Star Realty.

Should he go over to their office? What was the best approach?

He couldn't walk in and pretend to be looking for a house, since he already had one, and he had no intention of moving.

But maybe he could be looking for investment property.

And what if he ran into Renata while he was there? Well, she didn't know he'd been following her around. So it should be all right.

He took it a step further. What would he do at the realty office? Look at lists of properties for sale? Really, what he wanted to see was a list of men who had been shown houses by the agents who had been killed. Of course the police would already have done that. And eliminated any suspects who had been stupid enough to check in.

So what was Jacob going to do? Break in after hours and prowl through their computer records?

He was turning over his options when his cell phone rang.

The caller ID said that it was the Central Maryland

Animal Alliance, a privately funded organization that accepted strays and dogs and cats who had lost their home.
Unfortunately, their space was limited, so they did have to
euthanize some animals.

As soon as he answered, he found he had the bad luck to
be talking to Doug Davenport, the assistant director.

He and Jacob had clashed on a number of occasions,
because Davenport wanted to be the big expert in animal
behavior; only it had turned out that Jacob knew more
about the subject than the staffer.

"What can I do for you?" Jacob asked.

"We have a pit bull that chewed on a kid. We may have
to put him down."

Jacob had been primed to dive into the murder case.
Now Davenport was giving him a chance to think instead
of plunging recklessly ahead.

After turning off his computer, he got back into his car
and drove over to the facility, which was at the edge of an
industrial park in Columbia. Or what was called "industrial" in that city. Zoning laws didn't permit any large-scale
manufacturing plants or polluters, but there were modern
warehouse buildings with outlets for companies that sold
home products like kitchen cabinets, flooring, and furniture. There were also computer repair facilities, print
shops, and a couple of biotech labs.

Most of the buildings were lined up in long rows, with
truck loading docks next to customer entrances.

It wasn't an ideal place to keep animals, but it was the
best that the Alliance could afford.

Before he got out of the car, Jacob reached into the glove
compartment and took out a plastic bag that had some dog
biscuits. Then he got a light jacket from the trunk and
shoved the bag of dog treats into a pocket.

He knew the staff was overworked, but he was still annoyed when Davenport kept him waiting for several minutes. He was about Jacob's age, with sandy hair, brown eyes,
and a nose that was a little too big for his face.

"Appreciate your coming," the assistant director said.

"I'm glad I was available. Tell me about the dog."

"He was being kept in a townhouse in Owen Brown. The owner has a fenced backyard, but the dog got out and bit a kid. The owner said he had the dog for protection, and apparently, he'd trained it to attack."

"Too bad for the animal."

When they stepped into the back of the building, the odor of disinfectant, urine, and feces enveloped Jacob. It was too strong for a werewolf, but his only choice was to endure the mixture of odors.

Davenport led him down a corridor lined with cages.

Jacob hated seeing so many animals confined to what he considered prisons. It made him grateful once again that he was free to run in the forest. What would he do if that were impossible?

He shuddered and saw Davenport catch the gesture.

"What?"

"So many dogs in cages," he muttered.

Refocusing his attention, he began sending good thoughts to the animals.

A couple of barking dogs suddenly quieted, and Davenport turned toward him.

"How do you do that?"

"Do what?"

"Get them to settle down."

Jacob shrugged. "Maybe it's not me."

"It happens a lot when you're around."

Jacob shrugged again. There was nothing he could say that would satisfy the other man—or make him less hostile.

At the end of the hall, Davenport pressed the numbers on a keypad and opened a door. They came through into a room about thirteen feet square, with a cage in one corner.

As soon as they entered, a pit bull in the cage growled a warning.

"What's his name?" Jacob asked.

"Gunner."

"Okay. It's probably safer if you leave me alone with

him." He was thinking he didn't want the man to distract him when he needed his total focus on the animal.

Davenport gave him a long look. Jacob had made this request before, and he'd always managed to pull it off. He supposed the assistant director was waiting for the time when Marshall got so badly mauled that his reputation as a "dog whisperer" would be totally wrecked—and the shelter could finally take him off their list of consultants.

"Suit yourself." Davenport walked back out the door and stationed himself at the observation window.

Jacob blocked out everything else and turned toward the dog. It was a skinny creature, with ribs showing through its skin. As he watched the animal study him, he began to talk in a low, steady voice.

"I'm Jacob. I'm your friend. You don't have anything to fear from me. I'm here to help you."

He closed his eyes, listening. The dog's response didn't come in words. Or even thoughts, exactly. But in some strange way, he heard the animal's answer inside his head.

Nobody can help me.

Jacob felt pain coming off the dog in waves. Not physical pain, but mental anguish and despair that were almost too much for him to deal with.

No one had ever treated this animal with kindness. No one had ever cultivated its love of humans or its social instincts. If you gave a dog a chance, it would reward you with its devotion, but nobody had bothered to apply that simple truth to Gunner.

Still, Jacob tried to bridge the gap between himself and the animal's mind, carefully judging its reactions.

In a low even voice, he said. "I know what you've been through, Gunner."

The only answer was a low growl.

Jacob caught a flash of motion out of the corner of his eye. Davenport was talking to someone. Turning he walked rapidly away from the window.

A growl reminded Jacob to keep his focus on the dangerous animal. In the same even voice, he began to speak again.

"You're a good dog. You don't want to hurt people. You want to live with people—and other dogs."

It isn't possible.

Jacob struggled for inner calm as he crouched down beside the cage. "I'm going to unlock the door. I want you to come out here with me. I want you to understand what I can do for you."

The dog gave him a challenging look as it pawed the floor of the cage.

Slowly, Jacob stretched out his arm and reached for the latch on the cage.

With a metallic click, the latch sprang open—and the dog leaped out, teeth bared.

CHAPTER
TEN

GUNNER SHOT FROM the cage, lips drawn back, fangs ready to take a chunk out of the man who dared to get close to him.

Heart thumping, Jacob stood his ground, sending a powerful message to the animal—speaking aloud and also silently, beaming his words directly to the dog's brain, praying that he wasn't too far gone to listen.

"You don't want to hurt me. I'm your friend. I can save you. But you have to let me."

The dog went still, making eye contact. Not a good sign, under the circumstances. Its gaze was bloodshot and tinged with a frightening intensity. Its skinny body was rigid.

All the fear and pain rolling off it being coalesced into one terrible thought.

I am bad. And they're going to kill me.

"No."

You're lying to me. Just like everybody else.

Keeping his gaze on the dog, Jacob slowly shifted his position so that his back was to the window. He didn't want Davenport to see his next words, because they implied that he and Gunner were actually having a conversation. Which was impossible, of course, in Davenport's terms. Men might speak to dogs, but not in response to something the dog had said.

"I never lie to an animal."

The dog snarled, then blasted Jacob with a fierce message. *Why shouldn't I kill you first?*

"Because I can save you."

The animal tipped its head. *How?* Again, it didn't really speak. But Jacob got an impression from the pictures in its head—and from its false bravado. It was scared of what was going to happen to it, but it would never show that fear. Instead, it would go on the attack, because that was the only way it had been taught to respond.

When the jaws closed around his sleeve, it looked like Jacob's message hadn't gotten through. Then, at the last second, the dog stopped its attack and pulled its head back.

Jacob let out a little sigh. "Thank you," he murmured.

The dog stared questioningly at him.

Jacob resisted the urge to look over his shoulder and see how Davenport was taking the turn of events. Instead, he kept his focus on Gunner.

"I'm coming back for you soon, and I'll take you to a place where you can live."

There is no place.

"You have to trust me." The words were a cliché. In this case, they were the absolute truth. Jacob hoped the dog could sense his sincerity.

Thankfully, the animal's posture relaxed a little.

Jacob held out his hand to be sniffed. Then he reached into his jacket pocket where he'd put the plastic bag of dog treats. He took one out. Holding his hand flat and his fingers together, he offered the biscuit to Gunner.

The animal snapped it up and crunched it in his powerful jaw.

Jacob gave him another, staring at the animal's skinny flanks. When the dog had finished eating, Jacob held out his hand to be sniffed again, then he scratched behind one of Gunner's ears.

He felt the dog's pleasure at his touch.

"I have to go now. But I'll be back. All right?"

The dog's expression said he barely dared to hope.

"You have to go back in your cage now." He opened the door of the cage. "Get in."

The animal gave him one last look, then settled down against the back of the enclosure. "I'll be back," Jacob said, then left the room.

When he came out into the corridor again, Davenport was staring at him with a look that shuffled between awe and anger. "How the hell did you do that?"

Jacob shrugged. "I guess dogs trust me."

"That guy doesn't trust anybody."

"But I think he can be salvaged. I'd like you to hold on to him for a few days while I contact a facility that can handle him."

"I can't."

"What do you mean?"

"While you were in there, I got a call from the owner. He's relinquishing responsibility for the dog and under those circumstances, we can't keep him."

"What does that mean, exactly?"

"We're going to cut our losses and put him down."

"No!"

"Sorry. He may have responded to you, but he's a danger to everyone else."

"Then why did you have me evaluate him?"

"Like I said, I just got the call," Davenport said sharply.

Jacob fought to keep from answering with a curse. "Can you sign over the dog to me?"

"You'd take full responsibility?"

"Yes."

He saw Davenport weighing his options. This kind of thing wasn't usually done. The man would be releasing an animal that had proven dangerous. If this were a government facility, it would never happen, but because the shelter was private, Davenport had some discretion.

Long seconds ticked by. Finally, the other man spoke. "He has to be out of here immediately."

"I don't have any way to transport him. I have to go home and get a van and a cage."

"If you can do it before we close tonight."

"You're not giving me much time."

"I have to be rid of the problem today—one way or the other."

"All right."

They strode down the hall, and once again Jacob was assaulted by the sights, sounds, and smells of the captive animals.

He signed a statement, assuming responsibility for Gunner. Then, seized with the need to hurry, he stepped out into the fresh air. Blinking in the sunlight, he took a deep breath.

He'd like to release all the dogs and cats in there, but then they'd end up like the pack of dogs that had almost attacked Renata.

The thought brought his mind back to her. He'd been terrified when he'd seen the dogs confronting her. Now he knew she was putting herself in the path of a murderer.

"Dammit," he muttered.

He ached to throw himself back into the case, but first he had to take care of Gunner. He'd promised the dog he'd save his life, and he couldn't go back on that promise.

He wanted to speed home, but getting a ticket would only slow him down. So he kept to five miles over the speed limit, hoping he could get away with that.

RENATA waited on a side road near Jacob's driveway. Was he home? And if not, where was he?

She was thinking about getting out of her car and walking through the woods to his property when she spotted a car coming down the road at a fast clip.

She caught a glimpse of Jacob as he made the turn and disappeared up his driveway.

He looked like a pack of wolves was chasing him. No, cancel that image.

Not wolves.

But he was definitely in a hurry.

So now what? Moments later another vehicle came roaring down the driveway again. A minivan. And Jacob was driving.

He turned in the direction from which he'd come initially, moving just as fast as before.

She waited until the van was several hundred yards down the road before following. He drove to an industrial park on the east side of Columbia. Hanging back, she saw him pull up in front of an end unit. Still in a hurry, he climbed out and bolted up the stairs.

She drove past, noting that it was an animal shelter. At a discount carpet warehouse, she turned around and pulled into a space across the parking lot.

A few minutes later, Jacob came out. He had a pit bull on a short leash. And he was with another man. The dog looked dangerous, and the other guy was acting like he thought so, too.

The man opened the back of Jacob's van, then a cage inside. Jacob urged the dog inside, then locked the door and closed up the van.

After the two men shook hands stiffly, Jacob climbed back behind the wheel of the van and drove away.

Renata followed.

He turned up his driveway. She pulled off the road and followed on foot, in time to see him getting the dog out of the cage in the van and holding him firmly on a leash.

The animal still looked mean, but Jacob squatted down beside him and talked soothingly to him.

Then the two of them disappeared into the woods.

So now what should she do?

She wasn't exactly Hawkeye in *The Last of the Mohicans*. And she'd never tried tracking someone through the woods. What if Jacob spotted her?

Well, she'd keep far enough back so it wouldn't happen.

Which made it difficult to keep them in sight. Luckily, they seemed to be following a trail, not striking out through the underbrush.

She stopped short, staying well back as Jacob tied the dog to a small tree trunk.

After speaking quietly to the animal again, he got down and rummaged in a tangle of brambles, then pulled out a green plastic storage bin, from which he took a pair of leather pants and a homespun shirt. He held them up to the light, then shook out the wrinkles before taking off his jacket, then his shirt.

He was naked from the waist up, and her breath caught when she noticed the bandage on his arm.

The same bandage he'd had in the dream. In the same place where she'd thought she shot the wolf.

Only now she knew the wound was real.

Her throat clogged.

Scrambling for a logical explanation, she came up with one. He'd already been wounded when he'd come to the house she was showing the other day.

Somehow she'd realized that and incorporated the wound into her dream.

That made some kind of sense, and she clung to the rationale.

Her breath caught as he unbuckled his belt and shucked his jeans and his jockey shorts down his legs.

The dog growled, and he turned away from her to speak to the animal, then stood naked in the forest, obviously completely comfortable in the open air without a stitch on.

Maybe he *had* been toughening up his feet, like he'd told her.

She pressed her lips between her teeth, struggling not to make a sound. But it was impossible to watch him and not react.

The dream was too fresh in her mind. Memories from the night before flooded back. His kiss. His touch. The two of them frantic to get as close as possible.

And the feeling that it wasn't the first time. That they had made love before, thousands of times.

Her gaze dropped to his penis. It was large and thick. And she felt her stomach muscles contract as she stared at him, remembering how he had felt inside of her. How he had brought her to a fantastic climax. For a moment, the pleasure came back to her.

Then it was replaced by the pain.

Oh, Lord, the pain.

Where had that come from?

In answer, reality vanished, and she saw a hideous face shimmering before her eyes. An inhuman face, with scaly green skin and red eyes like glowing lumps of burning coal.

The lips were like a knife wound, dripping blood. The mouth opened and she saw fangs, like a snake. But she knew this creature was more deadly than any serpent.

And more powerful.

The monster filled the whole screen of her vision. It wasn't just a face, she suddenly realized. It had a head, a body, and a huge penis with a bulbous knot at the end. Although the creature was shaped vaguely like a man, it couldn't be human.

It was a fiend from the worst nightmares humans could conjure up. A memory from the primitive past that was more than a mere recollection. It was a terrible reality.

She had seen him before. Many times, she realized.

His name was . . .

She should know his name. It was there, somewhere at the edge of her mind. But it wouldn't come to her.

All she knew was that he had a job to do—to tear her and Jacob apart.

But she couldn't let him win. As if he knew her thoughts, he reached out and clawed his long nails over her hand, making terrible gouges that welled with blood.

She screamed, and the monster dissolved.

Leaving three women standing in a circle around her. They were beautiful, with long golden hair and delicate

features. Each woman wore a long white gown and a spar-
kling crown on her head.

And she knew them, too. The *señoritas hermosas* from
her childhood.

"You can't do that," one of them said in a loud, clear
voice.

"What?" Renata croaked.

They flickered out of existence, leaving her standing in
the forest, her fingers digging into the bark of a tree. Raising
one palm, she clamped it over her mouth. She had gone
into a walking dream. Now she was back in reality, expecting Jacob to come rushing toward her and demand to know
why she was spying on him.

But he was gone!

And cold fear tore at her. Fear that she was going mad.
Dios. No.

When she caught a glimpse of Jacob's back, she pushed
the fear away. She had to stay focused. She *would not* let
her mental problems interfere with her job. Jacob and the
dog were just disappearing into a cave in the rocks behind
where he'd been standing.

Now what? Was he going to kill the dog? Leave it there?

Another thought struck her. Maybe Jacob had been the
source of the strange vision. Maybe he belonged to some
primitive religious cult that engaged in animal sacrifices.

She tried to dismiss that idea out of hand, but it seemed
as likely as anything else.

Straining her ears, she listened for some sound that
would give her a clue. But she heard nothing.

As she stared at the cave entrance, she thought she saw
a flash of light. Then it was gone.

She stayed where she was for minutes, waiting for Jacob to come out. Or Jacob and the dog. Finally, she knew
she had only two options. She could go away, or she could
find out what was happening inside that cave.

But if she crept to the mouth of the cave and he saw her,
she was going to have a lot of trouble explaining what she
was doing there.

Finally, she moved cautiously forward, past the tangle of brambles and the plastic box.

At the cave entrance, she listened intently, then peered inside, straining to penetrate the darkness.

She saw nothing, so she waited for her eyes to adjust to the lack of light. Slowly she crept forward again, farther and farther into the recesses of the rock, expecting to come to a bend in the tunnel. And Jacob and the dog would be around the bend.

But the passage was straight. And all at once she came to the end.

A blank wall.

She gasped.

Jacob and the animal had disappeared, and there was nowhere on Earth that they could have gone.

CHAPTER
ELEVEN

JACOB AND GUNNER had stepped through the back of the cave. Actually, to be technical, through a portal between Jacob's world and a parallel universe where life was very different from twenty-first-century America.

He'd learned about the alternate reality from Rinna, his brother Logan's life mate.

Here, life was more primitive. But many people also had psychic powers, including healing powers, which was why he'd brought damaged animals through the portal to be cured. It wasn't a sure thing by any means, but it was a good enough bet that he was here with Gunner.

He felt the dog shiver as he took in the unfamiliar air, the barren plains. The shells of buildings that looked like a war zone. The two of them had literally stepped from the Maryland forest into another reality.

Jacob stooped down, laying his hand on the animal's back. "It's okay," he murmured.

Again, he and the dog exchanged thoughts. It wasn't a conversation he could recount in words. A dog's brain was different from a man's—or a werewolf's. And his silent communication with Gunner came to him in pictures. Still, he could translate what he was picking up into human terms.

Where are we? He felt the question rolling off the animal in a wave of fear.

Jacob kept his voice low and soothing. "Another place. Where they have people who can help you."

What happened back there? In the woods.

Jacob blinked. *Something.*

For a moment he had imagined seeing Renata watching him. Then he had realized he was making it up. "Nothing happened."

He spoke aloud, and the dog accepted his word.

For the first time since they'd arrived, Jacob raised his head, looking around. He'd been in a tearing hurry to get the dog to the other universe, before the shelter carried out its death sentence. Now he realized that he was pushing his luck. It was too late in the day for safety.

He spoke again to the animal. "We gotta get to the city of Sun Acres quickly. It's dangerous out here after dark."

He started off, and the dog kept pace, obviously still nervous. As the two of them trotted along, he thought about the people he knew here. His cousin Caleb. Caleb's wife Quinn. Griffin, a leader on the ruling council of Sun Acres, and his wife Zarah, who had taken refuge for a time in Logan's house.

Back in Jacob's world, Caleb had been a werewolf ghost, who had taken over a dead man's body. And to his horror, he'd found that he could no longer change to wolf form.

But Ross's wife, Megan, a doctor who specialized in genetic diseases and gene therapy, had treated him.

On Jacob's last visit, Caleb hadn't yet made the change from man to wolf, but he was still hopeful he could do it.

As Jacob thought about all that, he kept up a steady pace, the dog beside him. It would have been safer to travel to Sun Acres as a wolf. He could move faster, and he wouldn't be a tempting target for slavers. But that would give him no control over Gunner, and if the dog escaped, he'd end up in bad trouble.

So Jacob hung on to the leash as he jogged toward the city, all his senses alert.

He was just passing a crumbling building, when he heard a noise from above.

In the next moment, a net fell from a high wall, dropping over him. As he clawed at the webbing, his fingers let go of the leash and the dog bounded away.

Jacob fought to untangle himself, but before he could lift the net and slip out, men rushed out of the shadows and grabbed his arms.

In the dim light, he saw straggly beards. Long hair. Rough clothing. And he caught the odor of unwashed flesh.

There were three of them—and one of him.

"Well, look what we've got," a man with a missing tooth in the front of his mouth crowed. "You made a mistake, running around out here alone after dark."

The guy was right, but Jacob wasn't going to give him the benefit of agreeing.

"Get off me," he snarled, still struggling to free himself. He wanted to change to wolf form and scare the crap out of these guys. But what good would that do him? He'd only be a wolf caught in a net.

"You'd better get used to doing what you're told."

The man who spoke pulled Jacob's arms in back of him. As he did, a guy with straggly red hair drove his fist into Jacob's midsection. The pain made him double over.

RENATA wanted to wait for Jacob to come back, but it was getting late, and staying in the woods was a bad idea.

Quickly, before it got too dark to see anything, she started back down the hill, her mind churning.

She tried not to think about her daydream or whatever it had been. It was too much to cope with. Like the first night she'd awakened from a dream and found herself in the garden arranging natural objects on the stone bench.

Somewhere nearby leaves rustled, and she reached for the gun in her purse, slipping her fingers inside the trigger guard and wrapping her hand around the butt. The weapon made her feel better, until she felt eyes on her.

Red eyes. Like the creature she had seen in the vision a little while ago.

She clenched her teeth, fighting to hold on to sanity. Something was happening to her. Something she couldn't explain and couldn't control.

Shuddering, she fought to drive that image of the green monster off the screen of her mind.

That thing wasn't here. It wasn't real. Yet she couldn't shake the feeling that it was following her down the hill.

"One, two, three . . ." she counted aloud, shouting into the darkness. If she could get to her car before she counted to two hundred, she would be all right.

"DON'T be so rough on the new slave," the man in back of Jacob said. "If you rip up his guts, we can't sell him."

"Yeah. But he's got a mouth on him, and he's got to learn his place."

"Let his new master teach him. I want to earn our money's worth."

"Easy money," the one in back of Jacob crowed and gave his arms a yank.

One of the men looked around, his gaze probing the darkness. "He had a dog with him."

"Yeah, well, if the skinny mutt comes back, slit its throat."

Jacob winced. He was going to make these bastards sorry they'd ever been born.

The guy behind Jacob cut a hole in the webbing. Reaching through, he tied Jacob's hands behind his back before pulling the rest of the net off. The others stood ready to grab him if he made any trouble.

He hung his head and let his shoulders slump, acting like he was defeated, when his mind was churning, making escape plans.

He had come rushing into this universe without thinking

through the consequences, but he was damned if he was going to give up without a fight.

Biding his time, he let them march him away, to a campsite behind another ruined house. He drew in a breath when he saw a cage made of saplings lashed together. If they put him in there, he wasn't going to get out.

Jesus!

He'd have to act now and hope for the best.

One of the three walked forward to open the door of the cage. While he was occupied, Jacob began to chant.

"What the hell?" the red-haired guy said.

Jacob ignored him and kept saying the words that would change him from man to wolf.

"Shut up." The thug backhanded Jacob across the mouth, and he lost his focus for a moment, then had to start over.

"What are you doing?"

"Praying," he said, forcing a quaver into his voice. He hated to let them believe he was afraid, but really, it gave him his best chance.

The man gave a harsh laugh. "Go ahead. A lot of good that will do you."

Jacob ducked his head so the guy couldn't see his defiant expression, and he started chanting again, this time in a loud, fervent voice, as though he really were begging one of their gods to rescue him.

His arms were still tied in back of him, and he knew the bond was going to yank his shoulders out of their sockets if he changed in that position.

Tension gathered inside him as he waited for the exact moment when he could jerk his paws out of the rope.

CHAPTER
TWELVE

JACOB GRITTED HIS teeth. He was going to get away or die trying.

Just as his vision blurred from the change, he thought he saw a dark shape hurtle out of the night toward the men who held him captive.

Gunner.

Jacob couldn't see what was happening now, but he heard the scuffling. Heard the shouts of fear from the men who had thought only moments ago that they were in total control of the situation.

His heart leaped as one of the bastards screamed. Then screamed again.

Somehow, Jacob held his focus, feeling the change grab him. His timing had to be just right, or he was going to be in big trouble.

He had never tried to judge the moment of transformation so precisely. There had never been a need for it.

When he calculated he could slip from the bonds, he yanked his front limbs forward. For a terrible moment, his wrists caught on the ropes, and he thought he was trapped.

Then he yanked his paws free as his body made the shift. Relief flooded through him when he came down on all fours.

Of course, he still had a major problem. He had never changed with his clothes on. He leaped forward, managing to pull his lower body out of the pants that gaped around the wolf's middle. But there was no way to get out of the shirt. It hung around his neck and came down over his claws, seriously hampering his movements.

Still, his mouth was free. He sprang at the nearest thug, his powerful jaws closing over the throat of the slaver.

The man's gurgling sound was like a sweet song of victory ringing in Jacob's ears.

But he hadn't won yet. Where were the other two?

He heard a noise behind him and whirled to see one of the men charging him, a knife in his hand. "Fuck you, werewolf."

Jacob howled at him and ducked aside, then went for the knife hand just as Gunner landed on the man's shoulders, biting and growling.

Jacob kept his teeth on the man's wrist as Gunner chomped at his head and shoulders, screams filling the air—until the man suddenly went still.

Jacob raised his head and looked around. Three bodies lay on the ground. He trotted over to the nearest man and nudged him with a paw. He was dead. The next one was still breathing, but he was torn up pretty badly and would bleed out soon. The third one was also dead.

Gunner looked at him. *A good few minutes' work.*

I thought you'd gone for good. Thanks for sticking around.

You saved me. I came back to save you.

Gunner continued to stare at him, and he knew the animal was grappling with the creature standing in front of him.

I am the same being. I can change my form.

Yes.

He felt a wave of satisfaction come off the animal.

It was a good fight. I liked it. We fight well together. Have you killed men before?

Only to defend myself. Not for sport.

The dog stared at him, and he knew that the animal was still a danger to people. He had liked the excuse to kill. But without him, Jacob might be the one who was dead.

He walked to one of the men and picked up his knife in his teeth. With the hilt held in his mouth, he braced his paws on the edge of the shirt while he lowered his head to catch the knife in the fabric and slash downward. Once he'd cut a slit in the cloth, he was able to wiggle out of the shirt.

It's safer to travel like this, without my hand on the leash. Will you stay with me?

He heard the dog's agreement.

He stepped forward to loop the leash up and over the animal's shoulder and stopped when he encountered a red splotch on the dog's shoulder.

You're cut.

I've had worse.

I'm sorry. Can you run with me?

Yes.

Jacob wondered if it was better to change and examine the wound. Then he decided there was nothing he could do about it.

Carefully, he used his mouth to wind the leash loosely around the dog's neck. It wasn't a perfect solution, but it looked like the leash would stay in place.

He raised his head toward the sky. The moon was almost full, shining down with a silvery light that was bright enough to create shadows on the ground. And the stars were glorious. There were so many more of them than at home.

The air felt clean and fresh. Cleaner than it had ever been in Maryland, with the industrial pollution that hung over the earth.

He howled. For joy. For his freedom. And for his victory.

The dog barked his approval.

Then they started off, side by side, for Sun Acres, running toward the city with more speed than they had previously used. The dog following the wolf's lead.

They stopped once or twice when the leash slipped and Jacob had to pull it back into place. And each time they rested for a few minutes before continuing the journey.

Jacob watched the dog closely. He seemed to be holding up pretty well, considering his injury. Finally, they reached a spot where he could see the lights of the city not far ahead.

Now that they were near the city, going any farther as a wolf was not a good idea. Neither was going in as a naked man. But he and Griffin had talked about the possibility of his arriving in wolf form. Also, Griffin sometimes ventured out of the city as a wolf and needed to dress before he came back. So they'd stashed some clothing in a ruined house not far from the gate.

Jacob slowed his pace, searching among the old buildings and sniffing out the right one. Inside he dug in a corner of the front room until he uncovered the cache of clothing wrapped in oilcloth.

He dug it out and saw that there was more than one set of men's pants and shirts.

I'm going to change again, he told the dog.

The dog moved to the doorway of the house, standing guard. Jacob stepped back into the shadows, saying the chant in his mind.

When he stood up as a naked man, the dog gave a small bark.

"Yeah, I'm back the way you met me," Jacob answered as he pulled on a pair of trousers, a shirt, and sandals.

He also pulled a flashlight from the cache. In this world, it would customarily have been powered by psychic energy. But they'd brought batteries from the other universe.

Caleb had started teaching the soldiers Morse code. They were using it for long-distance communication over the radio transmitters that Caleb had "invented."

That was how he was making a living in this universe. So far, he was just adapting equipment that he knew about from the early part of the twentieth century back home.

Caleb was good with ideas and good with his hands. He'd made improvements in the equipment he'd sold, and Jacob was sure he would come up with some real inventions on his own.

He began flashing the light—giving his name several times. Before he could get a signal from the guards on the city wall, another animal stepped from behind the shadow of a nearby building.

IN the light coming from the moon and stars, Jacob stared at the newcomer, feeling the hairs on his arms prickle. It was a large wolf, an animal that he had never seen before.

His coloring was odd, at least as far as Jacob could see in the darkness. His coat appeared to be more blond than gray or silver.

As he caught the sight and scent of the animal, Gunner growled, and Jacob was suddenly aware of the dog. He could feel the animal coiling to attack. And the wolf was gathering his energy, preparing to defend himself.

"Don't," Jacob shouted aloud. He had never seen this wolf before. But he thought he knew who it was.

Caleb.

His wonder at seeing the other werewolf transformed was blotted out by the knowledge that if Gunner attacked, Jacob must go to the defense of his cousin.

The dog growled and bared its teeth. The wolf responded in kind.

"I know him." Raising his voice, Jacob stepped between wolf and dog.

Uncertain, Gunner stared from him to the wolf.

"He's a werewolf. My cousin," Jacob said, making every word count.

He saw Caleb's eyes flash to him for a moment before returning his focus to the dog.

"Yes, I recognize you," Jacob answered his unspoken question. "It's good to see you like this. Very good."

The wolf cocked his head toward the dog, his eyes questioning.

"This is Gunner. He got into some trouble back home, and I've brought him through for treatment with an adept."

The wolf nodded, then took a step back, his gaze still on the dog.

Jacob tensed. He knew Caleb was about to change, and he knew the other werewolf would be at his most vulnerable when he did.

But the dog stayed where he was.

Moments later, Caleb stood up on two legs, transformed into a blond-haired man.

Jacob reached out a hand, and they shook. "You made it," he said.

"Yeah," Caleb answered, his voice thick.

"How long has it been?"

"A couple of weeks. I tried a few times after Megan did that gene therapy on me." He sighed. "We thought the treatment might not have worked. But I kept at it."

Jacob nodded.

"Quinn's relieved. She's over the fear that I'm going to kill myself," he tossed off. He'd made a joke out of his life mate's fears, but Jacob suspected that it had been touch and go for Caleb.

He'd been reborn in another man's body, but when he'd found out he couldn't change to wolf form, he'd been devastated.

Well, he hadn't talked to any of them about it. But Jacob had no trouble imagining how that aching void would have felt.

Probably, Caleb didn't want to discuss the subject any further, because he looked at the dog.

"He's bleeding."

"Yeah. He needs medical treatment—as well as psychic treatment."

Gunner growled, and both men tensed. Then Jacob realized that a contingent of men was coming rapidly toward the building.

"It's all right," Caleb called out. "This is Caleb Marshall. And my cousin, Jacob Marshall. He's brought an animal with him."

The dog could have torn several of the men apart, but he moved next to Jacob, shivering.

Jacob leaned down and put his hand on the dog's skinny flank. "It's okay," he murmured.

The soldiers kept their distance from the animal, and the whole party started toward the city.

The gate was closed, but it opened as they approached. They had barely stepped inside when Gunner made a whimpering sound and fell over.

Jacob went down on his knees beside the animal. He could see the wound had opened up and was bleeding again.

And the dog hadn't let on. But he knew animals were like that. They endured pain that humans couldn't imagine—in silence.

"We've got to get him to Griffin's," Jacob said.

In this world, life was cheap. Not many men would care about saving one dog. But the soldiers pulled over a small cart, which they hitched up to a horse. There was a thick rug covering the bottom.

Jacob climbed in and two soldiers lifted Gunner in beside him. He stroked the animal's head and spoke softly to him as the cart rumbled through the streets toward Griffin's mansion.

Caleb rode on a horse beside them. "You care about him," he said in a low voice.

"He saved my life a few hours ago."

Caleb sucked in a sharp breath. "How?"

"Slavers got me. I thought he'd run off, but he came back to fight for me."

"Then we'll save him. I'm going on ahead to see if we can have a healer there when you arrive."

CHAPTER
THIRTEEN

JACOB LAID HIS hand on the dog's flank, and his heart clunked inside his chest when he felt that the animal was barely breathing.

He'd made a promise to Gunner that he would save his life. It could turn out to be a lie.

The cart clattered along the cobblestone streets. If he'd only had a car, they could have been at Griffin's house in fifteen minutes. But cars were not part of this world.

When civilization had broken down in this universe, modern progress had stopped. And in some ways, the people here lived as they would have before the industrial revolution.

Caleb might be able to bring them some modern improvements. But he was handicapped by not having an industrial base to manufacture things. Mass production was still a long way off. And so was the internal combustion engine. Caleb had gotten an old steam car going. But there was no way to manufacture more of them.

It was early in the morning and most people who lived in Sun Acres were sleeping, but Jacob saw candlelight flickering in a few windows. And a large dog darted out in front of the cart and started barking, then running beside them, keeping up the racket.

Gunner didn't stir, which was more disturbing than anything else. The other dog had challenged him, but he was too far gone to care.

Finally, to Jacob's relief, he saw the large gate of the compound come into view. As they approached, it swung open, and Griffin stepped out.

Jacob goggled at him. "I . . . I didn't mean to wake you," he stammered as he climbed down from the cart.

Griffin waved his hand. "Don't apologize. I owe a debt to the Marshall family. You sheltered my wife when she was with child and in grave danger. And I stand ready to do anything in my power to aid you."

He directed the cart to the side of the walled courtyard. Four soldiers came forward, lifted the rug up, and carried the dog into a ground-floor room that was illuminated by several oil lamps.

Two women were waiting for them.

One was dark and looked to be in her late fifties, although Jacob suspected she was really much older. Her name was Pamina. She had skills as an adept, and he knew that, with Quinn's help, she had brought Caleb back to the world—when he had wanted to die.

The other one was an ash blond and younger.

Jacob looked from one woman to the other. "I've met Pamina," he said.

"And I am Lydia," the blond one volunteered. "What happened to him?"

"He saved my life when I was attacked. I didn't realize he was so badly wounded, but I think he lost a lot of blood when we ran from the ambush toward the city." He swallowed and looked toward Pamina. "I was bringing him here because his mind is twisted. He was trained to kill, and he injured a child on the other side of the portal. If he gets his strength back, he might attack you."

The other woman, Lydia, knelt beside the dog and put her hand over the bloody patch on his fur. Then she pulled back his lips and looked at his gums.

"He may not make it," she said.

A noise in the doorway made Jacob turn to see Zarah, Griffin's wife, enter the room. She wore a rich robe, and her long golden hair was caught in a braid at the back of her neck. He saw she was holding what looked like a covered gravy boat. But he knew from previous trips that it was a small oil lamp.

He was as shocked to see her as he'd been to see Griffin.

"I came to help," she said.

The other two women acknowledged her presence, and she came forward, speaking to them in low tones.

Then she went to the dog and knelt down. He heard her suck in a sharp breath, then glance at Jacob, probably realizing that the dog was almost dead.

Still, her voice remained steady as she promised, "We'll do our best."

Jacob stepped out of the way, watching as Zarah stared at the mouth of the lamp. A flame sprang up, and she held the lamp in front of her as she bent over the dog.

The other two women came up on either side of her, and Jacob felt something. He couldn't say what it was exactly. Energy, gathering in the room and circling around the wounded animal.

He didn't know how much time passed. He heard the woman named Pamina murmur something. He heard the others answer. He saw the dog's body jerk.

Pamina turned to Jacob, and he felt her inside his head, prowling around, when her job was supposed to be curing the dog.

He didn't like the invasion of his privacy, and he tried to jerk back, to close his mind against her. Somehow she held him where he was.

It was as though he and Pamina were locked in a contest—until Gunner made a whimpering sound.

"How is he?" Jacob asked, relieved that the woman's focus was off of him.

"We're not finished yet. Come here," Lydia called softly to him. He came forward, kneeling down beside the animal.

"Send your mind to his. Tell him that his life will be different now. So much better."

Hardly daring to believe it was true, Jacob did as he was asked.

"Come back to us," he murmured. "Come back and live the life I promised you."

The dog's eyes blinked open and stared at him. He saw confusion. And something else. Joy.

An emotion he had never seen in this animal before. A pink tongue emerged from the dark muzzle and licked his right hand.

Jacob stroked the matted coat with his left. Then Lydia gave Gunner a bowl of water, which he lapped before laying his head down again.

"He's weak," Lydia said. "He must rest."

"I understand."

"Pamina made new connections in his brain," Lydia said.

"I think I can see that."

"Come outside," Lydia said.

Jacob did as she asked.

She pitched her voice low. "He may not live as long as he would have," she said. "But he will be happier."

"I see that already." He clasped her arm. "I thank you."

"I should get some herbs into him—herbs that will help build up his blood."

She went back inside, and Zarah and Pamina came out.

"Thank you," he said to both of them.

From across the courtyard, he heard a sudden cry, and at the same time, Zarah drew in a quick breath. "It's Marsh," she said. "He's hungry. You must excuse me."

"Yes. Of course."

She rushed to the woman standing in the doorway

holding a baby, leaving Jacob with Pamina. She was staring at him, making him want to squirm, but he kept himself still. He was exhausted, and he longed to find a bed and go to sleep, but he had a feeling that wasn't going to happen anytime soon.

Not when Pamina's gaze was so sharply on him. "You risked a lot to bring a dog here," she said.

He shrugged.

"Don't be modest."

"I wanted to save him."

"You did. But you must learn to save yourself."

"What do you mean?"

"We should talk—in private," the woman said.

He felt a shiver travel over his skin. He wasn't sure what this woman had seen inside his head, and he didn't want to talk to her about it. But she'd just done Gunner a great kindness, and he couldn't turn away from her.

She led him to another part of the compound, to what he judged was a reception area for visitors to Griffin's household.

It was nicely furnished with chairs and two couches grouped around a brass-topped table.

"Sit down."

He eyed the chairs, then sank into one of the couches, still unable to let go of his tension.

Pamina reached into a leather bag slung over her shoulder and took out a packet. Then she walked to the fireplace at the side of the room, where a pot sat on a metal stand over the fire.

She took off the top and let the contents of the packet drift inside. Then she used a cloth to hold the pot's handle and shake it gently.

He sat watching her, his heart pounding.

"What is that?" he whispered.

"Nothing bad. A kind of tea."

A pungent smell rose from the infusion.

Finally, she poured the brew into two small pottery cups, which she put on the table.

After giving him a considering look, she said, "It's been a long night. This will help relax us."

He reached for the cup, watching her pick up the other one and sit down.

When she sipped, he did, too, feeling the liquid fill his mouth, slip down his throat, and warm his stomach.

The warmth was good. But soon he felt a syrupy sensation spreading through him.

"What is this?" he said again, struggling to sit up and falling back against the sofa cushion.

"Something I designed."

"Why . . . did . . . you . . ." He stopped because he couldn't frame the question.

"You need to rest." She rose and walked toward him, then pressed her hand against his shoulders, forcing him back into the sofa cushion.

"Don't."

"I gave you the tea so you would listen to me."

"It didn't make your head fuzzy," he said, hearing his words slur.

She laughed. "I'm used to it." Her voice was low and even, almost a droning in his ears. She stopped and took another sip, which seemed to energize her.

"You could have left that dog to die. You brought him here—to this world. To this house. You risked much to come here."

He kept staring at her, struggling to keep her in focus when she threatened to split into two separate images. He was on the way to slipping into a drugged sleep when Pamina said, "You escaped the slavers, but you are still in danger."

That snapped his mind into focus, although his body still felt logy.

"From a woman named Renata?" he asked, wondering in some part of his mind why he had jumped to that conclusion.

The adept must have had the same thought, because she gave him an inquiring look.

Struggling to justify the question, he pushed himself up straighter and said, "She followed me into the woods. She's up to something." Even as he said it, he wondered if it was really true. But he knew one thing for certain. "She's . . . weird."

Pamina laughed and kept her gaze on him. He wanted to shift in his seat, but he held himself still.

"Why do you call her weird? Because she walks around her garden in the moonlight in her nightgown, gathering natural objects and placing them on an altar?"

"An altar!" He gasped. It had been a bench. He tried to sit forward. "How do you know about . . . the other night?"

"I picked it up from your mind. You didn't recognize the altar for what it was, but I did."

He managed a little nod.

"You are in danger. And she is in danger, too."

The words were like an arrow, piercing his flesh. He felt his heart leap into his throat. It was difficult to speak; but he managed to get a few words out of his mouth. "She's trying to lure a murderer out of hiding."

"That is a danger, yes. But there is more. An evil presence is making trouble between the two of you. A demon."

"No," Jacob croaked, hoping it wasn't true.

CHAPTER
FOURTEEN

RENATA'S DOORBELL RANG. And for one joyful, irrational moment, she thought it might be Jacob. But why would he be coming here?

He'd disappeared yesterday. And she hadn't heard anything about him since.

She'd driven by the animal shelter. And she'd driven to his house. But she saw no sign of him—or the dog.

She hurried to the door, but she wasn't reckless enough to open it without finding out who it was. When she looked out through the peephole, she saw Maxwell Sullivan, the head of the local Realty Association.

What was he doing here?

Quickly, she opened the door, then stepped back. "Maxwell?"

The look on his face made her chest tighten. "May I come in?"

"Of course," she said, wondering if she was making a mistake. She didn't know this man very well, and she certainly didn't expect him to show up at her home

When he stepped into the front hall and closed the door, she felt her tension rise.

Rounding on her, he spat out, "I've just found out you're practicing real estate without a license."

She blanched. "What do you mean?"

"You're working for Star Realty under false pretenses. Or, to put it another way, Dick Trainer let you join his company without any credentials."

"What makes you think so?" she murmured.

He hesitated for a moment. "I talked to Greg Newcastle."

She couldn't stop herself from sucking in a sharp breath. "How did that . . . come up?"

"I asked him how the investigation of the murders was going. And he told me that Star Realty had hired you."

"That was confidential information."

"Yes, well, I'm the head of the Realty Association. He didn't think it was appropriate to keep your role from me."

"Uh-huh."

"Practicing without a license is illegal."

"I'm not selling. I turn over any sales to Dick Trainer. Would you prefer that another woman lose her life?" she shot back.

"Of course not. I just want to be informed about what's going on in my own association."

"We were trying to keep the number of people who know as small as possible. Now that you're in the loop, I'll keep you updated."

He looked slightly mollified. "Do that."

"I can send you a report on the progress I've made."

"What progress?"

"Well, nothing concrete. But I'm presenting myself as a target. And if the killer is still in the area, I expect him to come after me."

"Do you have any suspects?"

The question made her go very still. What was she going to tell him, that she was investigating Lou Deverel, Jacob Marshall, Kurt Lanagan, and even Dick Trainer? "I'd rather not discuss that because I might be pointing the finger at someone who turns out to be innocent."

For a charged moment, she thought he was going to object. But he finally said, "Keep me informed."

"Of course."

He gave her a long look, as if he thought she might be lying. Then, without further conversation, he walked to the door and stepped outside again, leaving her vibrating with anger.

"*Dios mio.*" She swiped a hand through her hair, struggling to calm down. It wasn't going to do her any good to start screaming.

But what was she supposed to do now?

He didn't seem to care that she was putting her life on the line. In fact, it sounded like he was more concerned with licensing legalities than finding the killer . . .

What did that mean? That he was in on it?

Or maybe he had another motive. His own company was a rival of Star Realty. Maybe he wanted to make trouble for Dick Trainer.

Well, she'd get Barry to do a thorough background check on him. Too bad she couldn't speed up the damn investigation, but they were working on the killer's timetable, not hers.

Another thought struck her, and she went stock-still. Sullivan had gotten the information about the investigation from Greg Newcastle. Not a smart move on the detective's part.

So why had he ratted her out? Because he felt like he was on the spot? Because he wanted *her* off the case?

Or because he was too inexperienced to keep his mouth shut when he was cornered?

She clenched her fists. She wanted to confront him, but not when she was this angry. Because she'd end up saying something she'd regret.

She took a couple of deep breaths. She should call Barry. But not until she could speak to him more calmly.

*   *   *

JACOB'S eyes blinked open. Looking outside he saw the sun was high.

Someone had left him a basin of water that was still a little warm, soap, and a towel—along with clean clothes.

Jacob closed the door, then pulled off his shirt and pants and washed quickly. As he soaped himself, his eyes flicked to the fireplace. The teapot was gone.

So had the conversation with the adept been real, or had he conjured it up because he was so focused on Renata? Because he wanted explanations for what was happening between them, had he made one up—and attributed it to a woman with power? He shuddered. Or was it all true?

An evil presence was stalking them? A demon trying to make mischief between them? But why?

And did Renata understand what was happening?

He shook his head. He didn't want to believe it. He wouldn't believe it—until he had some kind of proof.

He pulled on his clothing, then hurried to the room where the women had treated the dog.

Caleb, Quinn, and Zarah were there.

When he saw that she was on the floor, showing the dog to her baby, he felt a dart of alarm.

He'd brought Gunner here because the animal had been dangerous.

Now he was lying next to Zarah and the baby, wagging his tail.

As soon as Jacob came in, Gunner's attention zinged to him.

Jacob squatted down beside the dog, stroking his head as he probed his mind. He felt the animal's gratitude and his wonder at being in this place.

"He has a home with us," Zarah said. "You don't have to worry about him."

"That makes him a very lucky dog," Jacob answered.

He spent a few more minutes with Gunner. But when Zarah left the room, he followed her outside. He was anxious to get back to his own world. But he knew he'd be missing an opportunity if he didn't speak to her.

When she realized he was behind her, she turned.

He shifted his weight from one foot to the other. "I wanted to ask you something."

"Of course."

"I know you use that lamp—that you use fire to cure. But you used it to kill once, didn't you?" he blurted.

Her face registered shock. "You know that?"

"I'm sorry. Yes." He didn't want to say that it was common knowledge in Griffin's household. But as he studied her expression, he realized that he'd gotten too personal.

"I overstepped," he muttered.

"You had a reason to bring it up," she answered in a tight voice.

"Yeah." Since he'd made her uncomfortable, he figured he might as well do it to himself. "I've been having dreams about fire."

She nodded.

"Can you tell me what it means?"

She shifted the baby in her arms. "Fire can symbolize a lot of things. Purification. Divine energy. Divine revelation. Hearth and home. In some cultures, the lighting of a new fire to begin the new year was a sacred ritual."

He nodded.

"Of course, fire is the only one of the elements—earth, air, fire, and water—that humans can make themselves. And being able to make fire was a breakthrough for primitive man. He could use it for warmth, for cooking, for light. But fire can also bring pain and death. Going all the way back to Greek myths, fire belonged only to the gods. And there are legends of man stealing it from them."

He nodded. He hadn't thought of all that. But it made sense.

"Fire can be the end of all things. Or the beginning. In your world, do you have the phoenix, the bird that is consumed by fire, then rises again from the ashes?"

"Yes."

"Does any of that help you?"

"I can't tell. Since I don't really know where I'm going

with this." He wanted to ask if she knew anything about demons and fire. But that would be giving too much away. And what did Pamina mean by a demon anyway? Had she meant the classic Christian definition? Or something else?

He didn't even know that.

"I can give you some books to read," Zarah said.

"Thanks." He was suddenly impatient to leave. Everything she'd said was in general terms, and he didn't know how it applied to him. Yet. "I can probably look it up on my own."

"I see you're restless," she said.

"I'm sorry. I'm the one who started the conversation, but now I can't help feeling like . . . I need to get home." That was a mild way to put the urgency he was suddenly feeling. Something bad was going to happen. And he knew he had to try and stop it.

"Maybe you'll find the answer in your world. But you must have a meal before you leave. Griffin has horses and an escort ready for you."

"Thank you. A small meal. And the horses will make the trip much faster."

He was relieved when the baby started to cry, and she excused herself to take care of her son.

RENATA drove to Jacob's house. It had been more than twenty-four hours since he and the dog had disappeared. Had he come home? Or had he taken off for good?

Her chest tightened. Why would he do that? Because he was guilty of something?

Clenching the wheel, she turned up the access road.

The sun slanted low in the west. The air was absolutely still as she strode toward the house, wondering what she was going to say if she found him at home.

No birds called in the trees. No little animals rustled in the underbrush.

Was that normal?

When she was almost to the front door, she stopped

short. She saw movement in the woods, and her breath
caught.

Jacob stepped out from under the shadow of the trees.
He was alone, and he was wearing the outfit that he had
left in the storage bin in the brambles.

Did he know she'd been poking inside?

Jacob's face registered surprise—then welcome.

"What are you doing here?" he called out.

She hardly knew how to answer. She had come to find
out what he was up to. Instead, gladness leaped inside her
as he started toward her.

All her attention was focused on him. But when something caught the corner of her vision, she turned her head.

Someone else was here.

At Jacob's house?

As she looked around and didn't see any vehicles besides his—and hers. Suddenly, fear leaped inside her.

"Watch out," she cried.

He stopped short, just as a shot rang out.

CHAPTER
FIFTEEN

JACOB HIT THE ground, ducking behind a bush as he rolled to his side and swiveled to see who was behind him. He caught sight of someone dashing away through the woods.

A man?

Well, someone standing upright. Not an animal.

Of course, not an animal! What did he think, that a bear had shot at him?

The guy's form was indistinct, like one of those fuzzy images on TV where they don't want you to know who the person is. But usually on TV, they just blocked out the face, and this was the whole man.

As he sprang up and took off after the guy, he heard footsteps behind him. Renata.

"Stay back," he shouted as he ran, but she didn't obey. Of course not.

"I have a gun," she answered.

"Stay back," he shouted again as he kept running after the shooter.

Even as Jacob kept charging ahead, he was thinking that the blurry image didn't make sense. This wasn't TV or a movie where you could manipulate a picture. It was real life—in the woods in back of his house.

He followed after the fleeing figure, feet pounding across the forest floor. These were his woods. He knew every inch of this ground because he'd prowled them as a wolf. He'd been here at night. And during the day. Yet somehow the man stayed ahead of him, ducking in and out of the shadows. And then he was gone.

Gone?

Jacob rushed to the spot where he'd last seen the guy. There was nobody there. Nothing.

Renata came up beside him, her gun drawn, looking wildly around. "Where did he go?"

Jacob dropped his gaze to the scuffed pine needles. "Hell if I know."

He'd like to change to a wolf and see what he could discover, but he couldn't do that with Renata watching.

Unwilling to give up, he tried to sniff the guy out. When he couldn't pick up the scent, he kept searching the woods, moving in a tight pattern through the underbrush.

RENATA did the same, her weapon at the ready in case the assailant jumped out of the bushes, which didn't seem likely at the moment.

She saw that Jacob was staying close to her.

"Don't tell me to go back," she said.

He gave her an assessing look. "I get the feeling that would be a waste of time. Do you always carry a gun?"

"When I think it's necessary."

"Which is?"

She lifted one shoulder. "When I'm showing a house by myself way out in the country."

"Did you have a gun when we met the other day?"

"Yes."

He nodded curtly. "Okay. That makes sense."

"I wasn't asking for your approval," she snapped, then was sorry she had reacted so strongly. Something about

Jacob brought that out in her—strong reactions. Good and bad.

She'd like to focus on the good. But the bad thoughts kept popping into her head.

He turned to face her. "You know that women real estate agents have been killed?"

She swallowed. "Yes."

"So you know you're putting yourself in danger by meeting clients in empty houses."

"It's my job," she answered, then immediately wondered if she'd given too much away.

He sighed.

"The women who were killed probably weren't armed. Or the man who killed them took them by surprise. That's not going to happen to me."

"Uh-huh."

When they came out to a side road leading along his property, Jacob stopped.

"I don't think we're going to find him."

"Why not?"

He flapped his arm in frustration. "This is my turf. I should have been able to catch him."

She nodded in agreement.

"Did you see him?" he asked.

"He was just a blur."

He turned to face her. "Then you saw it, too."

"What do you mean?"

"A blur. Like an electronically distorted image, only that should have been impossible."

She thought about his meaning. "I guess I thought the shadows distorted him. Or he was too far away to see clearly."

"Do you usually have problems with your eyes?"

"No."

"Neither do I."

An image leaped into her head. An image of a monster with green skin and a red slash for a mouth. She shoved it firmly away. This had nothing to do with that hallucination.

"Maybe he was wearing some kind of special suit. Something that distorted the light," she murmured, scrambling for an explanation.

Jacob shrugged. "We might as well go back."

FROM his hiding place, Questabaze spit out a string of foul curses as he watched Jacob and Renata turn around and head back toward the house.

"Fuck!"

None of this was going the way he expected.

Marshall should be dead now, and the crisis would be over. He *would have* been dead. But when Renata had shown up and shouted a warning, the bastard had ducked to the side and rolled to the ground. Then he'd come charging into the woods, and Questabaze's only option had been to shield his man form from recognition and take off—until he had enough of a lead to vanish.

A good thing he had that talent, because Marshall was fast, and he knew his way around this patch of ground.

Now the bastard was taking Renata back to his house, and there was very little doubt about what they were going to do there. Not when they had wanted each other for centuries. Not when their emotions were running so high.

Someone had shot at Marshall. Renata had warned him, and she was going to reap her reward.

Heat rolled off the demon. When the pine needles next to him started to smolder, he doused it with a blast of cold air and struggled to reign in his anger.

He came from a world so different from this one that any human being who found himself there would choke to death within minutes, if he didn't go mad first.

As far as Questabaze knew, no young demons had come into existence in thousands of years. He couldn't even say how he had been born—or if he had somehow sprung into being by supernatural means. He rarely thought about the irony that he knew more about humanity than about his own people. Probably that was a mercy.

He had read everything he could find about demons in the literature of men. And none of the stories had made any sense to him. He didn't even know when he had become aware of himself—or the others. He only knew that the numbers of his people were dwindling because they had hunted each other and eliminated their rivals. Many of his kind had come into this world to try and kill him. But he had always vanquished them.

Sometime soon, there would be only one demon left, and he meant to be that one. Because he would prove himself the strongest and the most cunning. No human could ever understand the urgency he felt. The wings of fear beat at his back. He had tasted human life, and he craved more. He could live forever in this world. Live in the comfort denied his kind.

But the great game of power had never presented this many problems, and he felt panic choking off his breath.

Were the Fates taking a hand because he'd tried to change the rules with those damn dogs? Tried to use them to disable Renata before she established a relationship with Jacob? Luring them to that vacant house had seemed like a good idea at the time. Now he wished he'd been more prudent. But his long life had taught him to take chances. Over the years, he had gambled everything again and again. And won.

This time it had been bad luck that Renata had spotted him and shouted a warning.

He watched Jacob tip his head toward her as they walked down the hill.

As Questabaze thought about what he might do to make trouble between them, another idea struck him. A very elegant idea. And this time it was going to work.

JACOB walked back to the house, with Renata beside him.

"Who do you think that was?" she asked.

"I have no idea."

"Who wants you dead?" she challenged.

He answered with a harsh laugh. "Damned if I know. Maybe Doug Davenport."

"Who's he?"

"The assistant director of the shelter where I just evaluated a dog. He hates my guts."

"Why?"

"Because I communicate with animals better than he does."

"You communicate with animals?" she asked.

"After a fashion. That's why I'm good at my job."

He'd given her the opening she'd been looking for, and she didn't have to admit that she had been snooping. "What about the dog you evaluated?"

"He had been trained to be vicious. It wasn't his fault. I took him where he could be cured."

"Where?"

"A facility that's not well known," he clipped out. "And I'm afraid I have to keep the information confidential."

"Okay. Sorry."

They stepped out of the woods, and she glanced around, surprised that the scene hadn't changed. It looked just the same. But she didn't feel the same.

"The shooter could have killed you," she whispered.

"Yeah. If you hadn't warned me."

They stood facing each other, and she wasn't sure which of them made the first move.

Maybe they each took a step forward, then another, until they were so close that she could reach out and pull him into her arms. Which she did.

It felt right. And good. And natural. Like coming home to a lover after a long journey.

He looked down at her, and the expression on his face made her heart turn over.

"Renata?"

"Yes," she answered, meaning it in so many ways that she couldn't even follow her own reasoning.

"We'd better go inside," he said.

She nodded. Somebody had shot at him. Focusing on each other out here was dangerous.

But breaking the contact between them seemed impossible, and maybe he felt the same way. He slung his arm around her as they hurried toward the house, swaying slightly on their feet.

He walked to a rock near the front door and took out a key. So did that mean he was just coming home from wherever he'd gone with the dog? Or had he come back earlier, then gone out again?

She couldn't hold on to the thought, not when he led her into the house, closed the door, and took her in his arms again.

His mouth came down on hers for a greedy kiss, and she found herself kissing him with equal lust. Too many emotions were bottled up inside her. She couldn't hold them back, and they came pouring out, unchecked and uncensored.

He slanted his mouth one way and then the other, eating from her like a starving man who has just discovered a feast.

It was the same for her. She worked her mouth against his as her hands slid under his shirt so that she could splay her fingers against the warm skin of his back.

She didn't know what the two of them meant to each other.

No, that was a lie. The two of them meant everything to each other. Would always mean everything.

She couldn't work her way through that, either. She could only kiss him, and stroke her hands up and down his back, before bringing them around to his chest.

She loved the crisp hair she found there. When she encountered his flat nipples, she drew circles around them, making them hard. Making him growl into her mouth.

He followed her lead, reaching under her knit top and unhooking her bra.

He pushed it up and out of the way, taking the weight of her breasts in his hands.

They felt full and aching.

When he stroked his thumbs across her tightened nipples, the pleasure of it shot downward through her body.

He stepped back to pull his shirt over his head, then strip away her knit top and toss it on the floor, along with her bra.

"Lord, you're lovely," he said, his voice thick as he caught her breasts in his hands again, his fingers playing over the nipples. Then he bent his head, taking one aching tip in his mouth and sucking sharply as he used his thumb and finger on the other.

She cried out, pressing her center against him, frantically moving her hips.

Standing right there, wedged against him, she came in an explosion that took her utterly by surprise.

Her eyes blinked open, and she stared up at him, feeling a flush spread across her face.

"I'm sorry," she whispered.

"Why?"

"That was a little premature."

"It was very sexy." He stroked his hand down her arm, then knit his fingers with hers, swaying her body against his, arousing her all over again.

She let him lead her down the hall to a bedroom at the back of the house. It was large and very masculine, decorated in earth tones, with a king-sized bed covered in a forest green comforter.

He pulled the comforter and the top sheet aside, before turning back to work the hook at the top of her slacks, then her zipper. Reaching inside, he discarded the pants and her panties in one quick motion.

"Yes, beautiful," he repeated as she stood naked in front of him.

Wanting to make up for her lack of finesse a few minutes ago, she reached for the snap at the top of his jeans. After undoing it, she lowered his zipper, and reached into his shorts, curving her hand around his cock. He felt wonderful. Full and hard and totally ready for her.

He gave her a smoldering look, then covered her hand with his, pressing her more firmly against himself for long seconds. Finally, with a sigh, he lifted her hand away.

She pushed his jeans down, and his cock sprang free, as magnificent looking as it had felt. And she knew that she had to have it inside her—soon.

He took her in his arms and brought her down to the surface of the bed. They wrapped their arms around each other, rocking together, increasing the friction of body to body.

She had always been a sensual person, and she had denied that part of her for so long. Now she was finally acknowledging her true self.

When he put a little space between them, she cried out in protest. But he was only moving away so that he could cup her breasts, then bend to kiss her there, circling her nipples with his tongue before sliding downward, his tongue tracing a hot trail down her body.

He paused at her navel and then kissed his way down to her throbbing core, using his lips and tongue on her with the skill of a man who knew exactly how to please a woman.

She had come a few minutes ago, and he made her ready to do it again.

Tugging on his hair, she pleaded. "Not that way."

He lifted his head, grinning at her. And then he covered her body with his.

She opened her legs and reached for his erection, guiding him into her.

They both cried out as he filled her. She stared up at him, wondering if her own expression mirrored the dazed look on his face.

That look meant something. Making love meant something. More than joining her body with a man's had ever meant before.

The fulfillment of a prophecy.

"Finally," she breathed.

He echoed the word.

Did it mean the same thing to him as it did to her? And what did it mean, exactly, to both of them?

She lost the thought—lost all thought—when he bent to press his lips to hers. As he began to move, it seemed like there was nothing else in the universe but the two of them.

Together again, after all the years of loneliness.

She knew that she was approaching climax and felt herself holding back. In the dream, the final pleasure had ended in a blinding headache.

But they had both gone too far to stop now.

His thrusts became harder, deeper. And she rose up to meet him with equal force.

This time they exploded together. Both of them crying out with the intensity of it.

This time there was no pain. Only pleasure. Glorious pleasure that rushed like a freight train through every cell of her body.

He stayed where he was, and she stroked his back, kissed his shoulder.

When he rolled to his side, he took her with him, and they snuggled together in the big bed.

The air-conditioning was on, and the house was cool. She lifted her hips so he could pull the sheet and the comforter over them.

She felt wonderful. Better than she had in years. And she wanted to tell him how much making love with him had meant to her.

Instead, to her horror, she started to sob.

CHAPTER
SIXTEEN

RENATA TRIED TO stifle the sobs that wracked her body. But once she had started, it was impossible to stop the wave of doubt—and guilt—from washing over her.

She had felt so good, and now reality had come slamming back to claim her.

She had been a fool. She had let her guard down. She had . . .

When she tried to roll away, Jacob pulled her close.

"Come here," he murmured, stroking his hands over her back and shoulders.

There was pain in his voice when he said, "I thought . . ."

She struggled to speak, because she couldn't let him believe this had something to do with him. Well, it did, but not the way he thought.

"It was . . . wonderful." That was all she could get out before the tears overwhelmed her again.

He rocked her in his arms, kissed her cheek, spoke to her in a low, reassuring voice. And finally the storm passed.

He reached around her to pull out a wad of tissues from the box on his night table and hand them to her.

She blew her nose, but she couldn't look at him.

"Tell me," he said, his voice so tender that she almost started to cry again. But she managed to keep from embarrassing herself a second time.

Finally, she raised her face to his. "It's been a long time since I made love with anyone."

"Why? I can't believe a lot of men haven't tried to get close."

"They have. But when I get mixed up with someone, he dies."

"What do you mean?"

In a shaky voice, she told him about James and Miguel. And about her parents.

"I'm sorry."

"So I've kept to myself."

"Nobody's going to kill me," he said, his voice hard and sure.

She kept her gaze on his face. "I'm afraid they almost did," she managed to say.

He laughed. "Yeah, I forgot about that. But you saved me. Maybe that's broken the bad-luck cycle."

She thought about that. "Maybe it was my fault."

"What do you mean?"

She hitched a breath, then said, "Two men are angry with me. The head of the Realty Association, Maxwell Sullivan." As soon as she'd said that, she was sorry she'd mentioned his name. "And the guy who takes care of repairs for Star Realty," she added quickly. "Lou Deverel. What if one of them followed me here and came after you?"

"What's their beef with you?" Jacob asked.

"Deverel was angry about the deck collapsing."

"*That's* supposed to be your fault?"

"My thought exactly. But I've had other run-ins with him. About repair work. And I've looked into his background. He was convicted of domestic violence."

"Nice guy. What about the other one?"

She swallowed. "That's confidential."

"Why?"

"Realty Association business. I can't talk about it."

"But you think either one of them would try to kill you? Or me?"

"I don't know. Maxwell Sullivan's pretty respectable."

Jacob looked like he wanted to say more, but he only nodded.

She lay back and closed her eyes, wishing that the two of them were back in San Rafael, where life was simple.

They'd be safe there. Or was anywhere safe?

Jacob stirred beside her. "Did you have a dream about me?" he asked in a gritty voice.

Her breath caught. "What do you mean?"

"A dream where you called me to an altar. And we made love. It was us. But we were other people, too. If you understand what I mean."

She wanted to deny it, but she couldn't. "You had that dream, too?" she asked in a small voice.

"YEAH. And when we came, the world caught on fire and my head hurt like hell," Jacob muttered.

"Mine, too."

"I'd like to know what it means," he said, hearing the challenge in his voice.

"I'm not sure I do."

"You don't want to face it?"

"No." The word came out much too sharply, and he wondered what she was hiding—besides her PI assignment. He already knew she was hiding *that*.

Well, he could ease back into it later.

"Where are you from?" he asked and saw her relax a little.

"Costa Rica."

"Exotic."

"Where are *you* from?"

"Nowhere special. I grew up in Maryland. I've lived here all my life," he said.

"Your family's here?"

"Uh-huh." He didn't want to talk about the Marshalls, not yet. The implications were too loaded for him. So he said, "Tell me about Costa Rica."

"What do you want to know?"

"What's most important?"

"The environment. We're into biodiversity. And that attracts a lot of tourists. They're our number one source of income."

"I thought it was coffee."

"That's big, too. Also, pineapples. They're sweeter than the ones grown in Hawaii, so they're capturing the market. I think you'd like it. There's lush rain forest. With incredible birds in colors you wouldn't believe."

Her face took on a faraway look. And he heard the pride and the wistfulness in her voice. "And monkeys. There's a beach, Manuel Antonio. The forest comes right down to the sand. White-faced monkeys live there. If you leave your stuff on a blanket or a picnic table, they'll riffle through it." She laughed. "They even know how to open zippers."

He laughed with her, imagining the scene. "Are those the monkeys you see in the ecotourism advertisements?"

"Usually, that's *mono titi*. Squirrel monkeys. They're smaller and cuter." On a roll, she kept talking about her native country. "And in the interior, we have volcanoes."

"They erupt?"

"Arenal had a big eruption in 1968, and a village got buried." She sighed. "And now a huge tourist industry is growing up around the base of the volcano."

"Isn't that dangerous?"

"Yes, but it brings in cash. They probably won't ban it until a resort gets wiped out."

He nodded, thinking it was too bad that people chasing profits often ignored safety. And as that thought surfaced, a question *he'd* ignored popped into his head.

"What were you doing at my house?" he asked.

She moved back a little so she could look him in the face. "What—you're annoyed that I saved your life?"

"No. I just want to know why you were here."

She gave him a hard look. "Actually, I was wondering what you did with the dog."

He tried to follow her logic. "Huh?"

"You took it from the shelter. And then you disappeared with it."

"Are you saying you followed me?" he asked, suddenly remembering that he thought he had seen her in the woods. Then, somehow, he'd forgotten about it.

Her expression hardened. "What of it?"

"I don't much like that." He almost asked her if he was a suspect in her murder investigation, but he managed to stop himself. He wasn't supposed to know about her private eye business.

"Sorry," she said, getting out of bed. "I think I'll leave now."

"Fine with me."

They glared at each other while she found her pants and pulled them on. Her shirt and bra were in the living room. He didn't follow her as she flounced down the hall.

He lay in bed with his anger simmering, then heard the door slam.

As soon as she left, he wondered what the hell had happened. They had wanted each other. They had made love, and it had been wonderful. They'd been warm and cozy, talking to each other in bed.

Then everything had started going wrong.

He sat up and pressed his face into his hands.

He was sure they had bonded. Sure that she was his life mate. And while they were lying in bed, they'd started picking a fight with each other.

Jesus!

He was angry. With himself. And with . . .

Well, not with her. Strange as it seemed, he felt like he was being manipulated by some outside force that he didn't understand—a force bent on tearing them apart.

He went very still, remembering Pamina's warning.

She'd told him an evil force was hovering around them. A demon.

And he hadn't wanted to believe it. Was this part of it? But how?

Christ! He just wanted to be normal. Well, werewolf normal. And now he was coping with . . .

He didn't know what the hell he was coping with. Maybe he and Renata could figure it out together. If she ever spoke to him again. Or maybe he should give her some space. If he took an out-of-town job for a few days, that would give both of them time to cool off. Or was he thinking straight? He didn't even know.

THREE days later, Renata was still trying to put Jacob out of her mind. She wanted to forget about him—about making love with him. About the mind-blowing climax. No . . . climaxes. Don't forget about the first one, when they were standing in the living room and he was playing with her breasts and she was pressing her clit against his hip.

She squeezed her eyes shut, struggling to banish that image. Just at that moment, her cell phone rang.

She saw it was Star Realty.

"Hello?"

Dick Trainer came on the line. "You must have made an impression on Kurt Lanagan."

"Oh?"

"He was looking at listings online. He wants you to show him another property."

"Okay. When?"

"Now. After you pick up the key, can you meet him at 225 Stone Creek Road?"

She was already in the car. She strapped on her holster and reached for the jacket that would cover it. Then she headed to Star Realty, where she took a quick look at the listing.

It was one of the mini-mansions that had sprung up in

the county. Now someone needed to unload the six-bedroom, seven-bath monstrosity on a wooded lot. The price was just over a million.

She picked up the key and got directions from Trainer.

"It's just after that new development. Chatsfield."

"I know where that is."

"Take the next right. That's the driveway."

"Okay."

She took Route 144, heading for the fairgrounds, then turned off on Stone Creek. When she pulled into the driveway, Lanagan was walking around to the front of the house from the backyard.

He folded his arms across his chest while he waited for her to park.

She didn't like the look on his face as she got out and came over.

"What took you so long?"

"I had to get the key to the lockbox."

"This is the kind of lot I'm looking for. I like the four-car garage."

"Yes."

To avoid turning her back on him, she gave him the key to the lockbox while she pretended she needed to get the spec sheet out of her car.

When she came in, he was in the huge kitchen, checking it out. Then he toured the bedrooms.

She followed, offering a few comments.

Finally, he went down to the lower level, which had a finished game room and two more rooms that could be used for sleeping, although their windows were small.

"This might do," he said.

"Really?" she asked, surprised. She had expected him to make some objection.

"If I can get it at the right price," he said.

She looked at the spec sheet. "It's been on the market for four months. Maybe they're willing to come down on the price."

"Offer them nine hundred thousand," he said.

"Okay," she said, not bothering to explain that she'd turn the job over to Dick Trainer.

"And if they won't take that, we can negotiate."

They walked back outside, and she watched him drive away. She'd been on edge the whole time they were in the house.

Still trying to settle down, she pulled out her cell phone and called Barry. "Did you do a background check on Kurt Lanagan?"

Barry chuckled. "Sorry, I should have gotten back to you on that. I think he's looking for property to use as a gentleman's club. As in high-class bordello."

"So that's why he wanted privacy and so many bedrooms. Should we tell the cops?"

"I don't think it would make much difference, given the way he's operated in the past."

"Should we take him off the suspect list?"

"Let's hold off on that."

"Okay," she agreed, then asked, "Did you get any more information on Jacob Marshall?"

"He's supposed to be up in Pennsylvania, at a center where they train dogs for the blind. I haven't confirmed that, though."

"Okay," she said again, then hung up.

Her heart started to pound. Jacob wasn't home. This was her chance to do some snooping. Without giving herself time to back away from that idea, she drove to his house. Fifteen minutes later, she pulled up his long driveway.

The van was outside. But not the car. Which meant he probably wasn't home. Still, she knocked loudly at the door and waited with her pulse pounding, wondering what she was going to say if he answered the door.

That she was sorry about starting a fight? She *was* sorry. Yet something compelled her to dig below the surface of his life.

When he didn't come to the door, she found the key under the rock, then picked it up with a trembling hand.

As far as she remembered, she hadn't seen an alarm

system in the house. Still, she fought a sick feeling in her throat as she shoved the key in the lock.

She had never done anything like this in her life. She shouldn't be doing it now. It almost felt like some outside force was compelling her to break the law.

If she were a cop, this course of action would be out of the question, but she wasn't working for the police department. She was a PI, and if she discovered something incriminating, she'd find a way to let the cops know.

A shudder went through her. What was she expecting to discover, exactly?

Or maybe she was doing this so she could put her suspicions to rest. Yes, that was a better reason. She clung to that as she twisted the key, then stepped inside. In the front hall, she breathed in the aroma of the house. It smelled like Jacob—that blend of man and outdoors that was so unique to him.

The air-conditioning was off. So did that mean he was away for several days?

In any event, she didn't want to stay here long. Because she was prying into his personal life. And because she didn't want to get caught.

SHE knew how to conduct a methodical search. Starting with the floorboards and the baseboards and working her way up. But she couldn't find any floorboards that were obviously loose.

The house was neat and tidy. Apparently, he liked order in his life.

One bedroom was set up as an office. She shuffled through the bills and junk mail on the desk and thought about booting his computer. But that would be a waste of time. If he had anything to hide, it would be password protected, wouldn't it?

She tried to keep her hands from shaking as she checked the desk drawers, the closet, the kitchen cabinets, the refrigerator, and the pantry. His eating habits were strange.

No cereal. No sweets. No fruit juices. No coffee. But he did have a big stock of herbal tea. And the side-by-side freezer was stuffed with packages of meat.

She checked her watch. Every minute she stayed made her blood pressure go up another couple of points.

Sprinting down the hall again, she stopped short when she reached the bedroom. Her gaze bounced off the bed. They'd made love here, and the feeling of betraying him was so strong that she almost turned around and left.

But she forced herself to cross the room and pull open a dresser drawer.

Tee shirts and sweaters were neatly folded. He even laid his undershorts in a flat stack. Closing the drawer, she turned to the closet and stared at the few dress shirts, jackets, and pants he possessed. Obviously, he wasn't a guy who got dressed up very often.

A pair of hiking boots drew her eye. Hadn't he said he was toughening his feet? So why did he need boots?

Beside the boots was a small portable file box that looked out of place among the shoes and clothing. Sitting on the floor, she lifted the top. Inside were neatly filed newspaper articles—stories about the murders she was investigating.

With trembling hands, she shuffled through the clippings. He had documented the murders, and in the last file folder was something that made her hands tingle. With numb fingers she lifted out a plastic bag. It contained hair—women's hair.

There were three bags. One with blond hair. One with black and one that looked dyed red. As she pictured the women who had been murdered, she started to shake.

This was their hair. Jacob had their hair.

The only conclusion she could draw was that he must have murdered them. And she had slept with him.

She crammed her fist against her mouth and bit on the side of her index finger.

Oh, God. She had slept with a murderer.

Pivoting, she looked toward the bed again, remembering

the two of them there. It had been so good, and it had all been a fake.

A sliver of doubt assaulted her. He'd showed up when she was alone at a house out in the country. Why hadn't he already killed her?

Because he enjoyed the game of getting close to his victims? Had he made love with the other women, too?

She bit back a sob, then fought to keep herself from going to pieces. Jumping up, she knocked over the box, then sternly ordered herself to calm down.

Going into panic mode wouldn't do her any good. She had to act rationally.

And what was the rational thing to do?

Call Barry.

No, call Greg Newcastle. He was her police contact. He was the one who needed to know.

She stood up and fumbled for her cell phone. Should she use it? Or the house line? Maybe that was better, because that would provide an automatic record of her location.

She looked at the box again, then walked to the phone on the bedside table and took the receiver from the cradle, but her hand was shaking, and she couldn't remember Greg's number.

She slammed the receiver into the cradle. Then spoke out loud to herself. "You're okay. Don't go to pieces. The number is programmed into your cell phone. All you have to do is go into your contact list."

Pressing the retrieve button, she scrolled down to the Ns.

When she heard Greg's voice, she breathed out a little sigh. In the next second she realized she was listening to his answering machine.

"This is Greg Newcastle. I'm out of the office. Leave a message and I'll get back to you as soon as possible."

"*Mierda!*" She didn't want to leave a message. But she waited for the beep, then started talking rapidly. "Greg, this is Renata Cordona. I've found the murderer. It's Jacob

Marshall. I'm at his house. You've got to get here right away."

Before she could finish the sentence, she heard the front door open. Then footsteps were pounding down the hall.

CHAPTER
SEVENTEEN

JACOB SPRINTED INTO his room, then stopped short. When he saw Renata standing beside the bed, he felt a surge of joy. He'd been miserable since she'd left, and he hadn't even been able to figure out what had happened between them. He'd longed to talk to her about it; but each time he'd reached for the phone, something had stopped him.

Now she was back.

Then he saw the look on her face and the gun in her hand, and he knew she wasn't there for the reasons he'd assumed.

"What?" he managed to say.

"Stay away from me."

"What in the hell is wrong with you?"

Her voice was flat and dead. "You murdered them."

He shook his head, because the words didn't make sense. "Murdered who?"

"The women. It was you."

"You're crazy!"

She gestured with her gun toward a box that lay half out of the closet. Newspaper clippings spilled out. Beside them lay plastic bags of hair.

"Jesus! Where did that come from?"

"Don't pretend it isn't yours." She glared at him.

"Of course it isn't mine. Somebody put it there."

She gave a bitter laugh. "Who would do that?"

He came up with the only answer that made sense. "The murderer. To frame me."

"You expect me to believe that?" she challenged.

"I expect you to believe I didn't do it."

She shook her head. "I called the police. They're coming."

"Shit!"

"You killed them," she repeated. "With a knife. And you tortured them first. With screwdrivers, pliers, and other tools. You're sick."

"It wasn't me," he said, emphasizing every word.

"You can prove that in court."

The words and the look on her face sent blind rage coursing through him. Somebody had deliberately gone to a lot of trouble to set him up. Somebody who wanted him out of the way.

"Think," he said. "Think about the guy who was here the other day. The guy who took a shot at me. He was trying to get me. He missed, but now he's found another way."

A look of doubt crossed her features, but she didn't put down the gun, and he knew he didn't have much time.

He'd heard her talking to the cops, and they were on their way now.

Recklessly, he played his trump card.

"If I were going to kill anybody, I wouldn't use knives and tools. I don't need them."

"What do you mean?"

"This," he answered as he pulled his tee shirt over his head.

"What . . . what are you doing?" she gasped, taking a step back. "Stop or I'll shoot."

"Proving it," he spat out as he began to say the chant, his hand fumbling with his belt buckle.

"Taranis, Epona, Cerridwen."

"Stop," Renata cried out, backing up against the wall. Her eyes were wide with terror. From her point of view, he probably looked like he'd gone crazy.

Maybe he had.

"Stay away."

Still chanting, he held up his hands and took a slow step back, then another. Away from her.

She might still shoot him, but at that moment, he knew it didn't matter.

RENATA stared at Jacob, her heart pounding and her throat so tight that she could barely breathe.

She wanted to scream. Her hand tightened on the trigger.

"Stop or I'll shoot," she managed to say. She didn't understand what was happening. She only knew she had to kill him.

Yet something kept her from doing it.

He was saying strange words that she didn't understand. They raised goose bumps on her arms and made the hair at the back of her neck tingle.

Dios.

She said a prayer to the Virgin. "*Ayúdeme. Por favor. Ayúdeme.*" And maybe the prayer was what kept her from pulling the trigger.

JACOB kept chanting, rushing the words.

"*Ga. Feart. Cleas. Duais. Aithriocht. Go gcumhdai is dtreorai na deithe thu.*"

"*Dios.*"

He heard her exclaim in Spanish as his vision blurred. Then he heard her scream as he leaped out of his pants and came down on all fours. As he sprang at her, he knocked the gun out of her hand. It clattered to the floor.

Ignoring the terror in her eyes, he snarled at her.

His own anger surged. He was a primitive being, and he

wanted to strike out with his teeth and his claws. He wanted to punish and maim.

But he had enough logic left in his brain to know that she wasn't the one he wanted to hurt. It was the bastard who had done this to him—to them.

Because he knew that planting the evidence here wasn't aimed only at him. The idea was to tear him and Renata apart. And it had worked.

Even as he tried to reason through what had happened, he was acting on instinct.

He knocked Renata to the ground and kicked the gun away, under the night table.

Then he said the chant in his head, speeding through the transformation again, fighting the pain that came from changing so rapidly.

But he had only minutes to get the hell out of here.

He was a man again. Naked, crouching over her.

Another woman might have been paralyzed with fear. She had the guts to raise her head and glare at him.

"It was you. The wolf. It was you."

"Yeah. I chased the pack of dogs away. I saved your life." She swallowed.

"Think about that."

Still, she lifted her chin and ordered, "Get away from me."

"No. We're leaving, whether you cooperate or not."

He yanked her up and pulled her to the closet where he grabbed a tie from the rack and used it to secure her hands behind her back. Then he tied her feet and used a tee shirt to gag her.

She stared at him with wide frightened eyes, and he knew that he was making her think of murder again.

But he couldn't leave her here.

He pulled on his pants and shoes, then his shirt. After he was dressed, he grabbed a backpack from the closet shelf and swept the clippings and the bags of hair inside before slinging the backpack over one shoulder.

"Come on."

When she dug in her heels, he yanked her across the room so he could pick up the gun and shove it into his waist-band.

Miraculously, her purse was still slung over her shoulder. Good. Because he didn't want to leave any evidence of foul play.

Of course there would be fingerprints. But that was only evidence that she'd been in his house.

When he heard sirens in the distance, she looked up hopefully, and he knew his time was up.

"We've got to split."

She shook her head.

He answered with a harsh laugh. "You think I'm going to leave you here so you can tell the cops I'm a werewolf? Think again."

The word made her cringe. Too bad. She'd get used to it. She was his life mate.

The knowledge made his throat close. His life mate. And they were in hell together. She'd put them there.

No, that wasn't fair. He'd just used caveman tactics to overpower her.

With clenched teeth, he untied her feet, then kept a firm hold on her as he dragged her toward the back door.

But as soon as they were outside, she sat down on the step and glared at him.

The sirens were coming closer.

"Damn you!"

He picked her up and slung her over his shoulder, then ran into the woods. It was hard to run and carry her and the backpack with the evidence. But he did it, making for the only place where he knew he'd be safe—the portal.

When they were three hundred yards from the house, he set her down and pulled the gag out of her mouth. She dragged in a huge breath.

"You have to walk."

"What if I just sit down again?"

"You won't. Because you're going to give me a chance to prove that I'm innocent."

"You have a funny way of doing it." She glared at him.

"You changed the rules by calling the cops. I can't save myself if I'm in jail."

She turned her head away.

"Come on. You wanted to know where I took the dog. I'll show you. You can meet him. He loves his new life."

He didn't know if he'd convinced her, but she started walking. Maybe she was waiting for him to untie her hands, so she could get away. But he wasn't planning to do that until he knew he had her secure in Quinn's world.

GREG Newcastle roared up the driveway and screeched to a halt. He'd been in the can, of all places. Then he'd gotten back to his desk and checked his messages.

As he climbed out of his unmarked, a couple of patrol cars pulled up in back of him.

He looked at the house. The front door was open. And when he sent one of the officers around to the back, it was open, too.

Which made it look like whoever was there had come in in a hurry—and left the same way.

Well, Renata had called for help. They could go in and look for her. He took the back door. One of the officers took the front.

After they'd quickly checked out the rooms, he called Renata's name.

Nobody answered.

He sent the two uniforms into the woods.

Meanwhile, since he'd had a legitimate reason to come in, he'd have a look around the place. Which would give him some time alone here.

JACOB took Renata's arm. "Come on."

She looked behind her as he pulled her along.

"Are you trying to slow me down? So the cops can catch up with us?"

"What do you think?"

When they reached the cave, she stopped short. "You went in there, and you didn't come out," she whispered.

"You followed me all the way *here*?"

"Yes."

"So it was true."

"What do you mean?"

"I thought I saw you. Then I thought I was imagining it. What else have you been up to?" he asked, his voice sharp.

"Nothing."

"Oh, yeah. Well, I know you've been lying to me."

She fought to keep her voice steady. "How?"

"You're a private eye. I know you were putting yourself in danger, investigating those murders." He laughed harshly. "And I was trying to figure out how to protect you. Jesus!"

She focused on the first part. "How did you know what I was doing?"

He flapped his arm. "Would you believe, *I* followed *you*? After I saw you outside in your nightgown, I wondered what was going on."

"Great," she muttered.

QUESTABAZE felt his satisfaction growing. But also his tension.

Each time in this cycle, when he thought his mission was accomplished, something went wrong.

His vision had been blocked when Renata and Marshall had been inside the house. Now she was outside again, and he was following them perfectly well.

This was it. His plan was working out, but maybe not exactly the way he'd expected.

He had found a fault line in the fabric of the universe and exploited it.

He was sure Renata had discovered the evidence he'd

planted and called the cops. Lucky he had saved the women's hair. It would match up when the CSI guys did the lab work.

That and the clippings made Marshall the prime suspect in the murders. But when it came time, he wouldn't go quietly. The guy was a hothead. It was a good bet that he'd end up dead.

Of course, his coming home and catching Renata in the act had changed the dynamics.

Marshall was angry. They were fighting now, and he was dragging her into the woods, where he could do whatever he wanted with her.

Good. That was excellent.

Marshall had tied Renata's hands behind her back and marched her into a cave. Questabaze strained to see what was happening in there. But the rock walls blocked his sight.

JACOB answered Renata's question.

"I heard you talking to Barry Prescott. He must be a real pussy, letting a woman put herself in danger while he sits in his office."

"He's the finest man I ever met!"

Jacob snorted. "We can debate the merits of Barry Prescott's character later." He turned and gave her a direct look. "Are you afraid to come with me?"

"Yes."

"At least you're being honest now."

"I'm always honest."

"I don't think so. You think it's honest to break into someone's house and search his stuff?"

"I was doing my job."

He made a frustrated sound. "This isn't getting us anywhere."

Jacob took her arm, leading her to the back of the cave, where he pressed his hand against the trigger spot on the rear wall.

She gasped when the rock began to thin, gasped again when she saw another place shimmering on the other side of what had been a solid wall.

Without giving her time to think about what was happening, he took her arm and pulled her forward.

THE demon strained to see into the cave. When he couldn't do it, his emotions swung wildly between elation and fear.

Almost. He had almost won.

Or had he?

He tried to call on his connection to Renata. But the massive wall of rock blocked his sight.

He spewed out a string of curses. Were the Fates screwing with him again?

"Not fair." He spat the words out.

He had powers beyond human imagining.

Ancient powers granted to him long ago.

He fought his own panic as he tried to forge the connection to Renata. He couldn't see her. That was bad enough. Worse, it felt like she had vanished.

Where in hell was she?

He didn't know, and he screamed his rage.

AS they stepped through the barrier between the worlds, Jacob dragged in a breath and let it out.

When Renata whirled around to charge back the way they had come, he grabbed her arm and held her where she was.

She might have turned into a trembling mass of fear as the doorway between the worlds vanished. Instead, she channeled the fear into anger.

The way she'd done before. Because that was the way she coped. He was learning that no matter how rational she wanted to be, she couldn't stop her emotions from taking over.

Her eyes blazed. "Where are we? What have you done?"

"We came through a portal. Into another universe."

Her features hardened. "You expect me to believe that?"

He shrugged. "It's just as likely as my being a werewolf, don't you think?"

Raising his head, he looked around, sniffing the air, trying to judge whether there were slavers in the area.

Once again, he had come here too late in the day for safety. This time Renata had forced the reckless course of action on him.

She must have sensed that he was distracted. Tearing herself away from him, she took off running.

CHAPTER
EIGHTEEN

JACOB'S CURSE FOLLOWED Renata as she darted away, heading toward one of the crumbling structures that dotted the landscape.

Once again, she had taken him by surprise.

But her hands were still tied behind her back, unbalancing her and making her gait awkward.

Putting on a burst of speed, he caught up with her quickly and grabbed her arm again.

"Stop. This place is dangerous."

"Thanks for bringing me here."

"It's your own damn fault. You turned me into a murder suspect, and this is the only place where the authorities can't find me."

She glared at him.

"It's time we both faced reality."

She snorted. "Really? Here?"

"Yeah. You're trapped here with me, until we figure out who is trying to screw us up."

"And what if I don't want to talk to you?"

"I think you will," he said, hoping it was true.

* * *

RENATA looked away, toward a half-wrecked house.

If she needed proof that they were in another universe, the landscape did the trick. This looked more like a war zone than the Maryland woods they'd been tramping through a few minutes ago.

She didn't want to be here, but it was her own damn fault. When she'd found the box of clippings and the bags of hair, she'd jumped to the logical conclusion, panicked, and called Newcastle.

Now that she had time to think, she saw that Jacob had a point. She'd gotten into his house very easily. Someone else could have done the same thing—and planted the evidence before she arrived.

"All right," she whispered.

"All right what?"

"Someone could have put the hair and the clippings in your closet."

"Thank you."

"But that doesn't change the fact that you scared the shit out of me with that werewolf act."

"It's not an act. It's who I am."

"You made love with me!"

"What do you think I'm going to do—tell every woman about my genetic defect before I take her to bed?"

She gave him a dark look. "Is it a defect?"

"It's a trait. We have an extra chromosome. Genetically, that usually means the person will die—or be defective. In our case, it gives us the ability to change into a wolf."

"Who's us?"

"My brothers and cousins."

"What about your sisters?"

"I don't have any. They died at birth because it's a sex-linked trait, and they lacked the proper hormones for survival."

She winced.

"But my cousin Ross's wife is a geneticist. They have a little girl. The first one born in the family in a thousand years," he said, and she caught the strong emotion in his voice.

He kept his gaze on her as he untied her hands. "But we're getting off the track. The most important point is that someone is screwing with both of us, and we have to figure out who."

She gave him a small nod, because she knew it was true. They had to settle this, and then she might end up walking away from him.

That thought made her throat clog.

"What?"

She shook her head and looked away. Her luck with men had been terrible, and this was part of the pattern.

Death and destruction followed her around. But Jacob was still alive.

She shuddered, imagining him lying dead and lifeless at her feet. Blood staining the front of his shirt.

"I almost shot you."

"You didn't."

"But you're supposed to die. Every man I hook up with dies."

"James and Miguel?"

"Not just them," she whispered.

She'd fought to hold the other images back, but they crowded in on her. Her lover with his face smashed. Or the hair torn off of his scalp. Or his body lying broken at the bottom of a cliff.

Squeezing her eyes shut, she tried to banish the terrible pictures that were playing through her head like clips from all the horror movies that had ever been made.

Her own private horror movies.

But she couldn't make the sickening images go away. And somehow she knew they were true. It had happened again and again, down through the ages. She turned her head away.

"Tell me," he insisted.

She didn't want to say the words aloud, but she forced them past her lips.

"It's happened before," she whispered.

"What?"

"I killed you. Or you died, because of me."

He stared at her with a kind of horrible fascination.

"You think I'm crazy," she whispered.

"No. An adept warned me. It's not just about *you*. It's about *us*."

Before he could explain, a flicker of movement to her right made her head jerk up. Two men dressed like barbarians had stepped out from the shadow of a nearby ruin. When she focused on them, they started running. Not away—but toward her and Jacob.

One held an axe. The other had a long knife.

JACOB thrust Renata in back of him and whipped around to face the attackers. But she had no intention of hiding behind him. As the wild-looking men charged forward, she reached her hand into the purse that was still hanging over her shoulder.

Jacob had pulled the gun from his belt. Holding it in a two-handed grip, he shouted, "Stop, or I'll kill you."

The men only jeered at him and kept coming. She got the feeling they didn't know that Jacob held a deadly weapon in his hands.

But their axe and knife would be just as deadly if they got in close enough to strike.

Her heart blocked her windpipe as she saw them leaping forward, their confidence evident.

Jacob waited, and she knew he was trying to ensure a close shot.

The men were thirty feet away when he fired. One of them looked astonished as a bullet hit him in the shoulder.

He must have had the constitution of an ox, because he

kept up the charge as though the bullet had been a bee sting.

Jacob fired again, hitting the man in the chest.

He dropped to his knees, leaning on the handle of his axe as he tried to stand again.

But his buddy kept coming.

When he was almost on them, Renata held up the canister of Mace she'd pulled from her purse and pressed the trigger.

Liquid shot from the nozzle. As a cloud of burning spray hit the attacker in the face, he screamed. Dropping the knife, he started coughing and clawing at his eyes.

But he kept staggering forward.

Jacob took the opportunity to shoot him in the head. He flopped onto the ground like a dead fish on a dock.

Renata watched blood frothing from his lips. Then he went still.

Jacob took in her reaction.

"Yeah. That's the way it works around here. The law is usually the stronger guy. Lucky for us we had your gun— and your Mace."

She stared at the man's ragged clothing, then at the jeans and tee shirt that Jacob was still wearing. "I guess I can see why you had different clothing in that storage box."

"Right. We don't fit in. We'd better find some shelter." His gaze flicked to the Mace canister in her hand. "You had that with you all along?"

"Yes."

"You could have used it on me a little while ago. Why didn't you?" he asked.

"I don't . . ." From the corner of her eye, she saw the first man Jacob had shot rise up and swing his axe at her.

"Watch out."

Jacob pushed her out of the way, putting himself between her and the attacker. As he did, the axe hit him in the side.

It all happened in seconds. As Renata gasped and whirled around, the man flopped back onto the ground.

She sprang at him. He had used up his strength attacking Jacob, and she was able to wrest the axe from his hands and chop down on his neck.

His mouth gurgled as blood spurted.

"*Cabrón*," she shouted, then leaped to the other guy to make sure he was really dead and wasn't going to attack them again.

When she turned back to Jacob, he was lying on the ground, blood spreading from a gash in his side.

Fighting her own fear, she knelt beside him. "Jacob. *Dios mio*. Jacob."

He tried to raise his hand toward her, but it fell back against the ground.

Tears blurred her vision, and she fought them back. His face was so pale, and his eyes were clouded. He had taken the blow intended for her, and she was terrified that he was dying.

Because it was destined to happen, no matter what. He'd saved himself from the police only to die here.

Everything inside her fought against that fear.

"Jacob," she said again as she rummaged in his backpack and found a shirt he'd left there. Wadding it up, she pressed it against his bloody side.

He spoke her name, but the sound was the barest whisper.

With her free hand, she stroked back the dark hair that fell across his forehead, feeling the clammy sweat on his brow.

Not so long ago, she had thought he was a killer. Now the world had turned upside down. How could he be a killer when he had leaped to save her without hesitation?

Her throat clogged as she crouched over him. And she knew that if she lost him now, her spirit would die.

No, it was more than that. It didn't just matter for the two of them. Some important pattern in the fabric of the universe would crumble. She didn't even understand exactly what that meant. But she understood deep inside her soul that his life and death mattered—and not just to her.

She reached for Jacob's hand, and his fingers were even colder than his forehead.

"Jacob."

His lips moved, but this time no words came out.

MILES away in Sun Acres, Gunner was dreaming. And in the dream, he felt a jolt of sensation. Joy leaped inside his doggy brain.

The man was back.

The knowledge came to him as a picture. And one word.

Jacob.

In some dim recess of his mind, Gunner remembered the way he had been before the man had brought him here.

Angry. Fierce. Dangerous.

He had been trained to kill, and his life had been miserable.

Pictures filled his mind. Himself outside in the heat and cold. Scratching fleas. And the terrible thirst when his water bowl was empty.

He could picture the horrible dirt pile where he had lived with his crap and piss all around. He saw himself digging a hole under the fence. Behind a bush where the bad man couldn't find him. He saw himself wiggling out. He was free. But then he bit the little boy. And he didn't even know why.

More memories leaped back at him. Men in uniforms dragging him away and putting him in a cage. Death had hovered over him then. Until Jacob had come to rescue him.

Now he lived with Griffin, Zarah, Marsh, and all the people of their big house.

They petted him. They kept his water bowl full. They made sure he had enough to eat. They threw a stick for him. And a ball.

He loved being here. He loved his new life. And it was all because of Jacob.

He could talk to Jacob in a way he could talk to no one else. But that was all right.

He was happy, and Jacob was coming back.

Or was he?

Gunner's eyes blinked open, and he looked around.

He was on his comfortable bed, under the overhang at the side of the courtyard. And the man, Jacob, was coming.

No. Something was wrong.

Gunner stood and stretched, then shook himself. He looked around at the courtyard. It was his home now. The best home he could imagine.

He was a good dog. And they let him live here because he was good. Not like . . .

He shook his head, shutting himself off from the old days. This was better. He must not do anything to make them send him away.

But fear gnawed at him. Fear for Jacob.

He looked around again. The courtyard was quiet.

If he tried to leave this place, would they let him back in?

RENATA felt a surge of panic—and anger. Anger was her friend. She had always used it as a protective mechanism when the world closed in around her.

She had to *do* something. Not just crouch over Jacob, pressing a wadded shirt to his side, watching the life ebb out of him.

But what could she do?

Pulling up his shirt, she looked at the gash in his side. When she saw it went all the way down to his ribs, she stifled a cry.

How could he survive *that*? Out here in the middle of nowhere—with no medical attention.

"Stay with me," she whispered urgently. "Stay with me."

CHAPTER
NINETEEN

DESPERATION FORCED RENATA past some barrier of time and space that chained her to the physical world.

There was a kernel of power deep inside her. A kernel that had always been walled off from her reach. Now she felt its shell cracking open.

As the barrier disintegrated, a strange warmth spread through her. She felt energy gather inside herself. Energy that she had never been able to access before.

It came from the earth and the sky. It came from a force outside herself. But at the same time, she was one with that force.

She wasn't even sure what that meant—or what she was doing. But she knew she had to channel that newly found energy to Jacob, if she wanted to save his life.

She stared down into his face, her whole focus on this man who was meant to be her friend. Her lover. Everything that she had always wanted and always been denied. Her life mate.

She didn't even know where the word life mate had come from.

No—she did. From Jacob. Somehow she had picked up the words from his mind. It was what he called her. And she knew it was true.

They belonged together as few men and women could belong to each other.

And she must save him.

But she still didn't know how to do it. All she could do was throw herself on the mercy of the power around her.

"Help me," she whispered. "Great Mother, help me."

She knew she called to an ancient deity. She didn't even know where she had gotten that name. Certainly not from her Catholic childhood.

Still, dim memories tapped at her mind. Memories from when she was very young, memories that had been lost to her as she'd matured.

She didn't have time to puzzle through that now. She had to focus on the power flowing into herself—and figure out how to use it.

She felt—or was it heard—a soft fluttering around her, like someone was beating on a drum.

"Thank you," she breathed as the force of it came pouring into her, bringing a wonderful warmth. But it didn't just seep into her being. Energy enclosed her—and Jacob, walling them off from the world.

She felt the air around them vibrate, then take on a fiery hue. And at the same time, she caught the scent of something she couldn't name. All she could say was that the air smelled different. Richer. Full of life-giving power.

She marveled at the unearthly phenomenon, then gasped as a wall of flame sprang up around them.

She shrank back, but the fire stayed in a ring, enclosing them. Inside the ring, small particles of light began to dance and shimmer in the air like a moving, golden fog. They hung there for long seconds, then began to rain down, not on the ground, but only on Jacob, making a delicate blanket over him.

Her heart leaped as her gaze traveled to his face. Slowly,

as she watched, the horrible pale tone of his skin changed. Little by little, pink color came back to him until he looked almost normal.

He coughed and his eyes opened, then focused on her.

"Renata."

"I'm right here. Right here with you," she answered, her fingers tightening on his.

"What's happening?"

"You were hurt."

"I know . . ." He kept his gaze on her. "I think I was dying. I was up above, looking down at us. I was sad that it was happening all over again. That we failed again."

"No."

He lifted his hand, watching the thin coating fall off. "What's this?

"I don't know. But I can tell it made you better."

"How?"

"Something happened. I can't explain it." She turned her free hand palm up. "I called energy to us. And the Great Mother granted me the power to . . ." She swallowed. "I guess you'd say—work a miracle."

He nodded. "I felt it."

"What was it like?"

"Warm. Comforting. It's still . . . happening."

"Yes. Lie still. Just let yourself heal."

She saw the shadows of the flames burning around them. Leaning down, she gathered him to her, in a tender and protective embrace.

She wasn't sure how long they stayed that way. But after a while, the fire and the energy faded away.

Jacob stirred.

"How are you?" she murmured.

"A lot better. You brought me back," he whispered.

He tried to push himself up, and flopped back against the ground.

"Don't move."

"We can't stay out here in the open."

She nodded. They'd been attacked a little while ago.

It could happen again, and if it did, they might not survive.

"We have to get to shelter," he said, forcing his body to a sitting position. Although he wavered, he remained upright.

"Help me stand up."

She wanted to refuse, but she knew he was right. She'd found out how dangerous it was to stay in the open, so she helped him to his feet.

Leaning heavily on her, he staggered across the ground to the nearest building.

It wasn't a lot of protection, but it was the best they had.

"Can I leave you for a minute?" she asked.

"Yes."

She ran back to the battle scene and grabbed the axe, the knife, the gun, and the bloody shirt, which she carried to the shelter where Jacob lay.

"Good idea," he said as he eyed the weapons.

After sitting down beside him, she looked out over the barren plain. "I could go for help," she said.

He shuddered. "It's too dark and dangerous."

Gingerly, she pulled up his shirt and looked at the terrible wound that had frightened her so badly. Instead of a deep gash that bared his rib bones, she saw pink skin.

Her indrawn breath had him turning his head and trying to follow her gaze. "Bad?" he whispered.

"No. It's getting better."

He nodded and closed his eyes again. "The worst time in the badlands is at night," he muttered.

"That's what you call this place?"

"Well, the land between the cities. Where there's no law."

"We'll stay very quiet. And I'll stand guard," she answered, hoping that would keep them safe.

She knew that he was weak, and he needed something to eat. But she was hardly equipped to go out and shoot him a rabbit—and cook it. She was fighting frustration when she remembered her purse again.

"Will you eat a candy bar?" she asked, remembering she'd seen nothing sweet in his house.

He made a face. "I *can* but I'd rather have chicken soup."

"Sorry."

She fed him the chocolate, peanut, and caramel energy bar she'd packed, in case she got stuck at a house waiting for a client.

As the sun dropped low in the sky, she lay down beside him, clasping her arm over his chest. They had been lovers, but this was different. A closeness to another human being that she had never experienced before.

Words of ancient prayers came to her. Prayers she didn't even realize she knew.

But she asked the Great Mother to protect them. And maybe it worked.

Jacob reached for her hand.

"I'm sorry I got you into this."

"I didn't give you much choice," she answered, her own emotions forcing her to brutal honesty. "You had to get away." In the darkness, she added. "I'm glad I'm here."

"Really?"

"Well, I'm not glad that we're in danger. Or that you almost got killed. But I'm glad that we're . . . closer," she whispered, conscious that they had to keep their voices low so that they wouldn't carry across the plain.

"Yeah."

There was an intimacy in the darkness of this place that made her able to talk.

"I had a great childhood, *gracias a Dios*. Because after that, bad things started happening. I told you, people I love die. James was killed by a hit-and-run driver. After that, it took me a long time before I could reach out to anyone again. I was so closed up. But Miguel was from a Latin culture, and he knew how to work his way into my life. He died of carbon monoxide poisoning. I found his body in bed."

He gripped her hand. "I'm so sorry. That must have been horrible."

"It was." She swallowed. "There's something I realize now. I started fighting with both of them. The way I did with you. I didn't know why. Now I think I was being . . . manipulated."

"The way *we've* been manipulated."

"Yes." She forced herself to say the next part. "By the monster."

"What monster?"

She made a low sound. "You were right. When you took the dog into the woods, I followed you. And while I was watching you get undressed . . ."

"Oh, yeah?"

She laid a hand on his shoulder. "Let me get this out before I lose my nerve. I was watching you, and suddenly, I was seeing something else. A horrible green creature, with a bloodred mouth, red eyes, and claws."

"An animal?"

"No. He stood upright. He had two arms and two legs. He attacked me. But then . . . three beautiful women made him stop."

"Jesus. What does it mean?"

"I've seen the ladies before. They used to come to me when I was a child. I think they were there to protect me." She hitched in a breath. "Too bad they weren't around to keep me from going crazy."

"You're not crazy!"

"What would you think if you kept sleepwalking—and ended up in the yard arranging flowers and rocks on a stone bench? What would you think if you saw that . . . hallucination?"

"I'd be worried. I'm sorry. No wonder you were . . ." His voice trailed off.

"What?"

"Off balance. Ready to believe I was the murderer."

"I think that monster has been hanging around me for years. When I was a little girl, I think he took an animal shape. And now . . ." She shrugged.

"Pamina, the adept, told me evil was hovering around us. A demon. But I didn't want to believe it."

"A demon! What does that mean?"

"I don't know."

"Well, whatever it is, it's been around me for years," she admitted again, "and I didn't want to believe it. So your reaction was the same as mine. I tried to cope. Maybe in the wrong way. After Miguel died, protecting myself was my main motivation."

"I understand."

"I didn't want to be hurt like that again, and I didn't want anyone else to die because of me."

"Not because of you!"

"Well, that's what I believed, and I needed to come up with a new way of thinking. Something where I was the aggressor, not the victim."

"Is that why you took up PI work?"

"Yes. But partly I wanted to help other people, too. I didn't want anyone to feel as helpless as I had." She hitched in a breath. "It didn't work out, did it? I thought I had changed, but I fell back into old patterns."

"Not exactly. You kept putting yourself in danger."

Again, she was glad of the darkness. "Maybe I had a death wish. Or maybe I knew disaster was closing in on me, and I wanted to get it over with."

He winced and brought her hand to his lips, moving his mouth against her knuckles with a familiar sensuality. "You're not alone anymore. We'll solve the problem together."

He sounded so confident, and she knew she had hooked up with a remarkable man. Maybe the man who would break the curse hovering over her. "I hope so," she dared to answer.

He ran his tongue along the edges of her fingers, and she closed her eyes, enjoying the sensations.

He aroused her, even when she knew there was no way he was going to make love to her now. She let the feeling of connection with him make her bold.

Before she could stop herself, she whispered. "I picked up something from your mind."

"You did? How?"

"I don't know. Maybe because you thought it was important. You called me your life mate. What exactly does that mean?"

GUNNER crouched low, moving toward the gate that closed off the courtyard from the city outside the big wall.

Jacob needed his help. And he had to get past the wall.

The gate opened when people went in and out. When it opened, he could slip out, into the city. He had been in the city a few times, always on a leash with one of the people who lived in the household. He didn't know the place very well. But he could go along the streets. Then to Jacob. If he could keep from getting caught.

He heard voices coming from outside. Then the guard talking to the men on the other side.

Keeping low to the ground, he waited until the barrier opened, then darted through.

"Come back," somebody shouted.

"It's the kid's pet."

"Get him."

Gunner heard footsteps running after him, but he kept charging ahead, through the city, and he was in a whole different world. Different from the courtyard.

He caught the scent of something good. Someone had dropped a piece of greasy meat on the ground. He scarfed it up. And caught a whiff of more.

Then he remembered what he was supposed to be doing—going to help Jacob.

He kept running, ignoring the smells of cats, goats, and cooking food. He was getting closer to Jacob . . . until he saw another wall—and another gate.

*   *   *

JACOB kept his lips against Renata's hand as he spoke in a voice that was heavy with emotion.

"In my family, a werewolf mates for life. Once we find that woman, we're bound together."

"And you think that's me?"

She heard him swallow. "I know it is. I know because of the way I feel about you."

"Even after I turned you in to the police?"

"Yes."

"*Dios.* That must have been horrible for you . . . when you knew I'd called the cops."

"Yeah. I didn't care if you killed me."

"Wanting you so badly frightens me," she whispered. "I think that's why I was ready to believe the worst."

He dragged in a breath and let it out. "I fought it, too. I didn't want to be tied down. Now it feels so right."

"I guess I should have paid attention to the numerology," she murmured.

"Huh?"

"The morning after that dream where we made love—I used a chart to figure out the number of your name."

He laughed. "Quite a morning after."

She laughed with him, then said, "Well, I look for ways to feel some kind of control. Numerology was a way to try and understand you."

"What did you find out?"

"That your number is nine. There's a profile for you. You're smart. Idealistic. Charming. Romantic."

"Charming and romantic. I like that."

"You like to travel."

"Yeah. I brought you *here*. What's the downside of being a nine?"

"Well, you can be judgmental. You crave freedom and passion—two things that are hard to balance."

"Hum. Right."

She swallowed. "You fall in and out of love easily."

"No. I've never been in love before."

Her breath caught.

"Only with you," he said, but his voice was fading.

Overwhelmed with emotion, she murmured, "You need to sleep."

"Um hum."

To her relief, he settled down beside her and closed his eyes.

She had intended to keep watch. But she was so emotionally and physically exhausted that she finally fell asleep. And her eyes didn't blink open until she felt Jacob stir against her.

Raising her head, she looked down at him. "I'm sorry. I was going to stay awake. Lucky for us, nobody bad showed up." She kept her gaze on him, trying to make a critical evaluation.

He watched her assessing him. "How am I?"

She grinned. "A lot better."

"Yeah. I feel almost human." Sitting up, he looked around. "I want to get to Sun Acres."

"You need to rest."

"Later." He used the wall to help himself up, then wavered on his feet.

She watched him with concern.

"We'd better do it, while I have the strength. There are thugs and slavers all over the place out here."

He looked down at the backpack. "I don't think we can carry this."

"Maybe we can get it later."

When he started walking, she slung her arm around his waist and they moved together.

She watched him grit his teeth as he struggled to keep going. Every moment, she expected him to fall over, but he doggedly put one foot in front of the other. From the look on his face, she didn't know how he stayed upright, much less walked.

She kept glancing around—right and left and also in back of her, in case someone like the barbarians attacked.

To her relief, they appeared to be the only ones on the plain.

He made for the next crumbling structure. When he reached the wall and stumbled inside, he sat down heavily.

"You can't go on," she whispered.

"I'll be fine." He leaned his head back, sucking in air. She had cured the wound, but he had lost a lot of blood, and that had sapped his strength.

After a few minutes, he pushed himself to his feet and started off again.

"Stop."

When he ignored her, she caught up with him, supporting his weight as he stumbled onward toward the next building. He hardly made it inside.

This time, after he'd rested for a few minutes, he was unable to rise again.

"Shit!"

She sat down beside him and laid her head on his shoulder. "It's okay. We'll stay here."

"We can't!"

"Then I'll go for help."

He gave her a dark look. "You don't know how to find the city."

"Give me landmarks."

He closed his eyes, and she saw him trying to gather his thoughts.

"You look for a dead tree," he muttered.

She'd seen a lot of dead trees, and she had no idea which one he meant.

"To the north? South? West?" she asked.

"North."

"Okay."

She could use the sun to guide her. But going north wasn't exactly like having a GPS—or a road map.

"What else, after the tree?" she asked.

"A broken building. Big. It must have been four or five stories. After that, it's only a few miles."

"Okay."

He made an exasperated sound. "This isn't going to work."

"It will! You just have to keep yourself safe until I get back."

She was just gathering herself to stand when a flash of movement made her freeze.

"What?"

"Another guy who looks like he crawled out of a Baltimore heating grate."

"Shit."

She sucked in a breath. "Sorry. There are three of them out there."

CHAPTER
TWENTY

AS RENATA WATCHED, one of them looked down at the ground and pointed, then up again and gestured toward the partially standing house where they had taken cover. She realized they had probably stopped at their first shelter and were following the trail that she and Jacob had left in the dirt as she'd helped him stagger along.

It was a good bet that they'd already seen the dead men on the ground and figured that their adversaries couldn't be in very good shape.

Did she know that bullets had killed one of the men? Or did it just look like a knife and axe fight?

Well, she still had the gun and the knife she had taken away from one of the assailants. The axe had been too heavy for her to waste the energy on it.

"YOU take the knife," she whispered, sliding the weapon toward him. "I'll use the gun."

He answered with a grim nod because both of them knew that in his condition, she was better equipped to shoot.

As they waited tensely for the attack, the silence stretched.

What the hell were the men out there planning?

She'd seen three of them. When they finally made a move, only one of them came boldly forward.

So where were the other two? Probably sneaking up on them from another direction, while the boldest one provided a distraction. Luckily, he didn't know that the gun gave her a big advantage.

She waited until the guy was twenty feet away—then fired.

Somehow she missed the first shot.

Steadying her hand, she pulled the trigger again and hit him in the chest. He went down, his face registering astonishment.

"How many shots do we have left?" Jacob asked.

She made a frustrated sound. "I'm not sure."

Beside her, Jacob tightened his grip on the knife, ready to make a last-ditch defense, but the other two men had seen their friend fall and had taken cover.

The air around them was still and silent. Long seconds ticked by, and she wished she knew what the *cabrónes* out there were doing.

Finally, she saw a rush of movement as two men came running toward them, dodging and weaving to avoid the fate of their companion.

She fired, then fired again, but their technique was successful, and she missed.

When the trigger clicked, she knew the gun was empty.

HOWARD County Police Detective Greg Newcastle pulled up in front of the two-story red brick house.

He could have conducted this conversation on the phone, but he wanted to see Barry Prescott's reaction when they talked. He'd checked up on the guy. He was in his late sixties but looked younger. He'd been in the PI business in

Maryland for the past thirty years, but he was starting to slow down, and he'd taken on a younger partner who could do the legwork for him.

Greg pulled up in the driveway, climbed out of his unmarked, and walked up to the front door.

It took several moments after he rang the doorbell before he heard footsteps inside.

Prescott was probably looking out through a peephole. When he opened the door, his face was a study in surprise.

"Detective Newcastle."

"Can I come in?"

"Of course." The PI stepped aside.

Greg followed him into a small foyer.

"Let's go to my office."

"Sure."

They walked down the hall to a wood-paneled room that looked like it had come from a Hollywood set for a detective movie. With an upscale private eye.

Prescott sat down behind his desk, giving himself the home-team advantage.

"What can I do for you?"

"I want to talk about Renata Cordona."

"Okay."

"Did you send her to Jacob Marshall's house to look for evidence?"

Prescott looked surprised. "Did she go there?"

"Yeah."

"Did she do something illegal?" the PI asked.

"Let's get back to the original question. Did you send her there?"

"No."

"Did you talk about Marshall being a possible suspect in the real estate murder cases?"

Prescott shifted in his seat. "We talked about several possibilities."

"Such as?"

"That's confidential information."

"We're working on this case together. No information is confidential."

"All right. Lou Deverel. Dick Trainer. Maxwell Sullivan. Kurt Lanagan."

Greg blew air out of his mouth. "Whooee. That's quite a list. Who's Lanagan?"

"He's had Renata show him a couple of properties. She thought he was fishy."

"You haven't mentioned that to me."

"Not yet."

Greg got out his notebook. "Give me the names again." As Prescott recited the list, he wrote the names down. He'd been checking in with Renata every few days, but she hadn't discussed any of these men.

They were supposed to be cooperating with each other. Now he realized he'd been out of the loop.

Before Greg could gather his thoughts, Prescott took the offensive.

"You started off by asking about Renata going to Jacob Marshall's house. What about it?"

Greg kept his gaze fixed on the PI's face. "Apparently, Renata broke into his house."

Prescott winced.

"Did you send her over there?" he asked again.

"Of course not!" He lowered his voice. "I didn't tell her to do it. But sometimes she's impulsive."

He sounded sincere, but that could be an act.

"She called me to say that she had evidence linking Marshall to the crimes."

The PI sat forward. "What evidence?"

"We don't know, but both of them are missing. I was hoping you'd have some insights into where they went."

"Nice of you to mention that."

"I just did."

Prescott ran a hand through his salt-and-pepper hair, his face distressed. "You think he kidnapped her?"

"It's possible. Or they're working together on some kind of scheme."

The PI's expression turned to outrage. "Absolutely not. She's gung ho. I can believe she'd put herself in danger. But I can't believe she'd work with a guy she thought was a killer."

"They might have taken off into the woods. I'm bringing tracking dogs out there now. Do you want to come along?"

"Yes."

JACOB put his hand down beside him, hiding the knife from view. He didn't have much strength, and he was going to have to let the guy get close enough for a surprise strike.

He could pull one of them away from Renata. Unfortunately, there were two of them.

And they both had knives, held in fighting position.

Would Renata's Mace stop the other guy?

Just as the first man was about to leap on Jacob, he heard a deep growl. In the next second, a brown and white body hurtled out of nowhere, landing on the man's back.

It was a dog.

"Gunner!" Jacob shouted.

The guy screamed and flailed with his arms, trying to get the dog off his back. His friend dashed forward, intent on slashing the animal.

Before he reached him, another four-legged attacker leaped into the fray.

A wolf.

Caleb.

He brought the second thug down.

Renata grabbed the knife out of Jacob's hand and sprang to defend them.

"No," he shouted, but she ignored him, bending low so

that she could slash at the leg of the man who was trying to get Gunner off his back.

He screamed and struck out at her.

ROSS Marshall pulled into the driveway leading to Jacob's house and stopped short. He had some information about the PI, Barry Prescott. And he'd wanted to deliver it in person.

But yellow crime scene tape blocked his entrance to the property. Up ahead of him, several cop cars were pulled up like pioneer wagons drawn into a defensive circle.

His heart started to pound. He could see Jacob's car parked up by the house. His van was also there, along with another car.

While he was jotting down that license number, a uniformed officer came trotting over.

"What's going on?" Ross asked.

"Who are you?"

"Ross Marshall. Jacob Marshall's cousin. What happened?"

"I'm not at liberty to say."

"Is Jacob all right? Is he hurt?"

"You'll have to leave."

"I have a right to know if he's all right."

"We don't know," the cop answered, and maybe that wasn't a lie. Something had happened here, but this flunky didn't have any information.

Ross gritted his teeth, aware that he wasn't going to pry anything out of the patrol officer.

He was about to turn around, when another car came up the driveway and pulled around him.

It looked like a Howard County detective was driving. And beside him in the passenger seat was none other than PI Barry Prescott.

"You'll have to leave," the uniform said to Ross again, "unless you want us to take you into custody."

"On what charge?"

"Interfering with a police investigation."

"Okay, I'll get out of your way," Ross said, holding his anger in check when he saw the officer's look of satisfaction.

The guy might have pulled rank, but that wasn't the end of it. Not by a long shot.

CHAPTER
TWENTY-ONE

RENATA DANCED BACK, out of the way of the slashing knife blade.

Gunner took advantage of the opening and went for the man's throat.

He screamed, and the scream turned into a gurgle.

Meanwhile, Caleb was mauling the other guy, who finally went limp.

Gunner ran to Jacob, his eyes pleading, and Jacob held out his arms.

The dog leaped into them.

He heard the animal's confused thoughts. His joy mixed with panic. Agony poured off of him.

I didn't want to kill. I didn't want to fight again. But I had to do it to save you.

"It's okay. It's all right," Jacob crooned as he stroked the dog's head and neck and buried his face against the short, stiff fur.

"It's okay. You did the right thing. It's all right to fight if . . . if it's to save someone you love," he finished, feeling the thickness of his voice.

The dog lifted his head, and large brown eyes searched Jacob's.

He continued to speak to the animal in a low, reassuring voice. "You saved my life. And Renata's." He looked around. "How did you get here?"

Again, the answer wasn't in words, but Jacob could follow it.

I felt you coming to me. From a long way off. I was glad you were coming. And then I felt your . . . trouble.

He kept stroking the dog, wanting to reassure Gunner that he'd done the right thing. "Lucky for us."

"Renata, this is Gunner, the dog I brought here a few days ago."

"He seems . . . different now."

"The adept I told you about fixed his mind. He's got a good life now."

The wolf made a throat-clearing sound.

"Right, where are my manners?" Jacob answered. "The other canine is my cousin, Caleb," he told her.

"Hi," she said in a strained voice.

Caleb nodded, then looked from Renata to Jacob. Trotting over to one of the thugs, he tugged on the leg of his ragged pants, before looking back at Jacob again. Then he pawed the ground.

It took several repetitions for Jacob to figure it out. Turning to Renata, he said, "Caleb wants to change to human form, but he doesn't have any pants. If it was just us guys, he'd go naked. But . . ." Jacob shrugged, acknowledging this classic werewolf problem.

Renata got up on shaky legs and went to the nearest dead man. With a grimace, she stripped off his pants and stepped back.

The wolf darted in and picked them up in his mouth. Then he disappeared behind the wall. In a few minutes, a blond-haired man stepped into view.

His nose wrinkled as he looked down at the pants he had pulled on. "These are disgusting."

"Better than being bare-assed," Jacob said. "Caleb was

born in 1907 or thereabouts, so he's pretty comfortable here."

Renata goggled at him. "You don't look old."

"I was dead for seventy-five years."

"Oh," she managed.

"This isn't the body I was born with. I got it from a dead man."

When she tried to take that in, Jacob added, "You'll get used to the Marshalls."

"Uh-huh."

He threw her another curve by saying, "Caleb, this is Renata. My life mate."

She caught her breath, and some of the color drained from her face.

He felt the same rush of feeling. Well, maybe not the same, because he'd known he was going to make the declaration to the rest of the pack.

"Yeah, there's no point in keeping it a secret." Jacob swung his head toward Caleb. "But there are some complications. She ratted me out to the cops on a murder charge."

Renata made a strangled sound.

"You're joking," Caleb said.

"Unfortunately not. Somebody planted some pretty convincing evidence at my house."

"And I fell for it," Renata added in a gritty voice.

"But we'll get it straightened out," he finished, hoping it was true. Then he said to his cousin, "What the hell are you doing here like this?"

"Gunner brought me. He escaped from Griffin's house."

The dog whined as he huddled against Jacob, who continued to stroke him.

"He had a nameplate on his collar. They caught him down by the city gate and sent one of the servants to bring him back. But he kept whining and lunging toward the gate. I came down there and saw that he was really upset, so I changed to wolf form. I couldn't talk to him the way you do, but I knew he thought that getting out of the city was important. So I went with him."

"Thanks."

"I wondered if it had something to do with you. He's pretty devoted to you."

Renata jumped into the conversation again. "Jacob was hurt. He lost a lot of blood, and he can't make it to the city on his own."

She had barely finished speaking when the dog jumped up and began to bark again, then took off running, toward a spot where Renata saw dust rising from the plain.

ROSS started down the driveway, giving every impression that he was slinking off with his tail between his legs.

He drove back to the road, then through a wooded area until he could turn off onto an unused lane.

After hiding his car under the trees, he gritted his teeth in frustration. He didn't want to waste any time, but he needed information.

So he pulled out the laptop he kept under the front passenger seat, booted up, and hacked into the Maryland Motor Vehicle Administration computer.

Then he typed in the license plate on the car he didn't recognize.

It belonged to Renata Cordona, the PI who worked for Prescott.

Very interesting.

Something was definitely going on. So was she there? Injured? Dead? What?

He hadn't seen any vehicles from the Medical Examiner's office. Or an ambulance. That didn't mean they hadn't already been to the scene and left.

Grim-faced, he got out of his car and looked around to make sure he was alone, then started taking off his clothes, which he stuffed into a pile of nearby leaves.

Standing naked in the woods, he said the chant that turned him from man to wolf, pushing through the change because he knew that every second counted.

When he was down on all fours, he started back toward Jacob's house.

He arrived to see the police detective talking on the phone.

"Okay. We'll be expecting them. No, I don't have anything from the kidnap victim, if that's what she is. Yeah, I'll have some of Marshall's clothes ready."

Clothes? Kidnap victim?

Prescott spoke to the cop. "And you have no idea what evidence she found that led her to believe Marshall was involved in the real estate murders?"

"No."

Ross sucked in a sharp breath. Renata had found evidence linking Jacob to some murder?

He knew Jacob. The guy might be a hothead. But he was no murderer.

Ross's mind raced. He did remember something about women real estate agents getting killed.

He tried to stay focused on the conversation, to pick up as much information as he could.

Prescott was shaking his head. "I'm worried about her. She'd check in with me if she could. We've got to find her."

Ross sorted through what he'd heard and concluded that they were bringing in dogs. More than one, from what he knew of police procedures.

Shit.

They thought Jacob kidnapped Renata Cordona and murdered several others. And they were going to try and follow his trail.

Unfortunately, maybe the kidnapping part was true. If Jacob had caught Renata in his house with what must be planted evidence, he might have dragged her away while he tried to figure out his next move.

Would he hurt Renata?

Ross doubted it. He'd picked up some interesting vibrations when Jacob had talked about her. Like his cousin cared about her in the way a werewolf could only care about his life mate and his children.

As those thoughts went through his mind, he circled around the house, then went into the woods.

He could follow his cousin's trail as well as the dogs, and he had a pretty good idea where Jacob had gone—toward the portal.

He moved his thinking several steps ahead. If Jacob had gone into the other universe, the dogs would come to a dead end, but then their handlers would start poking around in the cave. And they'd have a mystery on their hands.

In the distance, thunder rumbled. Ross cocked his head to the side. With any luck, they'd get a storm, and the handlers would have to get the dogs out of the woods where they wouldn't get hit by lightning. Unfortunately, with good tracking dogs, rain wouldn't put them off Jacob's trail. But maybe a werewolf could scare them away, especially if one of the dogs was young and inexperienced.

Ross started off toward the cave, crossing and criss-crossing the trail that Jacob had made, hoping to at least confuse the issue—and make the dogs nervous.

He could tell there was another person with Jacob, and it was definitely a woman, from her scent. Probably Renata.

What he needed now were another couple of werewolves, but he didn't have time to go and get them. Thunder rumbled again. Closer.

He was on his own, and he'd better decide what he was going to do now.

RENATA took in the men's tension as they followed the progress of the approaching riders.

Caleb was the first to relax. "It's Quinn," he said. Then he explained for Renata's benefit, "My life mate. I guess she wasn't going to let me wander around out here alone. It looks like she brought soldiers with her."

"Good thinking," Jacob answered.

The woman was in the lead, and Renata saw that five men followed her. If she'd had to describe them, she would have said they were dressed like Roman legionnaires, with light body armor, bare legs, and sandals.

As soon as they reached the group, Quinn dismounted and ran to Caleb.

"Are you all right?"

"Yes."

She looked down at his pants and made a gagging sound. "You smell like you spent the night in a garbage dump."

"Well, I took these off a dead man."

She grimaced, then ran back to her horse and opened a saddlebag. Moments later, she came back and handed Caleb a bundle of clothing.

He disappeared again, then reappeared wearing leather pants, with a shirt that looked like it had come from an outfitter back home.

But he'd also put on the standard footwear: sandals.

Turning to Jacob, he asked, "Can you ride?"

"I hope so."

"We'll go slow," Quinn said, then looked at Renata and said, "I'm Quinn. You're from Jacob's world?"

"Yes."

"I've been there," she said, a note of pride in her voice. "I guess this place is kind of strange for you."

"Yes. I'm Renata." She cleared her throat and said, "Jacob's life mate."

Quinn's face lit up. "Congratulations!"

Renata gave Jacob a quick look. "We've still got to work out some issues."

The other woman nodded. "But you will."

"I hope so."

"We'd better get out of here," Jacob said. "We've already been attacked twice."

The others murmured in agreement.

The soldiers helped Jacob up onto one of the horses. Another got down and offered Renata his mount.

She climbed into the saddle without help. Back in Costa Rica, when they'd lived out in the country, she'd ridden bareback down the road to the neighbors to pick up baskets of eggs, which she'd carried carefully back to her mother.

She hadn't been on a horse in years, but the skill came back to her quickly. And the exhilaration. She loved riding, and she wished she could take off and gallop across the plain, but she knew that was dangerous, so she stayed with the others as they started off toward the city.

The horses walked. Since there were now three extra riders, three of the soldiers also had to walk.

The dog trotted beside them and occasionally raised a wave of envy in her by dashing off when he spotted something interesting, then darting back.

The soldiers stayed alert for trouble, probably worried about the slow speed of the party. But she knew that Jacob couldn't go any faster. She kept glancing over at him. His face was pale, and he tended to lean forward.

When he caught her watching him, he sat up straighter, and she knew that he didn't want her to see him looking weak.

Finally, Quinn gestured ahead of them. "There's Sun Acres."

Renata squinted and made out the shape of buildings. But what she saw wasn't like any city she'd ever seen. Not even back in Costa Rica.

Well, that wasn't entirely correct.

It reminded her of medieval hill towns she'd seen in Europe. Walled towns of low stone buildings and narrow streets, designed so they could be easily defended. The only difference was that Sun Acres occupied a gentle rise, not a real hill.

She kept her eyes on the city as they approached. The highest buildings were only three stories tall, poking up above the massive stone wall.

They stopped at a gate, which was open but well guarded.

Apparently, the men stationed there recognized Caleb and Quinn, because there was no problem about entering.

As they rode through the streets, she looked around at the shops with signs that showed pictures of the products rather than words. The shops gave way to houses that sat shoulder to shoulder.

Leaning toward Jacob, she whispered, "It feels like I've dropped into a historical movie."

"Yeah. I hadn't thought of it that way, but now that you mention it, that's a good description."

The houses grew bigger, with walled land around them.

When they rode through a massive gate into a large courtyard, servants rushed forward to take their horses. And children came running toward Gunner, who greeted them with wags and licks.

Then a man dressed something like the soldiers only in richer clothing came striding out of a doorway. A young woman with long golden hair and a long gown was behind him.

She ran toward Quinn, drawing up beside her horse. "I was worried about you. You should have stayed here."

Quinn shrugged. "You know I couldn't hang back when Caleb might be in danger. And I had the soldiers with me. They wouldn't have let anything happen."

"You should have taken a bigger guard."

"We're fine."

"Thank the Great Mother."

Quinn turned to Renata. "This is Griffin, the master of the house and the leader of the city council. And Zarah, his wife."

"Hello," Renata answered, wondering how she was going to be received by the dignitary and his wife. When she saw Zarah give her a startled look, she caught her breath.

CHAPTER
TWENTY-TWO

ROSS HEARD THE dogs coming closer, following Jacob's trail toward the cave where the portal was hidden.

He could keep away from them easily, because he had several advantages. He knew this neck of the woods. And he was more intelligent than any dog.

The sky was filled with a mass of storm clouds. Thunder rumbled again, and the wind picked up.

Bring it on.

But though he could feel the storm quivering in the air, the rain held off.

Partly in frustration, and partly because it was his best strategy, Ross lifted his head and howled, then howled again.

In response, one of the dogs made a whining sound.

He couldn't see them, but he heard a man urging them forward.

"Come on, Ranger."

"Brando, good boy."

Ross howled again, and he knew from the shouts of the men that the dogs had turned and run.

They might be trained trackers, but that didn't mean they wanted to tangle with a wolf.

He could hear the men trying to control the animals and wondered what the handlers thought they had heard.

A few fat drops of rain fell, and Ross figured he was home free. If the storm broke, the men would have to take the dogs back.

Then someone came running through the woods. And he saw that it was the private detective, Barry Prescott.

He had an automatic weapon in his hand. And obviously he wasn't going to let any forest creature interfere with this search and rescue operation.

He caught sight of Ross and squeezed off a series of shots.

Ross turned and ran.

"Hold your fire," someone shouted. But the PI either hadn't heard or didn't care.

He fired again, and Ross dashed into the woods—just as rain came pouring out of the sky.

JACOB stood beside his mount, trying to keep from falling over. He wasn't sure if he would have succeeded if Caleb hadn't climbed down and come to his side.

Renata was on his other side.

Together they helped him into the house. It was difficult to climb the stairs, but he made himself do it. Then Caleb was leading him down the hall to the room where he slept when he stayed here. As soon as he was inside the door, he flopped onto the bed and closed his eyes.

RENATA stood looking at Jacob. She wanted to go into the bedroom with him and close the door behind her. But she knew that would be rude. She'd just met these people who were being so kind to her and Jacob.

And she had another reason, too.

She stepped back into the hall and found that Caleb and Quinn were there.

"You probably don't feel really comfortable here," Quinn said. "I know I had a lot of trouble adjusting to staying at Logan's house back in your world."

"Who is Logan?"

"Jacob's brother," Quinn answered. "I first went there because another council member tried to have Zarah killed, and she needed a safe place to stay."

Renata winced. "Is it always so violent here? I mean, I guess I can understand it out on the plains. But in the city?"

"It's a lot more stable since Griffin got the council members to see the advantages of not trying to assassinate each other," Quinn answered. "And Caleb's making improvements in the standard of living. That's helping, too. When people are more comfortable, they're more content." Quinn looked down the hall. "Come have something to eat. I know you've got to be hungry, if you spent the night and half the day out in the badlands with no food."

"Yes. Thanks."

They stepped into an interior courtyard where Zarah and Griffin were playing with a baby.

Renata stood looking at them with envy. It was such a warm domestic scene. Then she reminded herself that they'd earned their happiness.

Zarah left her husband and the child and came over.

"What can we get you?" she asked.

"Anything's fine." She looked down at her feet, then up again. "You looked startled when you saw me. What did you see?"

Renata held her breath, waiting for the other woman to answer.

Zarah spread her hands. "I saw power."

"What do you mean—power?"

"Come eat something while we talk."

Zarah led her to a table on one side of the courtyard, where food had been set out.

As soon as she saw it, Renata's stomach rumbled, and she looked with embarrassment at her hostess.

Zarah smiled. "Please help yourself. Our cook made an excellent quiche for you. We also have meat and cheese, and what I think you call crudités. And a bread pudding. I'm hungry all the time from nursing the baby. I'll eat with you."

"Good."

They both took food and water from a pitcher, then sat at a nearby table.

After they'd eaten a few bites, Zarah began to speak.

"I lived in your world for a few weeks, and I know it's not like ours. Here, a lot of people have psychic powers. On the other side of the portal, it's unusual. Did Jacob explain how we're different here?"

Renata chewed a piece of soft cheese and swallowed it before answering. "A little."

"Until 1893, your world and ours were much more alike. But we each had a World's Fair in Chicago that year."

Renata nodded. She didn't remember the year of the Chicago World's Fair, but she'd take Zarah's word for it.

"A man named Eric Carfoli set up a tent there. He told people he could give them psychic powers. And he did."

"I don't remember hearing anything about that," Renata said.

"I think he wasn't in your world. Or what he did didn't work there. But it worked here. Lots of people came out of his tent with mental abilities they hadn't possessed before. They were excited to have such strange new powers. But the people without talents were afraid of them, and the two groups started gathering together and fighting each other."

Renata tried to imagine what a mess that would have been.

"We used to have the United States of America—the way you do," Zarah continued. "But it didn't survive the fighting. The best we could do was gather together into cities for protection."

Renata nodded.

"We don't have industry. Elders go around to households testing children for psychic abilities. The ones with the most potential are put into special schools where they develop their powers. I went to one. We find out what we're best at. I'm certainly not one of the more talented. But I can use the flame of a lamp for communication over distances. And for healing."

"That sounds pretty impressive to me."

Zarah waved her hand in a dismissive gesture. "Believe me, my abilities are minor." She shifted in her seat. "Well, they've increased since I had the baby. I can recognize when a person has psychic talent." She cleared her throat. "I was surprised to see it in you—because I know it's not common in your world."

"I didn't know I had it," Renata said in a whisper. "But when Jacob was hurt, I was able to cure him. I don't know how I did it. I felt like I was calling on some energy outside myself. Do you think it happened because I came . . . through the portal?"

"I don't know. But I could bring someone here who could help you figure it out. A very strong adept who can sense things you can't."

"Yes, thanks," Renata answered. But when Zarah started talking about life in Sun Acres, she had trouble focusing on the words.

For weeks, she'd felt like she was losing her grip—with the sleepwalking and the strange ceremonies. Jacob had made her feel better. But suddenly, a disturbing phrase kept running through her head. *A danger to herself or others.*

That was the criterion they used when the cops or the medics came to cart someone off to a mental hospital. Did it apply to her? And how? Was she going to hurt someone the way she'd almost hurt Jacob? Or hurt herself?

Finally, she simply couldn't stay seated. Feeling awkward and ungrateful, she stood up. "Would you think I was rude if I went back to Jacob's room?"

Zarah also stood, studying her with concern. "Are you all right?"

It was impossible to explain what she was feeling when she didn't understand it herself.

"I'm a little shaky."

"You should rest. But you might want to wash before you lie down.

"Thank you," she answered, wondering just how grimy she looked. "Yes, I'd love that."

"There's hot water in the kitchen. I'll have some sent up."

Renata couldn't help feeling uncomfortable. "I'm putting you to a lot of trouble."

"Life is different here. It's not quite the way you're used to doing things. But let me enjoy playing hostess."

"If you're sure."

"Of course."

A maid came into the courtyard, and Zarah gave her some instructions before going off to get several gowns—similar to the one she was wearing herself.

Next she took Renata to a small bathroom and left her alone with a pitcher of water, soap, a basin, and a washcloth.

While she washed, she fought a sense of gathering dread. Other people had died because of her. Who was going to be the victim now?

Jacob. Dios. *Not Jacob.*

Quickly, she dried off and threw on the gown Zarah had given her. Then she flew down the hall to the room where Jacob was sleeping.

With a trembling hand, she reached for the door handle. As soon as her fingers connected with the wooden knob, a flash of flame erupted, enveloping her in a circle of fire.

She screamed in pain and terror, beating at the flames with her hands, but she couldn't put them out.

Through her own panic, she heard people shouting. A woman screamed. A baby started wailing. Several sets of footsteps came thumping down the hall.

Then Jacob wrenched the door inward and leaped toward her.

CHAPTER
TWENTY-THREE

RENATA HEARD JACOB call her name in horror.

Dashing back into the room, he tore the coverlet off the bed and wrapped it around her, trying to smother the blaze.

It should have worked. But she could still feel the flames scorching her flesh—and still see the fire licking through the covering.

Pain and fear enveloped her. "Stop! *Por Dios*, stop," she cried out.

She could hear people rushing around. Several maids came with buckets, throwing water onto her and Jacob where they lay on the floor, his body partially covering hers.

The water soaked through the coverlet, but it seemed to have no effect on the flames.

It was strange to feel cold water and fire at the same time. But the pain was no longer just on her skin. It felt like she was being consumed from the inside out. Tears streamed down her cheeks. Not just from the pain. There was so much she had never done. She had to tell Jacob she loved him. She had to tell the police she'd been wrong. She had to catch the real murderer.

But she wouldn't get to do any of that, because she would be dead. Very soon.

Someone else was crying. And she heard a man cursing. That was Jacob.

Strong hands tried to pull him away, but he shouted, "Get the hell off of me," and clung to her.

Shouldn't she smell smoke? And burning flesh. That thought flitted through her mind, but she didn't have the strength to hold on to it.

She tried to move her hand, to bring it up so that she could embrace Jacob—her love—one last time.

She would lose Jacob now, the way she had lost him over and over through the centuries.

All at once, as though the conflagration had finally run its course, the burning stopped, and she lay trembling violently on the floor, unable to control the movements of her arms and legs.

When she looked up, she saw tears streaming down Jacob's face.

"Don't. It's all right," she managed to say.

"No! Oh, Christ, no."

"It stopped," she whispered, shocked by the strength of her own voice.

"What?"

"It stopped. And . . . and . . . the blanket isn't even burned."

He looked down at her as though he couldn't believe what he was hearing.

Cautiously, tenderly, he pulled the coverlet away and looked in amazement at her clothing and her skin.

She heard his indrawn breath and followed his gaze.

There was no evidence of the blaze. When she held up her hand, she saw that her flesh wasn't burned. Neither was her gown. Or anything else.

It had been terribly real. The pain and the terror were as tangible as anything she'd ever experienced in her life, but it had swept over her and not left a mark that she could feel or see.

A circle of people had gathered in the hallway, all of them staring at her in hushed silence.

When she tried to sit up, Jacob pressed a gentle hand to her shoulder.

"Stay there."

Zarah knelt beside her, touching her face, her hands, her gown. "I was waiting to see if you needed anything. I saw you walk down the hall. Then I saw the flames."

Renata answered with a small nod.

"I thought you were on fire. I thought you were going to die."

"Yes."

"But there was no smoke. And no . . . smell. And I started wondering if it was psychic."

Renata swallowed. "Psychic? From where?"

"I don't know. Do you have enemies? Could someone have attacked you?"

She thought of all the bad things that had happened in her life. They had all had real, physical causes. Or had they?

"It could be an enemy," she whispered. "But how could an enemy follow me here?"

"If it's not from outside, then you have to consider that it came from within your own mind."

Renata stared at her. "From me? But why?"

"To punish yourself."

She didn't like that concept, but she could understand it. She'd hurt Jacob with her call to the police. She could have been punishing herself for that.

"But I never . . ." She stopped short, remembering an incident when she was little. Back in Costa Rica, in the community school where the children came from the farms and villages. The teacher was giving a prize for the best story. She and Juan Sanchez both wanted to win, and when she got up to go to the bathroom, she spilled ink on his paper. She was so sorry, she told him. He had to hurry to write his story again. And he had to cross out some words. So she had won the prize. A carved and brightly painted bird.

When she went up to the front of the room to claim it, Juan stared at her with sad, angry eyes.

She bowed her head as she accepted the prize. As soon as her fingers touched the painted surface, it burned her hand. She dropped the thing, and it had broken in half.

And Juan gave her a look that said, "Serves you right."

Was he the one who worked some kind of magic and made the bird burn her? Or did she do it to punish herself?

The pressure of Jacob's fingers on hers made her focus on the present again.

"Renata?"

"Um hum."

"Where were you just now?"

"Thinking about what Zarah said. Maybe I *was* punishing myself. For calling the cops on you."

"Don't!"

She gave him a wry look. "At least I had the sense to wait until we were safe—here."

Zarah came back into the conversation. "Don't make assumptions about what happened."

"We may never know," Renata whispered.

"In your world, it might be hard to find out," Zarah answered. "But I told you about our adepts. One of them can help you figure it out, if you want to."

"Of course I do."

"Then I'll call Pamina."

"Who is she?"

"She helped cure Gunner," Jacob answered.

"And she helped cure me," Caleb added. "When my body and soul separated."

She might have focused on that strange revelation, but Jacob was speaking to her again. "Can you stand up?"

"I think so."

He helped her to her feet, and she wobbled on unsteady legs.

"You'd better lie down."

She couldn't argue with that. The pain and terror of the fire had drained her.

Jacob led her to the bed where he'd been sleeping.

Gratefully, she flopped down and lay with her eyes closed. She needed to know what had happened, yet fear gnawed at her.

Jacob sat on the edge of the bed beside her as she lay with her heart pounding.

"I'm afraid," she whispered.

"I know. I am, too," he answered. "We're caught up in something that neither one of us understands."

"But I think we have to figure out what's going on, if we want to survive."

"Yes," he agreed, his voice gritty.

"How are you feeling?" she asked.

He laughed. "I should be asking *you* that question."

"I'm pretty good, considering I expected to be dead." She swallowed. "When I thought I was going to die, I wanted to tell you I love you. So much."

His hand tightened on hers. "I love you. You're the most important thing in my life."

"Is that enough?" she asked in a shaky voice.

"I hope so."

Still clasping his hand, she closed her eyes, wishing she could sleep. Some time later, a knock at the door startled her, and she realized she'd dozed off.

"Who is it?" Jacob asked.

"Pamina."

Panic grabbed her by the throat. She didn't want this woman to see her looking like an invalid.

"Just a minute," she called out. Quickly, she climbed out of bed, ran a hand through her hair, and pulled the coverlet up. Then she sat down in the chair near the window and nodded to Jacob.

As soon as she'd told him to open the door, she realized she was barefoot. But she couldn't do anything about that now.

A very attractive woman came in and closed the door behind her. She looked like she might have been in her late fifties, yet something about her made her seem older.

She nodded to Jacob. "I'm glad that everything worked out with Gunner."

"Yes, thank you. And thanks for coming back," he answered, moving to the armoire on the far wall and propping his shoulder against the corner.

Pamina looked at Renata, whose heart was pounding so hard that it felt like it was going to break through the wall of her chest.

"You're Renata, the woman Jacob mentioned when he was here before."

"Yes."

"Can I examine you?" she asked.

"Yes," Renata answered, checking to see if the woman had a medical bag with her. But she only had a small satchel.

The adept came over and looked into Renata's eyes, then picked up her hands, examining first the backs and then the palms.

"Will fire burn me again?" she asked in a shaky voice.

"That's up to you."

"What should I do?"

"I can't give you the answer. That has to come from you."

Oh, great. So what good was this woman going to do them? Feeling at a disadvantage, she climbed to her feet, then had to grab the arm of the chair to steady herself.

Pamina gave her a critical look. "The fire was quite an ordeal. You should lie down."

Giving in, Renata returned to the bed, where she plumped up the pillows, then eased onto the coverlet, propping her back against the pillows rather than lying flat. Jacob and the adept pulled two chairs close to her.

When Pamina gave Renata a long look, she had the uncomfortable sensation that her head was glass and the woman could see inside and read all her thoughts. She hoped it wasn't true.

Finally, after a long moment, the adept spoke. "When I met Jacob, I knew he was in danger. He thought the danger might be coming from you."

Renata glanced at him. "That was perceptive of him."

"It's okay," he whispered.

"Okay that I ratted you out to the cops?"

"We'll deal with it," Jacob answered.

"Together," Renata added.

The adept looked at her with satisfaction. "You have a strong will," she said. "And I think you have learned to admit when you have done something wrong."

"I hope so."

"When Jacob was here a few days ago, I gave him some tea that helped him understand some things. I can give you something stronger. A potion that brings back lost memories."

Renata felt a spurt of hope. "Can we do it now?"

"I must warn you. It could be dangerous. It has driven some people mad."

She couldn't repress a laugh that bordered on hysteria. "I've had a lot of practice fighting off madness recently."

Jacob turned toward Pamina. "Let me do it. Instead of her."

The old woman shook her head. "You have too much resistance. I found that out when I talked to you before."

He started to protest, but the old woman waved him to silence, and he closed his mouth.

"Let's get this over with," Renata said.

The adept set her bag on the chest under the window and brought out a small packet. Inside was a brownish powder, which she sprinkled into a glass of water she poured from the pitcher.

After stirring it, she handed it to Renata. She looked at Jacob, seeing the worry on his face. "It will be okay," she said, praying that it was true. Before she could lose her nerve, she lifted the glass to her lips and drank.

She had thought it might taste nasty, but it had the flavor of herbs and honey. Almost as soon as it went down her throat, she started to feel strange.

She tried to look at Jacob, but his face wouldn't come into focus. And all at once she felt like she was falling,

falling into the fury of a tornado. It caught her and spun her around, and she heard herself scream, heard Jacob curse.

"What have you done to her?"

"Pray she has the strength to see it through."

Did she?

She knew that her hands gripped the bedcovers as she tried to hang on to herself—to hang on to sanity. Pamina had warned her, but she hadn't been prepared for *this*.

She felt as if she were being torn apart. Memories leaped at her. She was a woman standing on a high, rocky bluff above the sea. She was in anguish, and when she couldn't take the pain a second longer, she flung herself off the cliff and into the sea. Before she hit the bottom, she was another woman, her arms wrapped around a dying man. Then she was yet another woman, tied to a stake waiting for a monk with a black hood to light the wood piled around. She leaped from scene to scene. And each time it was at the last moments of her life—or of the man she loved.

She heard herself whimper. Felt the cells of her brain tearing apart. Death followed her, clawed at her, stripped the flesh from her bones.

From somewhere she heard a woman's voice. "Go back. Go back to the beginning."

"I . . . can't," she gasped.

"You must. If you want to survive."

She screamed a protest. Then she was whirling away again, hanging on to consciousness by her fingernails.

She clawed herself into another woman's mind. And at last, the pain and death were gone. She was someone else. A woman with power she could never have imagined.

From far away, she heard Pamina's voice. "Tell us who you are."

"Rocanda."

"Ah. The earth goddess. She ruled long ago."

"Yes."

She sat in a beautiful white temple. In a garden of un-imagined beauty, bright with flowers. Butterflies flitted past her. And hummingbirds dipped into the flowers, sipping their nectar. The light around her was golden. From above, the sun splashed down on rocks arranged in a pattern on the ground. It was like the garden back home, only much more vibrant.

Some tiny part of her was still in the room back in Sun Acres, and she heard Jacob gasp.

"I rule over the face of the Earth," she murmured. "The rocks, mountains, and the soil, and everything that comes from the soil. The trees of the forest. The grasses and flowers of the plains. And the crops that men planted. When people wanted a fruitful harvest, they prayed to me. But I do more than watch over their crops. I help keep peace among nations. I help the seasons keep their stability."

A shiver traveled over Renata's skin. She had spoken the words. But were they true?

Oh, yes!

The power was intoxicating, and at the same time it threatened to overwhelm her. Yet she knew there was more. She clenched her fists, trying to drive away the pain that was to come.

"Speak," a woman's voice said.

She wanted to draw into herself, to savor the good memories. She wanted to bask in the glow of her power. But the voice from outside herself kept intruding.

"Tell us, so that we will understand. Tell us in your own words what went wrong."

She could flick the voice away with a wave of her hand. Yet a sense of duty kept her speaking.

"I fell in love with Jalerak, a man who was half god and half mortal." She swallowed painfully. "I had never shared that joy with a man before, and . . . and I got so carried away with my love for him that I neglected my duties. Harvests failed. Floods washed away the soil. The people began to look for another god to worship."

Renata caught her breath, struggling against the truth. She didn't want to go on, but she knew she must.

"My father, Thaodin, was one of the old gods. He had

once been powerful, but he had been foolish in his ways, and he had lost much of that power to his children. Once he had ruled the mountains and plains, and he wanted domain over the land again."

She stopped, unable to go on.

"Finish it," the voice urged. "You must finish it."

It was too painful to speak in the first person. On a sob, she began again, talking about herself as though she were someone else.

"Rocanda had weakened herself, and her father looked for a way to throw her aside. Then he grew worried, because she was starting to find her footing. She was starting to figure out how to manage her duties and her personal life. So he knew he had to act quickly."

Renata could barely breathe. She wanted to disappear into some dark place where she could hide from the terrible truth. Somehow she forced herself to go on. "Rocanda wanted the blessing of her father for her marriage, and he said he would give it if she and her lover would come to a sacred mountain temple. They were happy to receive his blessing, so they traveled to that temple—not knowing what he had planned."

Renata felt a terrible pressure inside her chest as the old reality dragged her under like a drowning swimmer. She tried to struggle back to the surface, back to reality. But she was locked into this nightmare, and she couldn't return to her own life until she finished.

"Thaodin had made a bargain with the dark forces. He had brought demons to the temple with him, demons who had promised to help him change his fate. And when Jalerak and Rocanda arrived he gave them food and drink. It was drugged, and it twisted their minds. They started to fight with each other." She sobbed, overcome with horror. "No. *Dios.* No."

CHAPTER
TWENTY-FOUR

FROM FAR AWAY she heard a voice cry out.

"What? What happened?"

It was Jacob, and she wanted to hide the truth from him. But she had to say it. So he would know the source of her pain.

"I stabbed Jalerak, and he fell dead at my feet." As she said the last part, Renata's whole body jolted. She felt shame and despair in every cell of her body.

"But that wasn't the end of it," she whispered. "The demons had lied to Thaodin. They had no intention of helping him. They killed him, because they wanted the Earth for themselves."

She felt sobs rack her body. Heard Jacob calling her name, trying to bring her back.

But she was caught up in Rocanda's tragedy.

"It wasn't her fault," Jacob shouted. "They drugged her."

She had been far away. In another life, but now when she raised her eyes, she could see him again—through a shimmering mist. But she was seeing Jalerak, too. "I couldn't cope with the truth. You were dead, and I had killed you," she murmured. "I killed myself, and the world went haywire. Volcanoes erupted and spewed lava over the land. There were great earthquakes and great tidal waves. The people were in despair. But the Fates came down from the heavens. They couldn't change things back the way they had been, but they could intervene because . . . because Rocanda and Jalerak were innocent victims. The Fates said the two of us must have another chance to get back together."

Renata blinked, seeing the room more clearly now. Seeing Jacob, his face a mask of horror.

"You hate me," she whispered.

"No. Of course not." Reaching out, he grasped her hand. "Come back to me now," he begged.

Ignoring him, she kept speaking, rushing through the last part. "The demons have partial power over the Earth. But they can't have absolute rule as long as we have a chance to reunite. We have been reborn in the bodies of humans hundreds of times over the centuries. The demons must let us meet each other and start to bond. But then they sow the seeds of mistrust between us." Her voice hitched. "They tear us apart. Jalerak dies. Then Rocanda dies, and the cycle starts all over again."

She gasped as the room came back into focus. She sat on the bed, clasping Jacob's hand. And Pamina sat in a chair watching them.

"*Dios, no*," she breathed.

"There are lots of old myths," Jacob argued. "Lots of different cultures. That story may just be a drug trip—from that potion she gave you. And you made up the whole thing because you want to explain what's happening to us."

Renata looked deep into his eyes. "I know why you don't want to believe it," she whispered, struggling to hold her voice steady. "But I think we have to." She dragged in a breath and let it out. "I was telling it to you, but I felt the truth of it. In my bones and in my blood. I *was* her. I *was* Rocanda."

Before he could speak, she went on, "All my life, even when I was little, I read stories of ancient mythology. From different cultures. I studied all kinds of strange arts. Numerology. Tarot. Astrology. And rituals were always important to me. Little things like counting my steps when I walked. And big things like doing a . . . purification ceremony when I moved into a new house. Or praying at my parents' grave on the same day of each month. I think I was trying to understand what I was. And trying to ward off the evil forces. Of course, none of the stories or the rituals really helped."

She saw emotions chase themselves across Jacob's face. Jumping up, he paced to the window and stood with his whole body rigid. She waited with her breath frozen in her lungs. Would he leave her now? Or was he strong enough to stay?

She saw him straighten his shoulders. Turning, he came back to her.

"I knew something was happening to us. Not just from what Pamina told me." He glanced at the adept, then back at Renata.

"I didn't want to believe it."

"Of course not," Renata answered.

"I guess we finally know the truth," he muttered.

Pamina gave them a long look. "I'm glad neither one of you dismisses it."

"Too much has already happened to me—to us," Renata answered. "I knew something bad was hovering around me. I finally understand."

"Recognizing what's happening means you are on the right track," Pamina said.

"But what can we do? How can we stop it from happening again?" Renata heard her voice quaver. "How can we fight a whole legion of demons?"

"I cannot answer that question."

"Yeah, that would be too easy," Jacob muttered.

The adept studied him. "Each time, over the years, the bond between Rocanda and Jalerak failed. But I think you are the key. You have more strength than the men who have received this gift and borne this burden before you. I think you have a better chance than the others because you are a man and also a wolf. And you will protect your mate as no other man can."

Renata saw Jacob's lip firm. But she had to ask one more question, the question that had brought Pamina here in the first place. "Why did the fire burn me?"

"The fire comes from deep in the earth. It feeds your power. But you must control it—or it will destroy you."

That wasn't exactly what she wanted to hear.

The adept stood and crossed the room. "You had the courage to bring forth the old story. Now you must solve this problem together."

Renata stood and reached for Jacob as Pamina swept out of the room, leaving them very much alone.

His arms tightened around her. "Jesus!" he breathed. "I don't like it."

All she could do was clasp him tightly, running her fingers over the strong muscles of his back.

"I feel like I don't have control over my own life," he muttered.

She nodded against his shoulder. "We have to take control."

"So what do you suggest we do?"

"I was afraid you were going to ask that."

QUESTABAZE wanted to scream in frustration. The seconds and the hours ticked by, and still he couldn't find Renata.

Once, he had been able to pass between the worlds. But that was long ago, before the great dance of power had settled into a stable pattern. Somehow, without his knowing it, he had been locked in place.

He had assumed that Renata was locked in this world with him. Now he wondered if she had somehow gotten to another universe.

"Where is she?" he cried out. "Is it my fault? Because I set the dogs on her? Have you hidden her from me?" he railed.

He was talking to the Fates again. But they didn't answer him.

He'd told himself he was playing by the rules, but maybe they didn't see it from that point of view.

For a few hours, he had thought the tracking dogs would solve his problem. They would find Jacob Marshall. And when they found the bastard, they would find Renata. But it hadn't worked out that way.

And there was one more piece to the puzzle that sent a shudder through him.

The police dogs had been following Marshall's trail. And then a wolf had showed up in the woods and screwed up the whole operation.

A wolf?

It seemed crazy. There were no wolves in the Maryland woods.

But somehow one had appeared.

Like the animal that had saved Renata from the dogs.

Through the centuries, he had heard stories of wolves. Not true animals, but unnatural creatures.

Was this one of them? Were there more?

And why would they be aiding Renata?

He tipped his head back and howled—like the wolf. Only his cry of anguish was impossible for any man or woman to hear.

TO give herself a little time to think, Renata slipped out of Jacob's arms and walked to the window.

Now that the adept was gone, it was hard to hold on to the feeling of certainty.

She'd just told Jacob and Pamina a fantastic story—that was supposed to apply to her. Was she really the reincarnation of a goddess? It seemed unbelievable. Yet she could remember the feeling of power. The feeling that she was more than a human being.

And the story fit with some of the memories from her childhood, when her mind hadn't been so tied to the world around her.

Sometimes in her imagination, she'd gone away to another place. A garden more beautiful than the one surrounding her house. A place where she felt safe and powerful. Now she was pretty sure that somehow she'd gone back in time to the beginning of the story. Or at least that was what it seemed like.

Of course, there was one piece of the puzzle she kept excluding. The horrible green-faced demon. Unfortunately, that also fit the story.

Demons. Who wanted the Earth for themselves. So they had tricked a god into betraying his daughter.

She hitched in a breath and let it out.

But a goddess could fight demons.

Careful. Don't get a swelled head. You haven't done a great job of it so far.

Yet if it were true . . .

She shoved away the bad part and let herself feel the power of ownership. This was her land. This planet belonged to her.

The excitement of that notion was like arousal pumping through her veins.

With a low sound, she clamped down on the seductive feeling. If she was the reincarnation of the goddess Rocanda, then she was thinking from the wrong angle. Her job was to serve the planet and its people, not take possession of them.

And so far, if she was a goddess, she had killed her lover. She had let her heritage slip through her fingers. She'd been granted chance after chance to reclaim her rightful place, yet she'd messed up every time.

A shudder went through her as she thought of the past few weeks. She'd almost screwed up *this* time. Because of her, Jacob would be in jail, accused of murder—if he hadn't brought her through the portal to this world.

Behind her, he cleared his throat. "What are you thinking?"

"That I was on my way to messing up again before you brought me here. Which brings up another question. Was I a goddess only in this universe? Or in the one where we came from?"

"The trouble for us started back home. I think we have to assume it's in both places."

She nodded. "Maybe it was ordained that we come through the portal—to fulfill our destiny."

"It hasn't changed our bad luck," he muttered.

Silently, she agreed, but she wasn't going to just give up. "Back home, when I was sleepwalking, I was doing some kind of ceremony. With natural things. Stones. Flowers. Maybe I was trying to get in touch with . . . the goddess part of myself. I was using things from nature, because that would be right for Rocanda."

"Um hum."

"Maybe now that I know about her, the ceremony would make more sense." She sighed. "Except that there's nowhere like my garden around here."

"Why don't I ask Quinn—or Zarah? Maybe they can suggest a place."

He crossed the room and was out the door before she could say anything else, and she wondered if he had been looking for an excuse to put some distance between them.

JACOB strode down the hall, hoping that Renata wasn't going to follow him.

He'd been struggling with his reaction to her past life regression, if that's what it was. It was a hell of a lot to deal with.

Unfortunately, maybe he didn't have a choice. The adept had said that he and Renata had met in different lives, over and over through the centuries. Each time, they had come to a horrible end.

This time they had a chance to make it come out right.

He stopped halfway down the hall, trying to make sure his facial expression didn't give away his inner turmoil before he strode to the courtyard. As soon as he entered, heads swiveled toward him.

The people he'd come to think of as friends were there. Quinn and Caleb. Griffin and Zarah, who was holding her baby tucked in a blanket against her chest.

He realized she must be nursing the infant and looked quickly away.

Should he be here? Well, she was doing it in front of the others. She must feel comfortable with it.

Maybe she saw his expression, because she said, "Come sit with us. How is Renata?"

He pulled a chair to the table and sat. "She's doing better."

"Was Pamina able to help her?" Quinn asked softly.

He wanted to be honest with them, but he hadn't totally come to grips with the idea that Renata was the reincarnation of a goddess and he was the reincarnation of her lover. So he only said, "We learned some things. I think we're going to have to help ourselves."

Quinn nodded. "She did that to me."

Caleb reached for her hand, and he watched the silent communication between them. Their start had been so rocky. Now they were rock solid. He wanted to have that with Renata.

Or was that possible? With a goddess?

While he was turning over those thoughts, Zarah asked, "What can we do to help you?"

He gave her a grateful look. "Renata wants to hold a ceremony. But it has to be outside. In a natural setting like a garden. And I don't think I'm going to find anything like that around here.

Griffin cleared his throat, and everyone turned toward him. "Maybe there is a place. A garden some women use.

They keep it looking nice, as part of their worship of the Great Mother. But it's outside the city, and I haven't allowed them to go there in the past few weeks, because there's been an unusual amount of trouble in the badlands. There seem to be several organized gangs of slavers operating out there."

"Yeah, we ran into a couple of them," Jacob muttered.

"If I send you outside the city, it will be with an armed guard, but I have to ask the women's permission first."

"Okay, I'll go tell R—" He almost said "Rocanda." But he changed it to Renata at the last moment, then excused himself to tell her the news.

In the bedroom, he found her pacing back and forth from the window to the bed, counting her steps in a low voice.

"Would you stop so I can talk to you?" The question came out more sharply than he intended.

She went still, and he told her about the garden. As soon as he finished, she started pacing again.

As he watched her march back and forth, he clenched his fists. He might have started screaming. Or changed to wolf form and started howling, but neither of those things would do him much good.

Finally, he said, "I'm going to see how Gunner's doing."

"Right. A dog is easier to deal with than people," she answered, her voice low and tight.

"This is a mess. We don't know how to treat each other," he blurted.

"When did we ever?"

"You have a point."

They stared at each other, tension crackling between them.

Before one of them could say the wrong thing, he turned and left the chamber again, taking the back stairs so he wouldn't run into the group still sitting in the courtyard.

Gunner jumped up, glad to see him. He found a stick and tossed it for the dog. Then settled down beside him, his eye on the gate.

He was still sitting with Gunner when Griffin came riding back into the compound.

When he caught sight of Jacob, he dismounted and strode over.

"The women agreed," he said.

"Thank the Fates," Jacob answered.

"The Fates? You believe in them?" Griffin asked.

Jacob shrugged. "They were part of the story . . . from Renata's past."

Griffin nodded, but he didn't ask for clarification.

"So how do we work it?" Jacob asked.

"As soon as I get a guard together, you can leave."

"We're putting you to a lot of trouble."

"No. I already have the system in place. Tell Renata to be ready as soon as she can."

"Right." Jacob turned and hurried back up the stairs. When he reached their room, it was empty, and his heart gave a lurch inside his chest.

Had she changed her mind? Had she left him? Gone back home?

His pulse was pounding as he ran down the hall toward the family courtyard.

ROSS Marshall drove toward his cousin Logan's house, which was almost as close to the portal as Jacob's. And Logan had another advantage in this situation as well. His wife, Rinna, was from the universe on the other side of the portal.

Ross had waited for the "kidnapping" incident to hit the news. So far, nobody was talking about it, which meant the cops were keeping it under wraps. It reminded him of that case at Camp Lejeune, where a pregnant Marine had been murdered, and nobody had started looking for her until a week later. Down in North Carolina, the Marines had stalled the investigation. Up here, it was the Howard County PD. Maybe because that PI, Barry Prescott, had asked them for some time.

As far as Ross was concerned, the quieter they kept it, the better.

When he knocked on the door, Rinna, Logan's life mate, answered. She was an attractive, dark-haired young woman who had started life as a slave in the other universe. Now she was happy to be living with Logan in a quiet corner of the Maryland woods.

Because she was from that other world, Rinna had a trait that he'd never encountered among women here. She was also a shape-shifter. She could transform into a white wolf—and into a white bird of prey as well.

When he took in her surprised look, he said quickly, "Is Logan here?"

"No. He's out on a job. What's wrong?"

CHAPTER
TWENTY-FIVE

JACOB SKIDDED TO a stop in the courtyard.

Renata was standing at the far end of the enclosure, wearing a white gown that emphasized her slim waist and full breasts and left her arms bare.

Zarah and Quinn were sticking flowers in a wreath that crowned the top of her head.

Jacob's breath caught as his gaze traveled over her. "You look beautiful," he murmured.

Raising her head, she searched his face. "I'm sorry I was giving you a hard time."

"I understand. We're both on edge. But Griffin just came back. He told me it's all set up. You're supposed to be ready as soon as possible."

"We decided to get started, just in case," Renata answered.

Zarah joined the conversation. "You should change your outfit, too."

"To what?"

She gestured toward a pile of clothing laid out on a side table.

"I picked them," Renata said. "I hope it's okay with you. It seemed like the thing to do."

He held up a short tunic, then sandals with long leather straps. He didn't tell her he was going to feel like his ass was exposed in that outfit. He just took it back to the bedroom and put it on, glad that he was almost back to normal after his near-death experience.

When he returned to the courtyard, Renata had put a long white cape over her dress.

Since she was still weak from the fire, Griffin had provided a small, light buggy designed to go much faster than the usual wagons.

Ten guards went with them. He hoped the number was excessive, and that they weren't going to run into any trouble. At the same time, he was glad of the escort.

They rode out of the city in a northerly direction, to an area he hadn't visited before.

Neither he nor Renata spoke. Or touched each other. He didn't see that as a good sign, but there was nothing he could do besides follow her lead. To his relief, it wasn't a long ride. Soon he saw a huge ruined building in the distance. It looked like it had been a church or a cathedral.

Just to the right was a stone wall that looked to be in better repair than the building. The wooden entrance door was closed with a stout padlock. And symbols had been painted on the wood.

Jacob pointed to them. "What are those?" he asked the nearest soldier.

"Warnings that something bad will happen if you enter."

Did that apply to him? Jacob guessed he'd find out.

As the cart stopped, Jacob climbed down and walked toward the gate. He was wondering how they were going to get inside, when Renata pulled a key out of the small white bag slung over her shoulder.

He hadn't noticed the bag before, because it hung flat and unobtrusive against her side.

She inserted the key in the lock and pulled on the hasp.

As they stepped inside, Jacob heard her draw in a breath. They were standing at the top of a little flight of steps, looking down on a series of stone paths that wound through carefully tended beds of shrubs and flowering plants.

Scattered through the beds were statues and stone benches. And off to the side was an open area with what looked like a grassy lawn. It was hard to believe that such a place existed in this world.

"This is amazing," Renata whispered.

"Yes."

"The women must care about this garden." She descended the steps and began wandering down one of the paths. As she did, she picked some of the flowers. When he saw a smooth white rock that looked like some of the ones she'd gathered in her garden back home, he picked it up.

"Yes," she murmured.

Was she giving him permission? Or asking for his help? He couldn't be sure, but he kept picking up rocks and small pieces of wood that appealed to him while she gathered growing things.

She turned to her right, to a place where a five-foot wall formed a sheltered niche. At the front was a stone platform that might serve as an altar.

Silently, she laid the flowers down on a bench at the side, then used her hand to sweep leaves off the altar.

When it was clean, she took off her cape and laid it on the bench, then brought the flowers to the altar and began arranging them in a pattern.

He could see that her hand wasn't quite steady.

"Should I put the stones there?" he whispered.

"Yes."

He came forward and set them down. "Do you want more?"

She turned, and he saw the uncertainty in her eyes. "Yes. Okay."

He was glad to do something useful. Hurrying down a path, he found a place where lots of rounded stones were piled around the base of a statue. He scooped up as many as he could hold and carried them back, then set them on the altar.

Moving out of her way, he watched her body tremble as she arranged the stones and the little sticks and the flowers.

Then she knelt in front of the altar and clasped her hands together.

He could hear the low murmur of her voice. She was asking the Fates for help. Asking the universe to grant her the boon of wisdom.

He felt very alone. Separated from her. A shadow hovering at the edge of her life.

Somewhere birds chirped. And a little wind stirred the branches of nearby bushes. But no flash of lightning came down from the sky. No Fates appeared before them to answer the questions that had been building up in their minds.

What did the Fates look like anyway?

Renata stood up again and started rearranging the objects on the altar, moving flowers and stones and twigs into a different pattern.

Still, nothing changed.

LOGAN had brought his brother, Lance, to the family conference.

"As far as I can tell," Ross told them, "Jacob escaped through the portal because he's wanted in connection with the murder of the women real estate agents."

"That's crap," Lance answered. "Why is he a suspect?"

Ross related that part of the story.

"This Renata woman really thinks he's guilty?" Lance asked.

"I think she found convincing evidence. I'm hoping she wouldn't make up some story to incriminate him."

The others nodded.

Ross looked at Rinna. "I'd like to go through the portal and find out what's happening over there, but I know the cops are keeping watch in the woods, hoping Jacob and Renata will come back."

"Are you thinking of driving them off with wolves?" Logan asked.

Before he could answer, Rinna gave him a hard look and jumped into the conversation. "The cops have guns. They can shoot wolves."

Ross sighed. "I was afraid you were going to say that." In fact, he *had* almost gotten shot when he'd tried to interfere with the search. But he decided not to mention that.

"What about a diversion?" Lance asked. "I mean, like an explosion that would draw them away. We did that when Rinna was kidnapped."

Ross shook his head. "Not a good idea. It would draw them away, but they'd probably think that Jacob was involved in some kind of conspiracy. That would make them start trying to figure out what he was up to besides murder— and who he was working with."

They were all silent for several minutes.

Then Logan looked at his wife. "You opened a portal once. Could you move this one?"

"You can't just move a portal. You'd have to close it and open another one."

"Could you do it?"

She dragged in a breath and let it out. "Not by myself. I'd need other adepts to help me."

"Like Olivia? And Sara?" Ross asked, naming his brother Sam's and Adam's wives.

She considered the suggestion. "They both have strong powers. Maybe we could do it together. Especially if we also had Antonia."

She was the wife of Logan's brother, Grant.

"Okay. Let's make some calls," Ross said. "We can say it's a family emergency, and we need them here. But they may not be able to drop everything and come in time."

JACOB'S insides clenched as he took in Renata's stiff posture.

When she made a small sound of frustration, he couldn't

remain where he was. Stepping forward, he clasped his arms around her, and the garden disappeared as though they had never been there. The world disappeared.

Renata cried out because they were suddenly in another place. The place where they'd met a week ago in a dream.

A land that was not of the world. A land where the rules of time and space had been suspended.

He was still standing in back of her, and he felt her body sag against him as she absorbed the change.

He held her upright, when it was difficult to keep himself vertical.

Mist swirled around them, but it felt like they were standing on a hard surface. A land of rock. In front of them he could see a massive stone building, looming indistinctly in the mist.

"What happened?" As he spoke, the mist around them muffled his voice.

"It was you," she gasped.

"Me?" he asked, not understanding what she meant.

She turned to face him, and her eyes were fierce and regretful. "I was supposed to be the goddess. I thought I had to make the connection to the Fates. And I was so focused on that mission that I was shutting you out. I guess it doesn't work that way."

Since the session with Pamina, he'd felt as though an invisible wall had sprung up between himself and Renata. But he hadn't thought it was his place to object, not after the goddess story.

Would Renata have listened to him back at Griffin's house? Or had it taken a supernatural event to change the equation?

She began speaking again. "Nothing was working. I was just moving flowers and stones around. And I didn't know what I was doing. Then you touched me, and everything changed. For the better, I think."

"I hope so," he answered, when he didn't know if she was only expressing her wishful thinking.

His wishful thinking, too. Because he wanted whatever happened to depend on the two of them working together.

Since he was feeling more confident, he gestured toward the massive building. "We should go in there."

"What's inside?"

He laughed, the sound turning hollow in the foggy atmosphere. "I don't know. But I think we need to find out."

"Okay," she said in a small voice.

He took her hand, and they walked forward across the hard ground, until something stopped them.

He could see into the shadowy interior of the building, but the entrance seemed to be protected by an invisible barrier.

When he put his hand up the way he did when he unlocked a portal between the worlds, he felt a transparent wall, but there seemed to be no way to get through it.

Then Renata put her hand up, too, and he felt the surface give. They stepped forward together, from the misty exterior into a large entrance hall.

As soon as they were inside, a whooshing sound told him that the invisible wall had snapped back into place behind them.

So were they trapped? Or could they reverse the process and get back out again?

And go where?

Renata clung tightly to his hand, and he held on to her just as tightly.

"Look," she whispered, as soft light began to illuminate the interior.

His gaze fell on a richly woven rug that depicted a scene of men with spears hunting lions. "I remember that."

"Yes. This was . . ." She gulped. "My father's temple. And that's where he received visitors," she said, gesturing toward a golden throne, with rich red upholstery.

Each thing in the room—the furniture, the rugs, the tapestries—looked like it had been made by skilled artisans.

A doorway loomed at the far end of the entrance hall, but the room beyond was dark. As he looked around, he felt goose bumps rise on his skin.

"Is this the place where it happened?" he asked in a low voice.

"I think so," she answered, her tone equally hushed.

"Your father brought us to this place. I mean, the first time . . ." He let the end of the sentence dangle.

"Not this time. This time we came here with the knowledge of the past—to face whatever's here."

As she spoke, he heard a sound from the interior room. Then a shadow rushed at them out of the blackness. It had the vague shape of a man with a knife in his hand.

The shadow was dark, like a black hole out in space from which no light could escape. But as it enveloped them, Jacob felt the prickle of fire on his skin.

Fire. Again.

CHAPTER
TWENTY-SIX

EVEN AS JACOB'S senses dimmed and the fire sent darts of agony to his nerve endings, he tried to fold his body and his arms around Renata to protect her, but he knew by her gasps and cries that whatever was burning him was attacking her in the same way.

Not just on his skin. It was in his brain, bursting inside his skull, making it almost impossible for him to put one thought in front of the other.

"We have to control the fire," he gasped out.

"How?"

He looked down, his eyes locked with hers, and in that moment of understanding, he knew.

Swiftly, he lowered his mouth to hers, moving his lips with a desperate need that came from deep inside his soul. When he focused on her, his mind cleared.

The fire receded to the background as he felt passion bloom between them. The passion he had held in check since before the two of them had come through the portal.

"Renata."

She trembled in his arms, running her hands over his

back, his shoulders, her touch telling him she felt the same desperate need for connection that swamped him.

As they cleaved to each other, the laws of their own private universe shifted. Now the fire sealed them off from everything but each other, the flames mutating to an element of their arousal.

Jacob knew they had done it together, through their need for each other. Because even when they had been angry, even when he hadn't known how to reach out to her, he had longed to make love with her.

Now, it felt as if he had been turned on for days, and no woman but Renata would satisfy his desire.

And, miracle of miracles, she was in his arms, silently telling him that she wanted the same thing he did.

Every nerve ending in his body sizzled as he drank in the heady taste of her, breathed in her scent, stroked his hands over the warm silk of her wonderful skin, touching her everywhere he could reach, letting the sensory input fuel his craving for her.

"I need you." She was the one who spoke, and the words transmitted themselves directly from her mouth to his. He drank them in, absorbing the passion and drawing strength from her desire.

His hand slid down to her hips, pulling her more tightly against his erection, letting her see how much he needed her—as if she didn't know already.

He stepped back long enough to drag the tunic over his head and toss it to the floor, then stooped to rid himself of the briefs he'd insisted on wearing.

When he looked up, he saw that she had pulled off the gown and sent it to join the tunic.

He grinned at her, then sobered as he took in the perfection of her body.

"You are so beautiful," he whispered, then said it louder.

With hands he couldn't quite keep steady, he reached out to cup her wonderful breasts, reveling in their soft weight before gliding his thumbs over the hardened tips.

The sound of pleasure he wrung from her vibrated through him.

Desperate to feel her body against his, he pulled her close, so that his cock nestled against her belly while his hands stroked over the rounded curve of her bottom, then reached downward to slip into the folds of her sex.

She cried out, pressing more tightly against him, rocking her breasts against his chest.

When she drew back, her eyes were regretful, and his insides clenched.

"What's wrong?" he managed to ask.

She reached to touch his lips, to run her finger against the stubble on his cheek. "I shut you out. I think because I was too used to being alone," she whispered. "And because I was afraid to embrace . . . us."

She dropped to her knees on the rug in front of him, and when she closed her mouth around the head of his cock, he shuddered.

She ran her tongue over him, finding the places where the sensation was greatest, teasing him before taking him more fully into her mouth.

He threw his head back as she began to suck and at the same time slid him in and out of her mouth, giving him more pleasure than he thought possible.

His hands braced against her shoulders, because he didn't know how much longer he could stand up on his own.

When he knew that the pleasure was going to make him explode, he touched her cheek.

"Stop. No more. I want to come with you, not like this."

She raised her head, her eyes glimmering with promise.

He came down beside her on the rug, gathering her close. He had never wanted a woman more. Yet his own satisfaction was only a small part of what he craved.

Tenderly, he laid her on the rug.

"Your turn."

Lowering his head, he caressed her breasts with his face, then turned his head so that he could take one pebble-hard nipple into his mouth, sucking on her, teasing her with his teeth and tongue, while he used his thumb and finger on the other nipple.

Then with a smile, he slid his mouth down her body, licking and kissing her as he went, traveling to the hot, slick core of her.

"This must be what they mean by the ambrosia of the gods," he said, as he lapped up the wonderful taste of her.

She reached down, gliding her fingers through his hair while he used his mouth on her clit and dipped two fingers inside her, stroking in and out, driving her to the high peak where he waited in trembling anticipation.

When she tugged at his hair and lifted her hips in a pleading gesture, he moved up her body and plunged inside her.

They both cried out at the joining.

Her arms came around his shoulders, clasping him to her as he began to move in an age-old rhythm.

They were Jacob and Renata. But, here in this place, they were also Rocanda and Jalerak, fulfilling their destiny at last.

He went still above her. Raising his head, he looked down into her eyes.

"Yes, it's you. And me," she whispered, as she circled his shoulders with her arms. "Finally, after so long."

They stared at each other, in perfect harmony now. For several heartbeats, he remained still. Then, when he could no longer help himself, he began to move within her again in a fast, hard rhythm.

She matched him stroke for stroke, her nails digging into his back, the intensity building quickly, spiraling out of control.

"Jalerak," she cried out as he felt her inner muscles tighten around him.

The spasms were like jolts of electricity zinging through him. She took him over the edge with her, climax roaring through him like a force of nature.

And while they both vibrated with the intensity of their

pleasure, it seemed as though time folded back on itself. Or went backward.

Or something that he couldn't name.

All the centuries came flooding through his mind. All the times they had reached out toward each other—only to turn away in fear and anger because the demons had driven them away from this perfect joining, this perfect understanding.

As he clasped her to him, he sensed something he hadn't been able to grasp before.

In his memory, he could see the demon who came to them again and again.

And a name zinged into his brain. Questabaze.

He felt her gasp, as though she'd been struck by a bullet.

"Questabaze," she whispered. "That's who he is. I almost remembered it before. But not quite." She shuddered. "I saw him."

He tightened his hold protectively around her. "Here?"

She hitched in a breath. "No, in our world. He's the monster I told you about."

"Does he know where we went?"

"I don't know. Zarah told me about how the time lines changed. Maybe when that happened, Rocanda was only reincarnated in our world. So the demon was with me there, and he didn't know how to follow us to the other side. At least I hope that's true."

Jacob still lay on top of her, his body joined with hers. She clung to him, her hands sliding over his hips and onto his ass, kneading and pressing him more firmly against her.

As she did, he felt his arousal building again.

And hers. He knew that from the little internal muscle contractions clasping his cock, and from the way her breathing picked up.

Lifting his head, he grinned down at her. "I think we have an advantage over him."

"You mean this?" she asked, deliberately contracting her vagina around him.

"Oh, yeah." He held her close and rolled to his side,

shifting their positions so that they were lying facing each other.

"Let's try to use this," he murmured.

"It feels good."

"Uh-huh, but it gives us deep communication."

He saw a smile twitch at the corners of her lips, as she thrust her hips a little, then pulled back. "Deep communication? Is *that* what you call it?"

He grinned again, letting himself enjoy the sensation for a few moments before he said, "We should talk about fire. Sometimes it's good. And sometimes it's bad."

"It's bad when it has control over us. And good when we control it," she whispered.

"We'd better remember that and not let it get the upper hand," he said, his voice thick.

He closed his eyes, kissing her cheek and stroking her arm. "I don't want to hurt you."

"How could you do that?"

"Because I'm going to ask you to do something you won't like."

He felt her body tense. "What?"

"I think you need to go back to one of the bad things that happened in your life."

She sucked in a sharp breath. "Why?"

"Because we need to know if he was there. But this time, I'll be right here with you."

She ducked her head and stroked her lips against his shoulder, and he could hear her breath coming fast and sharp. "Okay," she finally whispered.

He forced himself to ask, "What was the worst time you can remember?"

She answered immediately. "It was my junior year at the University of Maryland. But I had a feeling that I needed to come home and see my parents. When I turned onto our street, I could see the house was on fire. And I knew my parents were in there."

"Fire!"

"Yes," she breathed.

The pain on her face made his throat contract. "I'm so sorry."

Her grip tightened on his shoulders. "You're here with me—now."

Her touch gave him the strength to keep asking questions. "Was there a crowd around the house?"

"Yes."

"Can you remember the people who were there?"

"I wasn't paying much attention to them," she answered.

"Do it now."

She whimpered, and he felt her squeeze her eyes closed. When she gasped, all he could do was hold her close, praying that he wasn't making everything worse.

RENATA clung to Jacob as the terrible scene came back to her.

Fire. She knew about fire.

She saw the flames licking at the house in Baltimore where they'd lived. Not the first little row house from right after they came from Costa Rica. The big house off North Charles Street that her parents had bought when their furniture business was pumping out money.

With a feeling of doom, she sloshed through the water from the fire hoses, trying to run inside and find her parents, but somebody grabbed her and held her back.

"Let me go!" she screamed.

"You can't go in there. You'll be killed."

"What does it matter?"

Her life was crumbling before her eyes, and people crowded around to witness the destruction. They were on the sidewalk and in the street, in back of the fire trucks.

She turned her head, staring at them. They were blurry images in front of her eyes, but one man stood out from the rest.

Because even if they were blurred by memory, their

faces were normal. And his face was a gray blob like he was an innocent bystander in a police film, and the cops had blocked out his head.

When she gasped, she felt fingers digging into her shoulder. Her naked shoulder.

"It's okay," Jacob said, his voice low and urgent. "You're with me. You're safe with me."

She stared into his eyes. They were clouded with pain and worry. Pain and worry for her.

"What happened?" he asked.

She couldn't hold her voice steady as she whispered, "He was there."

"The demon?"

"Yes."

"You saw him?"

"He was one of the people in the crowd, watching my house burn—and watching me try to get to my parents."

"Right there out in the open? What did he look like?"

She hitched in a breath. "Do you remember the day I came to your house—and somebody shot at you?"

"The day we first made love," he said softly.

"Yes. And we saw the shooter. Only we couldn't *see* him. His image looked like it had been digitally altered. I came up with an explanation that didn't make a lot of sense."

"But we both wanted to believe there was a logical reason we couldn't identify him."

Her skin had turned cold, and he stroked her shoulders and arms, trying to warm her.

"The man standing in the crowd was like that. In the vision just now, I could see he was there, but I couldn't see his face."

"Christ!"

"I felt his satisfaction. He *wanted* me to be in pain. It served his purpose."

"I'm so sorry."

"Well, now I know."

"Now *we* know," he corrected.

"Yes. Both of us," she answered.

"You are so strong," he murmured.

"No."

"Of course you are. He should have destroyed you. But he could never do it."

"Almost. With all the strange stuff happening, I thought I was going crazy until you straightened me out."

He looked startled.

"Yes. You made the difference."

They clung to each other for a long moment. Jacob's mind was spinning, trying to absorb everything that had happened—and reaching for something that he couldn't quite grasp.

Finally, he began to speak again. "Each time we've encountered a demon—it's been only one of them. The creature you told me about with the green skin and a red slash of a mouth. The guy in the woods. The guy watching your house burn. When you were speaking as Rocanda, you talked about demons. More than one. So we thought we were fighting a whole legion of them, but maybe only one of them is allowed to screw with us."

Hope sparked in her eyes. "That would make it easier."

He swallowed. "Maybe. But the one demon has a lot of power. And he doesn't have to play fair. He can also be human. Well, not *be* human. *Look* human."

She nodded.

"So maybe he doesn't just show up as a bystander in the crowd watching the fire. He can be different people in your life if he wants to."

"*Dios.*" She sucked in a sharp breath. "Who?"

"We have to find out." A thought danced through his mind. "But we don't know how he does it. I mean—make himself human. Maybe he can change his appearance. Or maybe he takes over the body of someone else."

"Oh, great."

"We don't know anything for sure."

Her fingers closed over his arms. "Back in Costa Rica, when I was little, I used to feel like the animals were watching me. I remember looking up and seeing a green iguana on the rocks sunning himself. Only I'm pretty sure now that it wasn't a real iguana."

He stroked his hand through her hair, thinking that the deck was stacked against them. This demon had a lot of power. And what did they have?

"Each other," she whispered.

His eyes questioned hers. "You picked that up from my mind."

"Yes. Because we're so intimate."

He nodded, touching her cheek as he asked another question that made his insides clench. "If we defeat him, does it affect more than the two of us? Will it change the world?"

CHAPTER
TWENTY-SEVEN

RENATA MOVED SO that she could brush her lips against Jacob's finger. "Let's put it another way. The world can use all the help it can get."

He cradled her close, wondering what that would mean for him. For them. Would she still be his life mate? Or would he lose her again? For the final time?

Desperation clawed at him. He wanted to bring back the sexual feeling that had warmed them earlier. But the mood was broken.

"I don't think I can do this anymore. Not right now," she whispered.

He wanted to protest. But he couldn't find the words. So he eased away, slipping out of her. When she rolled to her back, he saw tears glistening in her eyes.

"Don't." Tenderly, he turned her onto her side again, this time with her back to his front. Moving up behind her, he held her close, rocking her in his arms.

"It's been so hard for you," he murmured.

"I tried to be strong."

"And you were. As strong as you could be, with the deck stacked against you."

"He probably loved watching me go to pieces." She stiffened. "Do you think he was the one who baited that property with meat?"

He thought about it for a moment. "That would make sense. I mean, if he wanted to hurt you."

"We don't even know the rules. Could he have killed me?"

"Maybe not. Maybe he had to let us get close, so the situation is like it was for Rocanda and Jalerak."

"Lucky for me you came along," she murmured. "Lucky you're Jacob Marshall. You're so strong. When I held a gun on you, you didn't let me win."

"I was angry as hell."

"*Gracias a Dios*. Maybe Pamina was right, and it took a werewolf to give Rocanda the strength she needed."

"I hope it makes a difference."

"We'll do whatever it takes to find out who he is. Together. I'm so used to being alone that I have trouble thinking like part of a couple."

"So do I. But I'm getting used to it."

"Tell me more about your life," she murmured.

He laughed. "I'm good at understanding dogs. At communicating with them. Like you said, I guess I felt more comfortable with dogs than with people."

"I said it because I was on edge."

"Yeah, but it might be true."

"Even with your family?"

"Especially my family." He made a low sound. "For years, the Marshalls didn't get along, until my cousin, Ross, got us together. I was still resisting, but having you makes me understand why family is important."

She snuggled against him. "I had a warm, loving family."

"That's something you can teach me." He swallowed hard. "But first we have to make sure that Questabaze doesn't win."

"He won't!"

He held her close. It was wonderful to simply lie there with her in his arms. Wonderful to fall asleep that way.

Some time later, his eyes blinked open again.

He craned his neck toward the doorway and saw that the mist outside hadn't changed.

Renata stirred next to him, then stroked her hand along his arm and his hip.

"Our first night together," she whispered. "Or do you think it really is night?"

She sat up, and he did the same. "How long have we been sleeping?" she asked.

"I don't know."

"And more importantly, how do we get out of here? Not just out of this building. Out of this world that isn't real?"

Jacob made his voice sound steady, although a kind of cold fear clawed at his insides. "Let's pretend we know how to get back to that garden."

"Okay."

They both stood and reached for the clothing they had discarded. When they were dressed again, Jacob took Renata's hand.

"We got here like Dorothy got back to Kansas in *The Wizard of Oz*."

"You mean when she closed her eyes and clicked her magic red slippers together?"

"Yeah. But I'd say she wished herself there."

"Do you think our bodies are still back in our world? Like at the end of the movie when Dorothy is unconscious in bed?"

"No. I think we're here now. And we'll be *there* soon," he said, again trying to sound confident. Taking her hand, he led her back the way they'd come. When they reached the barrier at the entrance to the building, they repeated the process they'd used earlier, flattening their hands against the invisible window.

Again, the surface turned malleable, and they stepped

outside, into the mist. Only this time, he could see sunlight glinting in the distance.

He pointed. "Let's go that way."

Their hands linked together, they walked toward the sun. And suddenly, from one step to the next, they broke through the mist and into the daylight. Into the garden, where Renata had been arranging natural objects on the altar.

"Thank God," Jacob whispered, because he hadn't been sure there was any way to get back. But here they were.

He looked toward the gate. "They'll be worried about us. We'd better tell them we're okay."

"Yes."

They hurried toward the entrance, and Jacob threw the door open.

The soldier in charge gave them a startled look. "I thought you were going to do some kind of ceremony."

"We did."

"When? You were only gone a few minutes."

Jacob and Renata stared at each other. A few minutes. No, it had been hours, but apparently, the time they'd spent in that other place hadn't happened here.

"We did what we had to," Renata answered. "We need to get back to the city."

The soldier looked disgruntled, like he'd been sent out here on a fool's mission, but he stepped back as they hurried to the carriage.

They'd brought the horse-drawn vehicle because Renata had been weakened by the psychic fire.

Now she looked like she wanted to grab one of the guards' horses and ride full tilt back to Sun Acres.

But she didn't try to pull rank because she was the reincarnation of a goddess.

He took that as a good sign.

When they arrived back at Griffin's house, their friends were waiting for them in the family courtyard, which was lit by lamps and candles.

"You should eat," Zarah said, and he was glad they could stall for a little while longer.

Everyone let them eat their meal before Zarah asked, "You weren't gone long. Can you tell us what happened in the garden?"

Jacob looked at Renata. "You're probably better at telling it than I am," he said, because he wasn't sure how much she wanted to reveal.

"I guess you need to know the goddess story," she said in a low voice, then backed up to the meeting with Pamina. As she talked, he could see various reactions from the other people around the table. Disbelief. Awe. And a distancing that he had been afraid of.

"A goddess," Quinn breathed.

Renata took her lower lip between her teeth. "I'm the same person I was this morning."

"You're . . . divine," Quinn breathed.

"I'm human," she answered. "The goddess died a long time ago."

Jacob wasn't sure it was true. If they defeated the demon, she would be different. Maybe very different. He could see the others were thinking the same thing as Renata related their experiences in the garden—skating over the parts that were too personal to talk about.

But he did see a bright side to the reaction of the group. Back in the good old U.S. of A., he and Renata might have been carted off to the loony bin. Or maybe they'd get on the cable news, like someone who'd claimed to have been picked up by a UFO. But here, the account of going into a place outside time and space was accepted for what it was.

Griffin leaned back in his seat, and Jacob could tell he was struggling to sound objective. "There are quite a few psychic elements to the story. Obviously, you both have powers. In this world, both of you would have been nurtured in your talents from an early age."

"I never thought of myself as having powers," Jacob said.

Quinn laughed. "You're a werewolf! That's a talent few people have. And don't downplay your ability to talk to animals," she added. "That's very rare."

He hadn't considered that skill as a "psychic power." But now he guessed that it was true. When he glanced at Renata, he saw that her gaze had turned inward.

"Actually, I think I could do more when I was a child. But it left me," she murmured.

"Children have more freedom to use their minds," Zarah said. "Nobody's told them the rules of life. So they make up their own."

At that moment, from inside the house, a baby started to cry, and he saw Zarah give a start. He'd seen that before.

She looked at him. "That's an excellent demonstration. I just got a little, I guess you'd call it, an electrical shock when Marsh started crying. It's his way of making sure I pick him up."

"He hurt you?" Renata asked.

"He reached out to me," Zarah answered.

She got up quickly and went to take care of her son. They continued discussing psychic powers for a few minutes until Zarah came rushing back into the courtyard, her eyes wide.

"You have to get back to the portal," she gasped.

"Why?"

"I don't know, but I know something's going to happen."

Jacob's stomach knotted. He'd been thinking they had time to do some planning. No such luck. Instead, they'd be crossing the badlands at night again, and when they got back to their world, they'd be facing a demon. Too bad they had no idea how to fight him.

CHAPTER
TWENTY-EIGHT

FOUR WOLVES AND their life mates moved silently through the Maryland woods, using only moonlight as their guide.

Well, one of the women wasn't using the moonlight. She was Antonia, Grant's life mate, and blind, so she held Olivia's arm.

The wolves had already scoped out the area and found a sheltered place where their wives could wait to find out the situation with the police.

At that agreed-upon spot, the women stopped, and the wolves went ahead to scope out the area. When they came back, one of them disappeared into the shadows and returned a few minutes later as a man.

It was Ross, and he had pulled on a pair of sweatpants and a tee shirt.

"What's the situation?" Rinna asked.

He made a disgusted sound. "They have guards near the mouth of the cave. Two guys who are leaving food wrappers and soda cans all over the woods. The place looks like a garbage dump. They must have shifts camped up there twenty-four hours a day hoping Jacob will come back to the cave."

"I thought the rain washed away Jacob's trail."

Ross sighed. "It did. But I guess the dogs kept looking, and they eventually found the cave."

"So if Jacob and Renata come through from the other side, they'll run smack into the cops."

GRIFFIN turned to Jacob. "I can send troops part of the distance with you. But they can't go all the way to the portal, because the location has to remain secret."

"I understand," Jacob answered.

They returned to their room to change their clothes, then rode to the main gate and out of the city. As they headed across the moonlit plains, Renata tried to make contingency plans. They'd come here because the cops were looking for Jacob—thanks to her. That was still probably true. So were they rushing headlong into disaster?

She tightened her hands on the reins. She'd like to have a gun. And then what? Was she going to have a shoot-out with the police? That didn't seem like a very good option.

And then there was the demon. He was walking around in human form. What if he was one of the cops? If so, she'd played right into his hands.

Another horrible thought struck her—one she should have considered before. What if the demon was the one who killed the women? To pull her into his plans?

When the lead soldier stopped beside a crumbling building, Jacob also reined in his mount. So did she.

The soldier gestured toward the house. "This is our landmark. It's as far as we're allowed to go."

In this world, she figured it was better to let the men do the talking.

"I understand," Jacob answered. "Thanks for coming this far with us. I hope you have an easy trip back to the city."

"We will," the man said with confidence. He dismounted

and pulled a long, thin, leather-wrapped package from his saddlebag. "You should not go unarmed. These are knives—in case you run into any trouble."

"Thanks," Jacob said again.

When he and Renata dismounted, she moved to his side. Her hand clasped his as the soldiers turned around and rode back the way they'd come.

Jacob unwrapped the leather and examined the blades. They looked like they were meant for fighting, not cutting steak.

When he passed her one, she hefted it in her hand, wishing again that it was a gun.

They stood where they were, waiting for the horsemen to disappear. When they were alone, they started walking the quarter mile across the plain to the cave.

"It's so quiet," Renata whispered.

"Too quiet," he answered. "I feel like I've got a target on my back."

"All we have to do is get to the cave."

"We hope."

They had crossed half the distance when a sound behind them made her stop in her tracks.

They both turned. In the moonlight, she saw five rough-looking men closing rapidly in on them.

"It's them," the guy in the lead growled. "The ones who killed Barth and Grove."

"Run," Jacob shouted.

Renata sprinted toward the portal entrance, expecting that at any moment one of the pursuers would grab her from behind and throw her to the ground.

She pushed herself harder, her breath coming in gasps as she dashed into the shelter of the cave and ducked behind a place where the rock bulged out.

Jacob also made it inside, and she saw the five men stop a little distance away. They could have rushed forward, but maybe they'd seen the guns during the earlier encounter, and maybe they were afraid they'd get killed by the unfamiliar weapon.

Renata watched the men take cover behind some rubble fifty feet away.

"Go open the portal," she said to Jacob.

"I don't want to leave you here."

"I can't do it."

He stopped arguing and ran to the back of the tunnel. Risking a glance behind her, she saw him press his palm to the rock wall.

She expected it to thin the way it had before. But nothing happened.

Maybe he had the wrong spot. She saw him move his hand to another position and try again. Then another. But nothing worked.

"Shit!"

"What's wrong?" she asked, her heart blocking her windpipe.

"The portal's gone."

"What happened to it?" she gasped.

"I don't know."

"What are we going to do?"

"Fight."

"There are five of them and only two of us. All they have to do is rush us."

"Maybe we've got an advantage," he said.

"What?"

"Maybe we can get into that other world like we did when you were working the ceremony."

"How?"

"The way we did last time."

He kept the knife in one hand as he wrapped his free arm around her.

"Think yourself back to Oz," he whispered.

She had done it before. No, *they* had done it before— together. Focusing her mind, she tried to get back to the safety of that strange place outside of time. She could feel it flickering at the edge of her consciousness. But she couldn't quite grasp it.

"Help me," she whispered to Jacob.

He made a frustrated sound. "If I take my focus off of them, they'll get us."

She understood what he meant. It was hard to concentrate on anything else when she could see the barbarians fifty feet away, conferring.

She should close her eyes. But she couldn't make herself do it, not when the men out there were getting ready to rush the cave.

She spoke low, urgent words—praying to the Fates, asking them to have favor on her and Jacob. Asking for their help.

She kept praying.

But nothing changed, except that the attackers separated from each other so that they were standing in a semicircle, all facing toward the cave, all holding knives, and she guessed that they were experts at using them.

"We've got you trapped," one of them jeered.

"That's what you think," Jacob called out, his voice amazingly steady.

The men looked at each other. Then on a signal from the guy in the middle of the group, they started running forward.

Jacob thrust Renata behind him and raised the knife.

CHAPTER
TWENTY-NINE

JACOB CALCULATED THE odds. Not good. Then a shout from his right had him jerking in that direction.

A man was running forward. No, not just one man. Two men and two wolves

Jacob blinked, hardly able to believe his eyes. Or his ears, as both men started firing guns.

Three of the attackers went down. The other two took off, running as fast as they could.

The man in the lead stopped at the entrance to the cave.

"Jacob?" he called.

"Ross? How the hell did you get here?"

"Long story."

Jacob looked back at Renata. "It's okay," he said. "It's my cousin Ross. And my brother Logan. And the wolves are my brother Grant and Ross's brother, Sam Morgan. Not Marshall. He changed his name when he moved to California."

He addressed the men and wolves. "This is my life mate, Renata."

She swallowed. "Nice to meet you."

"Come on," Ross said.

"Where?"

"To the new location of the portal."

"A new location? But why?" Jacob asked.

"Because the cops have staked out this one. So we closed it to keep you from running smack into them if you came back through. Then we opened another one."

"I thought that was hard to do."

"It is," Ross conceded. "Rinna's done it before. She had help—from the life mates with powers. Olivia, Sam's wife. Sara, Adam's wife, and Antonia, Grant's wife," he said for Renata's benefit. "Together they were strong enough to do it." He looked out over the plain. "This place is pretty dangerous. We should get back to the other universe."

Renata stepped forward. "You know we're in trouble with the law?"

"I was at Jacob's house. I heard the cops talking. The good news is that they've kept it out of the papers."

"And how did they find the location of the portal?" Jacob asked.

"They had dogs who tracked you there."

Renata cleared her throat. When she spoke, her voice was tight. "And you know I implicated Jacob in the murders?"

"I know about that. You can explain what happened when we get back to our world," Ross answered.

Renata stood with her hands on her hips. "You know about the cops. I don't think you know about the demon waiting for us on the other side."

"A demon? As in, a fiend from hell?" Ross asked.

"That's as good a definition as any," Jacob answered.

"So before we go through, we'd better talk about what's going to happen when we get back there."

"Yeah," Ross answered, then he led the group of wolves and humans through the badlands. They ended up beside one of the dilapidated buildings that littered the landscape.

"The trigger mechanism is right here," Ross said, pointing to a spot on a half-standing wall.

"Okay. Thanks." Jacob looked at the men and the wolves. He'd always wanted to keep to himself. Now he understood the power of his family connections. "I appreciate your help. But if the women are waiting for you on the other side, you should go back and tell them we're okay."

Logan nodded.

Ross turned to the others. "You go on. I've been thinking of a way Jacob can clear himself of the murder charges." He gave him a direct look. "You can reject the idea if you want."

Jacob lowered his gaze, thinking he was within his rights to ask Ross to leave with everyone else.

Instead, he met his cousin's eyes and said, "I'd like to hear it."

The others left, and Ross passed out weapons to Jacob and Renata. Then they all sat down with their backs to the wall.

"I'm a private eye, like Prescott," Ross told Renata.

"You know I work for him?"

"Jacob told me. But let's focus on you. I've been checking into your background. You took criminal justice courses at the University of Maryland, then applied for a private investigator's license, which was approved three years ago."

"Yes."

"Were you working with Prescott and the police to catch the guy who was murdering women real estate agents?"

"Yes."

"Well, I hope I've disproved your case against Jacob. I looked up when the murders occurred. October fifteenth of last year. December twenty-fourth of last year. And February first of this year."

"That's right," Renata agreed.

Ross turned to Jacob. "And I did some checking on your whereabouts on those dates. On October fifteenth and February first, you were at a dog training school in Pennsylvania."

Jacob nodded. "I didn't think of matching up the dates. I mean, I didn't even know exactly when the murders had occurred."

"I didn't think of that, either," Renata murmured.

"What about Christmas Eve?" Ross asked.

Jacob flicked a glance at Renata. He remembered the date very well. "That was before I met you," he muttered.

"And . . ."

"And I was with a woman. I'm sure she'll remember the evening."

"The murder was in the afternoon," Ross said.

Jacob was sorry he'd stepped into that trap. He'd just assumed Christmas Eve meant evening. But a sense of relief swept over him as he remembered what he'd been doing earlier in the day. "I was at the Central Maryland Animal Alliance most of the day. I remember because I was trying to help them get some animals ready for the people who were picking them up for Christmas presents. The staff will remember I was there."

"So that would mean you couldn't have been at the scenes of any of the murders."

"*Gracias a Dios*." Renata sighed.

"The cops may already know that," Ross said. "But they still want you for kidnapping." He turned back to Renata. "And what about the evidence somebody planted in his house? What was it?"

"A file box with newspaper clippings about the murders. And plastic bags with the victims' hair," Renata answered.

"I took them through the portal. They're out in the badlands," Jacob clarified. "We got attacked, and I was cut pretty bad, so we didn't bring them to Griffin's house with us. I don't know if we can find them again. Renata healed me. Or I'd be dead."

Ross looked at her with interest.

"We can tell you all about it later," she said.

"Right." Ross shrugged. "Either we find the evidence—

or we don't. But if it's really the hair from the murder victims, then the killer put it in your house."

"Yes," Renata whispered. She glanced at Jacob. "And
I'm thinking the perp is the demon."

Jacob blinked. He hadn't quite put that together yet, but
it made sense, since the murders had dragged Renata into
danger.

"Jesus!" Ross answered. "Can you tell me about that?"

"It's a long story."

"We've got time."

Renata sucked in a breath, then let it out. She reached
for Jacob's hand, held on tight, and started telling the story
of Rocanda and Jalerak. As she spoke, she kept glancing at
Ross, but he simply let her talk.

After relating the ancient tale, she talked about the
deaths in her life, then went on to tell him about breaking
into Jacob's house and finding the planted evidence.

When she finished, Ross remained silent.

"So do you think I'm a nut case?" Renata finally asked.

Ross put a hand on her shoulder. "No. It sounds like
you've had a pretty rough time. Someone else would have
cracked up."

"I almost did. I thought I was going crazy."

Jacob turned to her. "That's what the demon wanted.
But you're tough. Whichever way this comes out, I want
you to know how proud I am of you."

"You don't think we're going to win?" she asked.

"I hope we will."

She sat up straighter. "We will! The trouble is, right
now I don't know how we're going to have any freedom
back in Howard County until Ross proves to the police that
you can't be the killer. And until they drop the kidnapping
charges." She paused for a minute, gathering herself to say
something, and the expression on her face made him tense.

"If we get married, they can't say you kidnapped me."

He felt his heart clunk inside his chest. "Married?"

"You don't want to?" she asked in a small voice.

From the corner of his eye, he saw Ross get up and move

away, giving them some privacy. "I do. But I was thinking that we'd wait . . . until we had the demon off our backs."

Her voice was strong when she answered. "And if he's going to win—and we die, then I want to accomplish what we never did before."

His heart contracted. "He's not going to win."

"So let's start by getting you out of a jam. We'll tell the cops we went away together and tied the knot."

It was so tempting. This proud, beautiful woman was offering him the most precious gift he could imagine. He wanted to say "yes" more than he had ever wanted anything in his life. But that wasn't the word he spoke.

It was, "No."

CHAPTER
THIRTY

JACOB SAW THE shock on Renata's face. And the hurt. She looked like he had slapped her, and that was how he felt.

"You don't want to marry me?" she asked in a voice that she couldn't quite hold steady.

He made a low sound as he took her in his arms, feeling the stiffness of her body.

"Of course I do, but we can't," he whispered, as everything inside himself tightened and clenched.

"Why not?"

"Because it will change everything with the demon. He has to think that we haven't found each other. I don't mean physically. He probably knows we've made love. But he doesn't know we've figured out that we belong together. That working together is the only way we can defeat him."

When she didn't answer, his hands tightened on her arms. "Do you understand what I'm saying?"

"Yes," she whispered.

He let out the breath he was holding, then looked toward Ross. "The cops aren't our biggest problem. We've got to go back, but when we step through the portal, I have a feeling the demon is going to zero in on us."

"Unless we put up a force field."

The suggestion came from behind the wall.

Rinna stepped into view, and they all whirled toward her.

"How long have you been there?" Jacob demanded.

"Long enough."

Jacob felt his jaw tighten. "Maybe we didn't want you to hear all that."

"You weren't going to tell us?" Rinna demanded.

"We were."

"Then maybe I've done you a favor," she said.

THE great dance of power could not be over. Questabaze would not believe that.

If he had been defeated, he would know it.

He wouldn't linger here in this terrible state of uncertainty. Or was that the ultimate punishment—not to know?

No matter what he tried to tell himself, despair clung to him like particles of heavy smoke hovering above the ground.

All these years he'd reveled in his life on Earth. In many different bodies. In many different cultures. He'd gotten used to the pleasures and the privileges of being here. And in his mind, he'd earned them. Through his hard work. And his determination. And his absolute willingness to do anything it took to win.

This time he was afraid he would lose it all.

After so many years of working and scheming.

He and many other demons had fought over the privilege of battling Rocanda.

And he had always been the winner.

She hadn't come back in every generation. That had been part of the challenge. To figure out if she was on Earth—and then to go after her.

He'd always found her. Always been ready and able to fuck with her life. Until now.

For two days, he'd been searching for her. And his terrible anger had boiled over in a great volcanic eruption that had spewed lava and ash onto a small Asian country.

In his rage, he cursed the Fates—for all the good that did him. He was sure they were hiding Renata from him. They were on her side, even when they were supposed to be neutral. But he had no place to appeal the injustice. No court of last resort.

Then, just when despair threatened to overwhelm him, he felt a jolt of awareness.

Renata!

He had found her again, and his spirits leaped. He'd been worried and frightened, but he had control of the situation again.

With renewed energy, he started to send his mind out to link with her more firmly. Just as he was about to close the connection, a door slammed shut, and she was gone again.

"Fuck!"

He'd found her. And she'd gone away again.

He stopped his rant and tried to calm himself.

No, not gone. He could sense *something*. Not the total void when she had been completely hidden. If he kept his focus, he could reach out and find her once again.

THE portal was at the edge of another outcropping of rock, about a quarter mile from the original site. It wasn't as good a location as the previous one, because there was no cave to shield the entrance. But it was the best Rinna and the other women had been able to do on short notice.

As they stepped through into the Maryland woods, the women and the wolves formed a circle around Jacob and Renata.

For a long moment, they all stood perfectly still, prepared for an attack, but no monsters materialized out of the trees—or out of the air.

"I think the force field is working," Renata whispered as they started through the woods, walking quietly so as not to catch the attention of the cops.

Were they really protected from the demon? Jacob didn't feel any magic shimmering in the air.

He gripped Renata's hand, and she knit her fingers with his. She was holding tight to him—probably because her nerves were just as raw as his. Still, he knew he'd hurt her by not agreeing to marry her right now, even if he knew deep down that it wasn't the right thing to do.

Nobody spoke. Maybe they were all feeling spooked. When they got near the road, he saw two vans waiting in a spot screened by trees.

The wolves disappeared, into the woods. Then three men emerged.

Ross's brother, Adam, had stayed to guard the women. He and the other men took one of the vans. Jacob, Renata, Ross, and the four life mates climbed into the other van, and they sped off into the night.

"Where are we going?" Jacob asked as they headed down the road.

Ross laughed. "Since Renata was working for Star Realty, I got the idea of checking the real estate listings. There's a house that's been vacant for several months. When it didn't sell, the owners pulled it off the market. So you should be safe there for a few days."

"Safe from the cops or safe from the demon?" Renata asked.

"I was thinking about the cops," Ross admitted.

"But we can work on the demon problem when we get there," Olivia answered.

"How?"

"We have a shield around you now. We can do the same thing with the house."

"You mean you have to be physically there?" Jacob asked.

Olivia dragged in a breath and let it out. "I think so."

"Shit," he answered, then immediately added, "Sorry. I don't want to sound ungrateful."

"But anyone who stays around us is in danger," Renata finished and began to fill in the other women about the demon.

Jacob sat in the darkness, wishing that he was alone with Renata. He'd hurt her, and he wanted to explain his thinking—and not in front of a bunch of other people.

The house was only about ten miles from the portal, on a large, wooded lot where they'd have some privacy. To hide their presence, they pulled both vans into the three-car garage.

They had already put up blackout shades at the windows, so that the neighbors wouldn't see the lights. And the house was partially furnished.

The group of werewolves and their life mates gathered in the family room, where Jacob and Renata flopped onto the couch.

"You look like you need to sleep," Olivia said.

"We need to defeat the demon," Renata answered.

"But if you're so tired you can't function, then you won't be able to do it," Antonia put in.

Jacob nodded, thinking this was his chance to be alone with Renata.

"We put beds into all of the rooms," Rinna said. "You two take the master bedroom. It's got its own bathroom. And there's clothing in there for you."

"Thanks," Renata murmured.

Jacob was glad to disappear into the bedroom and close the door, until he saw the shuttered look on Renata's face.

"I want to be married to you," he said. "More than anything in the world. But I want to know we'll be safe first."

"Maybe we won't be."

"We're going to do our damnedest to get the bastard out of our lives."

"Okay," she said, but her voice sounded weary.

He looked from her to the bed. "Maybe we'll both feel

better after we get some sleep. Do you want to take a shower first, or shall I?"

"Let me go first." Her tone was brusque as she rummaged in a dresser drawer, found some panties and a tee shirt, and disappeared into the bathroom.

He sat in the chair in the corner in the dark, listening to the water run while she took a quick shower. When she came out, dressed for sleep, she walked to the other side of the bed and slipped under the covers without speaking, then lay with her eyes closed.

He stood looking at her for several heartbeats, then turned to the dresser, where he found shorts for himself.

After taking a quick shower, he closed the bathroom door partway so that some light drifted into the bedroom.

Sliding into bed beside Renata, he listened to her even breathing. He wanted to reach over and fold her into his arms. But maybe she was really awake, and maybe she would turn away from him. So he kept his arms at his sides.

He thought he wouldn't be able to sleep. But somehow he did. And then he was dreaming.

He and Renata were back in the place outside time, the place where they had gone after the garden. At first it was quiet and peaceful, and he was so thankful that they were together again, with no misunderstandings between them. They strolled arm in arm down a garden path, neither of them speaking.

They were heading toward the temple where they'd been earlier, and the closer they got, the more his nerves jumped.

When they'd broken through the barrier and stepped inside, Renata quickly walked to the altar. Heaped all around it were rocks, seashells, and flowers.

She started poking through them, making selections which she began arranging in patterns the way she'd done before.

He wanted to help, but he didn't know what to do, so he stepped back, out of her way. As he did, he could feel his tension growing.

Something was going to happen. Something bad.

As if to confirm his dread, lightning crackled far above them. Then the roof of the building burst open, and through the opening a terrible roar sounded. A great green lizard with wings swooped down, catching Renata in its talons, lifting her off the ground as it tore at her flesh.

It was Questabaze.

Jacob tried to jump up and catch her. But she dangled just out of his reach. He knew the creature was teasing him, gloating at its victory.

Jacob screamed in anguish and frustration, then screamed again as he felt strong hands digging into his shoulders.

"Jacob. Wake up, Jacob."

His eyes blinked open, and he stared up into Renata's face.

"Thank God," he whispered. "Thank God you're okay."

A sharp knock sounded at the door. "Are you all right?" Ross called.

"Yeah. I was having a nightmare. I'm . . . fine."

Ross went away, and Jacob flopped back against the pillows as he stared up at Renata. "I was dreaming about the demon."

She nodded.

He didn't want to tell her the rest, but he knew he had to. "I was watching him tear you apart, and I couldn't do anything."

She gulped. "I'm sorry."

He wrapped his arms around her and held on tight. "Thank the Fates you're all right."

"I'm here. I'm fine," she whispered.

He raised his head and looked at her, trying to put everything he felt into his voice and his expression. "Don't go away from me again."

She swallowed. "Oh, Jacob."

The look she gave him melted his heart. "We've been drawing away from each other," he said in a low voice. "I mean, even when we don't intend to—we get caught in the same behavior that . . . leads to destruction."

She nodded, then clasped him to her. "I'm sorry," she murmured. "I let myself get upset about that marriage thing."

"I understand why," he answered, as he gathered her closer.

"It's a familiar pattern. Because walling myself up is safer than being vulnerable to you. I won't do it again. I promise."

He kept holding her, wishing he didn't have to tell her the next part, but he did.

Finally, because he couldn't put it off any longer, he said, "I think the dream told me what we need to do."

RENATA watched Jacob sit up and press his back against the headboard.

She sat up, too.

"They said this house was shielded," he said, speaking quickly, and she had the feeling he wanted to get it over with. "I think we have to get the shield down, get everybody else out of the house, and work a ceremony. You have to do it, because you'll be totally vulnerable to him. But it won't end like the dream. When he swoops in here, I'll be waiting to connect with you, and we'll . . ." His voice trailed off.

"We'll what?"

He swallowed. "We'll use our joined energy to fry him."

"Do we know how to do that?"

"No."

"That's taking a big chance." She dragged in a breath and let it out in a rush.

"You have the power. I know it."

"So do you."

"Well, not like you. But when we join together, something happens that neither one of us can explain. Something that's more than you or I can do alone."

She reached for his hand. "It sounds great—in theory. Too bad we didn't get some training when we were kids."

"But we know how to connect with each other." He found her mouth, and they exchanged a long, greedy kiss.

"That's better," she said when they finally came up for air.

"A lot better," he agreed. "I can feel power . . . tickling at the edge of my mind."

"Yes."

They eased down so that they were lying together, holding each other. And her hands began to move over his back and arms and hips, drawing him closer.

As he dipped his head, pressing his face into the warmth between her breasts, she felt her arousal building.

He pulled up her tee shirt and turned his head so that he could find one nipple with his hot, wet mouth. As he teased her, he spoke, "Try to reach for my mind. Try to connect with me on more than a physical level."

She cradled the back of his head, stroking him as she opened herself to him, trying to make the connection with him on every possible level.

It was something like being in a dark room, trying to find objects that she knew must be there. But it was even harder, because she didn't know exactly what the objects were.

Yet as she reached for him, she felt him doing the same thing. Felt his touch not only on her body but in her mind.

"Yes," she whispered, striving to strengthen the link between them.

They touched and kissed, and opened themselves in ways that she hadn't dreamed possible.

And she felt the familiar flames flickering around them, the way it had out in the badlands when he'd been so horribly injured. Not the hot flames of pain that they both had feared. The warm flames of love and healing. And she knew that this time, he was doing as much of the work as she was.

"We're controlling the blaze," he murmured, his voice full of awe.

Once again, they were in a different time and place, the

only two people in a universe they had made where they could merge together, body and soul.

Until a banging at the door yanked them back to reality.

"Jacob. Renata," Ross called. "You'd better get out here."

They sprang apart, and Renata wondered if the door was locked. But Ross didn't come in.

"What's wrong?" Jacob called.

"There have been two more women murdered," Ross answered.

"*Dios*," Renata muttered.

CHAPTER
THIRTY-ONE

THEY BOTH CLAMBERED out of bed. Jacob had seen sweatpants in the dresser drawer. He pulled on a pair and tossed another one to Renata, who also yanked them on.

After dragging on a tee shirt, he threw the door open.

Ross's face was grim. "I've been listening to the police radio, trying to keep on top of the investigation," he said. "They got a tip from an anonymous source who said that two more women real estate agents had been killed. They went to the vacant houses where the caller said the women would be—and discovered the mutilated bodies. Not only that, another woman real estate agent has been reported missing."

"*Dios mio,*" Renata moaned. "What does it mean?"

Jacob felt his jaw tighten. "It means that he's trying to lure us into the open," he growled. "And it also means that he's going to torture and kill that woman unless we let him find us."

The color had drained from Renata's face. "Unfortunately, I think you're right." She turned to Ross. "Are the others up?"

"Yeah. I got everybody together in the living room."

They hurried down the hall to confront a group of worried faces.

Before anybody else could speak, Renata started talking, "You all have to leave." As she finished, she looked to Jacob for confirmation.

"It's too dangerous for you to stay," he agreed.

"When we leave, the shield will drop," Olivia said.

"We have to let that happen," Jacob answered. "We have to let him find us. And Lord knows what he's going to do. So I want everyone out of here. Now."

The others looked like they wanted to object.

"Please," Renata added. "Those women died because of me."

"Because of *him*." Jacob corrected her. "Never blame yourself for the evil he does."

She turned toward him. "Yes. Him. Questabaze. But he'll keep killing until he finds me."

"Before we clear out, I want to show you some stuff," Ross said. "There are surveillance cameras and a recording system, so you can get this on tape."

Jacob and Renata followed him down the hall, to a bedroom where several monitor screens showed views of the driveway, the home's exterior, and the living room. After a quick demonstration, Ross turned back to Jacob. "Did you follow that?"

"Sort of. But I figure this is going to end one way or the other pretty quickly. So I can just leave it on."

Ross nodded, then held out his hand. "I don't like running out on you."

"You're not running out. All of you are getting out of danger because we're asking you to do that. You and your life mates."

"Good luck," Ross said in a thick voice.

Jacob swallowed. "Thanks. And thanks for your help. I appreciate it."

Ross nodded.

They hurried back to the living room, where Renata embraced the women—and also the men. Jacob shook hands all around. "It means a lot that you did this for us," he said. "But the sooner you leave, the sooner we get this over with."

In the control room, Jacob and Renata watched the van speed down the driveway and turn onto the two-lane road.

"I want to hold you," Jacob whispered.

"But you can't," Renata said. "We have to let him think that I'm alone, until he gets here. We don't even know what's going to happen. Will he come in human form?"

Jacob shrugged. "Maybe if he thinks it will fool you into dropping your guard."

"And how long will we have to wait?"

"I wish to hell I knew. But you'd better go down the hall. At least I can see you on the monitor."

She gave him one last look, then turned with a jerky motion and walked out of the room.

Moments later, she appeared on the monitor screen and he took in her stiff posture as she began to pace back and forth on the rug, her lips moving as she counted her steps.

He kept watching the time display. Seconds dragged by at what seemed like the speed of glaciers forming. He was starting to wonder if he'd been wrong about his theory when he saw something change.

"A car's coming," he called to Renata.

The sedan pulled up a hundred yards from the house, and a man got out.

"Who is it?"

"I don't recognize him."

Renata ran down the hall, looked at the monitor, and gasped. "It's Greg Newcastle. The police detective I've been working with on the murders."

"Jesus! It's *him*?"

"I never liked him. I kept feeling like he didn't really want me to solve the case, but I thought he was just pissed that he had to deal with a woman PI."

Jacob could see Renata struggling to rearrange her thinking as Newcastle started walking toward the house.

"How close do we have to let him get?"

"Give it a minute," Jacob muttered as the man drew closer, a look of determination on his face . . .

Jacob had barely finished speaking when another man stepped out of the shadows under the trees and called out to the police detective.

"Newcastle."

"What are you doing here?"

"I could ask you the same question," the newcomer said.

Renata goggled at the screen as she stared at the other man. "It's Barry," she wheezed.

"There's another woman being held captive," Newcastle said. "I'm checking out empty houses."

"By yourself?"

"I figure the killer's left her somewhere. So I've got uniforms searching other properties."

"Good thinking," Barry said. Then he pulled out a gun.

Newcastle stared at him in surprise. "What the hell?"

"Stay where you are. Hands in the air."

Greg obeyed.

"Too bad you had to be so proactive, but this isn't where I left the other one."

Renata stood watching, a look of horror on her face.

"*Dios*. No! It's Barry. Questabaze is Barry." Renata made a moaning sound and doubled over, holding her middle. "I can't believe it. Not Barry. We have to stop him before he kills Greg," she gasped.

But it was already too late.

The PI didn't pull the trigger, but Greg clutched at his chest, a terrified look on his face as he crumpled to the ground. He writhed for a moment, then lay still.

"This ends your part of the investigation. And it will turn out that Renata is just going to be another victim of a crazed serial killer. Someone you'll never catch."

The PI stepped over the limp body on the ground and started toward the house.

Her face had drained of color. "All this time, he was playing with me."

"And now we're going to give him a big surprise," Jacob told her. He wanted to reach for Renata, but he didn't dare touch her. Not with the demon heading for the house. "We're going to kill him. But we have to do it together!"

Her gaze snapped into focus. "What should I do?"

He didn't know the answer. Not for sure. But he knew where to start. "Unlock the front door. Let him come in."

She turned and gave him a look that wavered between determination and desperation. Then she hurried down the hall.

Jacob grabbed the gun that Ross had left and followed, not that he thought a gun was going to do him much good against a demon.

Keeping Renata in sight, he stayed far enough back so that the focus would be on her. She had barely reached the living room when the front door blew inward, the explosion knocking them both to the ground.

CHAPTER
THIRTY-TWO

JACOB STRUGGLED TO sit up, but his head felt like a gong was ringing inside his brain.

He looked wildly around and saw that Renata lay a few feet away from him, crumpled like a broken doll on the floor. She'd been closer to the blast, and she'd gotten the worst of it.

When he called her name and she didn't answer, cold, sharp fear clawed at his insides.

Then he heard her moan, and he said a fervent prayer to the Fates, thanking them that she was still in this world.

His focus shot to the door as the PI stepped inside, a satisfied smirk on his fake human face.

"Got ya!"

Jacob could only stare at him, trying to summon the strength to reach Renata. If he could do that, he could change the equation.

As Jacob tried to push himself to his hands and knees, he saw Questabaze staring at him as a man might stare at a bug scuttling across the floor.

The demon raised his hand, preparing for another strike. The killing strike.

Before he could follow through, four dark shapes appeared in back of the demon. A wolf leaped out of the shadows, taking him down to the floor. Then two more seized his legs in their jaws. And another one clamped onto his shoulder.

It was Ross, Sam, Logan, and Grant.

"No!" Jacob cried out. They had lied to him. Well, not with words. They had left the house all right—and taken their life mates to safety, but they'd had no intention of clearing out of the area. They had been lurking around all the time he and Renata thought they were alone. And here they were, fighting an enemy that could demolish them in an instant, the way he had demolished Greg Newcastle.

Still, Newcastle was a man, and these werewolves were something that the demon hadn't counted on.

"Get away from me," he shrieked, flailing at them with his arms.

As the wolves kept Prescott occupied, Jacob crawled toward Renata, but he didn't seem to be making any headway. The living room had turned into an endless corridor. And if Jacob was moving forward at all, his progress was measured in millimeters.

As he struggled to reach Renata, he watched the fight from the corner of his eye.

Sharp teeth tore at Prescott as Jacob finally, finally reached Renata. His hand closed over her shoulder, shaking her, trying to bring her back to consciousness—with his touch and with the mind-to-mind connection they'd been trying to forge.

For long seconds, she didn't respond.

"Renata! *Por Dios*, Renata!" he shouted, hoping the language of her childhood would help center her.

Her eyes blinked open, and his heart leaped into his throat. She looked totally confused, her vision unfocused and her mouth slack.

His fingers tightened on her. "Renata, please. It's Jacob. Your life mate. You have to come back to me. It's our only chance."

At that moment, the demon must have realized he could fight the wolves on his terms—not theirs. The house shook again, and the werewolves were thrown back onto the porch.

"Get out of here," Jacob shouted. "For God's sake, get out."

To his profound relief, the gray shapes backed away.

Maybe the demon thought Jacob was shouting at him. He grinned as he stood up. Straightening his posture, he started closing in on them. Only now his face was no longer human. It had elongated and turned to a sickening green, with a red slash of a mouth and red eyes.

The thing was the sum of all human fears. Every nightmare from the dawn of human consciousness.

And it was right here in the room with them, preparing to wipe them from the face of the Earth.

If he intended to frighten them, to give them a look at his real self before they died, the change in his appearance had the opposite effect. It hardened Jacob's resolve as he reached for Renata with his mind.

She was still groggy.

"Renata, you've got to help me."

For a moment he was afraid she couldn't respond. Then he felt a spark leap within her.

He dug his fingers into her arm. "Renata!"

Prescott had pulled his gun.

"What? Are you going to shoot us?" Jacob jeered. "Is that the best you can do?"

To his surprise, the demon responded. "It's going to *look like* I shot you. Then I'll have my turn with Renata, like I did with the other women. They'll find you shot and her body mutilated." He raised the weapon and fired into the wall in back of them. Although the bullet didn't hit them, a fountain of fire seared them.

But the demon had done more than singe them. When Renata gasped, Jacob knew that the blast had focused her attention.

"Yes. Come back to me," Jacob whispered. He could

feel her resolve strengthen, feel her trying to forge the supernatural connection that they'd felt before.

All at once, he knew what he had to do. What he couldn't do before when they'd been under attack near the portal. With every fiber of concentration, he tried to wipe the demon out of his mind and focus all his energy on Renata.

When he did, he felt her body quiver. Then she gathered herself and leaped into his arms, holding on to him with all her strength, burying her face against his shoulder. As he folded her close, he felt something change in the air of the room.

The warming flames began to gather around them as they had before. At first the effect was so thin that he could barely see it.

But as he watched in wonder, the flames grew and thickened, enclosing them in a shimmering cloud of flickering light that created a shield around them.

Through the barrier, Jacob saw Questabaze's terrible face contort into a mask of anger—and desperation.

"No," he screamed as he raised his hand and sent another jet of heat toward them. But this time, instead of searing them, the blast flared up as it hit the barrier, then bounced back toward the demon.

He screamed in agony, as his own attack enveloped him in fire. Not the warm glow of the protective shield, but a searing blaze of his own creation.

Renata raised her head, staring at the monster. As she clung to Jacob, Questabaze sank to his knees, his finger pulling the trigger one more time. His face was fierce as he focused all his fury on them.

Jacob held on to Renata, feeling the protective shield around them part.

For a terrible second, he thought the demon had broken through to them. Then he realized that the opening was Renata's choice. A dangerous choice as the demon gathered himself for another strike.

"Help me now," she whispered as she held out her hand.

Jacob wanted to cling to their only defense against the demon, yet he knew that he must trust Renata. And he knew that trust had been the issue all along, all through the centuries when they had failed time after time to realize their destiny.

Rocanda had killed Jalerak. And he had never trusted her again—no matter how much he loved her.

But Jacob must let down every barrier to her. Or they were doomed, like all the other couples reincarnated through the centuries.

He struggled to drop every protective shield within himself. Struggled to make his own vulnerability an offering to her. As he did, he felt her reaching into his mind, merging with him in a way that he never could have imagined. In response, he opened himself to her more fully, giving himself to her—on every level of his existence. His past, his present. His future. And he knew she was doing the same thing, making herself so open to him that he could kill her with a mere thought.

At that perfect moment when they were truly one, a blast of fire shot from her fingers, creating a conflagration that blazed up around the monster in a geyser of flame.

At the same time, Jacob fired the gun in his free hand, hitting the man shape in the chest.

His screams were terrible as the fire consumed him, burning his flesh, turning it to ash and then to white powder.

But when the fire burned itself out, the white powder was gone and Barry Prescott was lying pale and still on the floor in front of them, a bullet wound in his chest oozing blood.

Renata gasped, staring at him.

Jacob leaped up and hurtled toward the creature. He felt for a pulse in his neck. And bent to check his breathing.

"He's dead."

Renata still stared at the monster, as though she didn't believe what had happened.

"Is it finished?"

"I hope so," he answered, praying that it was true.

"How can we be sure the demon is dead—and not just this body?"

"I don't know," he admitted.

THIRTY-THREE

SUDDENLY, THEY WERE no longer alone. Three women with gauzy dresses and long golden hair stood in the room with them. They were visible, but they weren't entirely solid.

"The battle is over," one of them said in a voice that rang out with authority.

"Who . . . who are you?" Renata asked.

The one in the middle took a step forward and spoke. "Don't you know?"

"The Fates?" Renata asked.

"Yes. We have watched this drama play out through the ages." She looked from Renata to Jacob and back again. "Well done. The two of you were finally strong enough and brave enough to defeat the evil hovering over you."

"We're free of the . . . curse?" Jacob asked.

"It was not a curse. It was an ancient battle between good and evil. And between Rocanda and Jalerak, too. But it is over now. You have won. You and your life mate are free to live your lives as you wish."

Renata looked stunned. Her lips quivered as she spoke. "But what about Rocanda? What about the goddess?"

"Her time has passed; she no longer holds sway over the Earth. She belongs to the ancient past. She will only be a spark inside you. But your defeat of the dark forces will make a difference for the world."

Jacob kept his arms around Renata. "Why couldn't the demon find us in the other universe?"

"It is as you suspected. When the time lines diverged, there could not be two representations of Rocanda. She stayed in this world, and the demon stayed with her. He couldn't go into the other time line."

The woman looked at Renata. "You would never have been able to go there on your own. You only crossed the barrier because Jacob forced you there."

Renata gave him a grateful look. "Your instincts were right."

"I did it to get away from the cops."

Renata grinned. "Let's not argue about it—or anything else."

"Right."

She turned back to the trio. "So you weren't helping us?"

The speaker smiled. "Only to work against the demon's trick with the dogs. He was . . . cheating when he tried to keep you from bonding. And that required a countermeasure."

Jacob wanted to ask more questions. But before he could form the words, the images of the women began to fade. And then, they flickered out, leaving Jacob and Renata alone with the body of Barry Prescott.

From outside, they heard a moan.

When they hurried to the door, they saw Greg Newcastle sitting up, looking dazed. Antonia, Olivia, Rinna, and Sara stood around him.

"What the hell?" he asked.

"You had some kind of attack," Rinna said. "And you were unconscious. We were out for a run and we found you here. Olivia knows CPR. She got you breathing again."

He looked wildly around. "Prescott, where's Prescott? He admitted to me he was the killer."

Jacob stepped outside. "He came here and started shooting at us. I nailed him," he said.

Newcastle goggled at him. "Where the hell did *you* come from?"

"I've been hiding out."

Newcastle nodded, then pressed his hand to his chest. "Prescott did something to me."

"What?"

"I don't know. I felt like I was having a heart attack."

"Well, he tried to kill us, too. With his gun. He's dead. In the house." Jacob gestured, thinking that he was going to have to get to the damn videotape and erase it before anybody saw all the weird stuff that had happened. "Do you have a cell phone? We'd better call the paramedics."

The detective still looked dazed. "Where are the women? And the dogs?"

"What women?" Renata asked. While they'd been talking, the four life mates had quietly left the scene.

"They said they were jogging. One of them gave me CPR," he said. His gaze probed the woods. "But they're gone."

Renata glanced at Jacob, then asked a question they'd already heard Newcastle answer. "And you were checking vacant properties? Looking for the missing woman?"

"Yeah."

"Good thinking. I'm glad you're all right," she said.

"We'd better pray that monster was keeping her on ice," Newcastle muttered.

"Monster," Renata repeated. "Yes, I guess he was."

Newcastle's eyes narrowed. "This is where you were hiding out?"

"Yeah," Jacob answered. "While I figured out how to clear my name. Well, I have an alibi for the times of the other murders. I was going to have my cousin, Ross Marshall, give you that information."

Renata looked back toward the house and shuddered. "I was working for Barry Prescott, and I didn't know he was the killer."

Jacob draped his arm around her and held her close, sure she was still coming to grips with what had happened.

A siren sounded in the distance, and Newcastle looked up, startled.

"Someone must have heard the shooting," Renata said. "Or maybe those women called nine-one-one."

"Be right back," Jacob muttered, dashing into the house.

When he reached the room with the video equipment, he found Ross already there erasing the tapes.

"There's going to be a malfunction," he said.

"Thanks."

"Prescott confessed to Newcastle."

"And Olivia saved him," Jacob finished.

When he saw Ross's expression darken, he asked. "What else?"

"Something that slipped my mind in all the excitement. The day the cops were looking for you and Renata, I was coming to your house to deliver some information about Prescott. I just remembered it." He gave Jacob a direct look. "Maybe I was using it as an excuse to check up on you. But I was coming to your place to tell you he didn't have a daughter. That was apparently a lie."

"To make himself more sympathetic to me," Renata said from the doorway.

Ross nodded. "As far as I can tell, he was never married."

"And I never checked up on him," Renata said.

Jacob crossed to her. "Why should you? He made you trust him."

"But . . ."

He pulled her close. "He killed everyone you ever loved. Then he put himself in a position to be a father figure to you."

She pressed her fist against her mouth. "I got the idea of working for him because he advertised a PI lecture in my neighborhood. I went to it, and he impressed me so much."

"Of course he did."

"He encouraged me to take those courses at the University of Maryland—and apply for a license. He even helped me qualify with a handgun."

She was about to say something else when Newcastle came in.

"I thought you were going to the ER," Jacob said.

"Later." He looked at the recording equipment. "What's all this?"

"We were going to try and lure the murderer here," Ross said. "I'm Jacob's cousin, Ross Marshall. I'm a private detective, and I was helping him clear his name."

"How were you going to get Prescott here?"

"We didn't know it was Prescott," Jacob said, improvising. "We were hoping to figure out who it was."

"Amateurs," Newcastle muttered. "What do you have on tape?"

Ross looked apologetic. "It all happened so fast we didn't get the tape going."

Newcastle snorted, and Jacob's gaze shot to Renata. He could see she wanted to punch him in the jaw. He squeezed her arm, and she settled back against him.

The police detective looked at Renata. "What was the evidence you found at Jacob Marshall's house?"

She tensed. "Newspaper articles about the murders," she answered. "And hair from the victims. I guess Barry put them there to make me think Jacob was the killer."

"Where are they?" Newcastle demanded.

Without missing a beat, Renata answered, "I burned them."

"Why?"

"Because I realized Jacob wasn't guilty."

Newcastle gave her a long look. "And how did you realize that?"

"Because he made me listen to him, and he could account for his time when the murders were taking place."

"Could we stop standing here getting grilled?" Jacob

said. "We're both pretty beat, and we need to get some sleep."

"After we take your statements down at headquarters."

Jacob nodded. He'd been afraid Newcastle was going to insist on that.

"I'll drive them over," Ross said.

The cop looked like he was going to object, then he cut them a break and said, "Okay."

Before he could change his mind, Ross led them out of the house. And on the way to the station, they got the details of their stories straight, so that when Newcastle put all three of them in separate rooms to write a narrative of the past few days, Jacob and Renata could start with hiding in the cave and go on to hiding in the vacant house while Ross worked on clearing Jacob's name.

While they were at the station, a call came in from one of the patrol officers that the missing real estate agent had been found, to Renata and Jacob's relief.

Three hours after they'd left the battle scene, they were back in Ross's SUV. Before pulling out of his parking space, Ross looked around at Jacob.

"My guess is that the cops tossed your house."

He groaned. "I'll need to clean it up."

"Later. For now let's go to my place," Renata said quickly.

"Good idea."

She gave Ross directions. When they reached her driveway, they all climbed out, and the two werewolves shook hands. "Thanks," Jacob said. "You could have left me twisting in the wind when the boys in blue were beating the bushes for me."

"I wouldn't do that."

"Yeah, you have great family loyalty."

Ross laughed. "Try not to hold that against me."

Renata hugged him. "We don't. We're very grateful."

"Then I'm expecting a wedding invitation," he said.

Jacob glanced at Renata.

"Yes," she answered, then looked upset.

"What?"

"I didn't get a chance to thank everyone else. After they risked their lives for us."

"We're all getting together at my house tomorrow afternoon," Ross said. "You're welcome to come."

"I'd like that," Jacob said, meaning it.

"And so would I," Renata added. "I'd like to meet the family—when we're not in the middle of a crisis."

Ross laughed. "We're a pretty staid lot. We don't drink liquor or coffee—or smoke. Stimulants play havoc with our delicate constitutions."

She snorted. "You just prowl the woods at night as wolves."

"Yeah."

Ross drove away, leaving them standing in front of the house.

"I've been waiting to be alone with you," Renata murmured.

"I'd say *burning* to be alone with you," he said in a thick voice.

When she started toward the front door, Jacob stopped her.

"How are you going to get in?"

"Same way you did. A key under a rock," she answered. "But the rest of my stuff, like my driver's license, is back at Griffin's."

"We'll get it later. Come around back before we go inside." He took her hand and led her around to the stone bench.

She stared at it. "My makeshift altar. But I don't need it anymore. I'm not a goddess."

He dragged in a breath and let it out. "I'm glad." Then he searched her face. "Is that okay with you?"

She turned toward him. "It's more than okay. I was afraid I was going to have to . . ." She shrugged. "Well, I don't know exactly what. But I don't want to be anything besides your life mate."

"And a private detective," he added.

She blinked. "You wouldn't mind?"

"I'd worry about you. But I wouldn't try to dictate what you could do. I think you'd be restless if you didn't have a job."

"You've gotten to know me pretty well."

He laughed. "I had more than a thousand years to do it."

"Yes. And thank the Great Mother this time it's worked out."

"Or thank the Fates. Let's not forget about them."

One more question teased the edge of his mind.

Catching his expression, she asked, "What?"

"I was wondering if we still have . . . powers."

"You mean, can we work magic together?"

He nodded.

"I guess we'll find out." She reached for him, and he clasped her tightly. Then he found her mouth with his, and they exchanged a long, hungry kiss.

"Better get that key," he said, his voice thick when he finally broke away to drag in air. "Because I don't want the neighbors gossiping about us."

"Maybe they already are. Maybe they saw me in my nightgown."

"Let's not give them anything else to talk about."

With that, he led her toward the house, his hand clasped in hers and his heart swelling with joy.

They made it inside the door, and he slammed it shut with his foot, then caught her in his arms, his mouth moving frantically over hers, his hands tearing at her clothing.

"You're picking up where we left off this morning," she gasped, her hands and mouth just as busy.

"Oh, yeah."

He got her tee shirt over her head and her sweatpants and panties off in record time. And she did the same for him, closing her hand around his cock when she had him naked, driving him toward insanity.

Naked, they swayed together near the door, both of them having difficulty staying on their feet.

She linked her hand with his and led him to the rug in the living room, where they sank to their knees, stroking and kissing, both of them so hot that he expected to see the flames spring up around them. And maybe he did. At least the room seemed to have taken on a familiar warm glow.

Dipping his head, he pressed his face against her breasts, then took one hardened nipple into his mouth, sucking on her as he slid a hand down her body, finding her wet, swollen folds. He dipped inside her, then stroked upward to her clit and back again, until she cried out with need.

"Now. Please now."

He tipped her to her back, then covered her body with his as she closed her fist around him again before guiding him inside her.

He had been frantic to join with her. Now he went still, looked down at her, meeting her gaze.

"Finally. After all these years," he murmured.

She reached up to touch his face, her eyes full of wonder.

"We did it. The two of us," she marveled. "Against all odds. No. You changed the odds. It took a werewolf to defeat the demon."

"A werewolf and his family," he corrected. "And a woman who didn't give up."

"I almost did—until I found you."

"And now we have our reward."

He began to move inside her, slowly at first and then with more force. He wanted it to last. But they were both too far gone to put off the ending for long.

He struggled to wait for her, but when her hands clasped his ass, he came in a great roiling climax. And he felt her exploding with him.

They hung on to each other as the storm swept them

away in time and space. To that place that only the two of them could enter.

And when they floated back to earth, he raised his head and stared down at her again, a grin on his face.

"I think we still have the magic."

"Oh, yes."

He rolled to his side, clasping her against him, kissing her sweat-slick cheek.

They lay holding each other, breathing hard.

"My life mate," she whispered. "It's a miracle to be together, like this."

"My perfect love," he answered, nibbling at her cheek.

She snuggled against him, but he was so tuned to her that he knew she wanted to say something. Something that made her a little bit nervous.

"What?"

She raised her head and looked down at him. "Remember when I did that numerology thing, I found out you liked to travel?"

"Um hum."

"Will you come to Costa Rica with me?" she asked, then held her breath.

"You were worried about that? Of course I want to go there with you. I want to understand where you came from. I want to see all the things you love—and find out what made you who you are. Not just from the ancient past. I want to understand the roots of Renata Cordona, because you are the most important thing in my life," he said with conviction, his hand stroking up and down her body.

"And you are mine. I want to know you every way we can." She laughed. "And not just through stuff like numerology. But I do like what I found out there. Freedom and passion. That's a wonderful description for a werewolf."

"A werewolf with his life mate."

She lowered her mouth to his, and they kissed again, this time knowing they didn't need to hurry.

"Um. And maybe before you show me Costa Rica, we can start with your bedroom."

"I think that can be arranged," she said, her hand linked with his as she stood and led him naked to the stairway.

Keep reading for a special preview
of the next book in the series,

DRAGON MOON
BY REBECCA YORK

Available soon from Berkley Sensation!

HIS NAME WAS Vandar, and he was a creature from an ancient nightmare. A creature who had lived for centuries relying on his psychic powers, his cunning.

Now he lifted his massive head and roared for the pleasure of feeling his slaves cringe.

In his present incarnation, he was a huge, scaled being with glittering red eyes, a reptilian body, and wings shaped like those of a bat—only infinitely larger. But he was just as likely to take human form.

Leaping into the air, he circled his lair, looking down with a feeling of satisfaction as he churned up the chemicals in his belly, then spewed out a blast of fire that singed the already blackened landscape below.

His huge mouth stretched into a parody of a smile as he looked down on the circle of destruction. It was a warning to any enemies who dared approach this blighted place. And a warning to the slaves who lived in the huge cave he had blasted out of a mountainside. If any tried to escape, he would turn them to ash as easily as he charred the land spread out below him.

In his long life, he had seen many changes. The world

of men had climbed from primitive existence to a rich civilization. Then, in the space of a few years, everything had spun out of control when thousands of people had developed psychic powers, throwing civilization into chaos.

Governments had been wiped out as the ordinary people fought the psychics. And when the fighting was over, the people were left huddled together for protection in city-states.

He had almost lost his life during that terrible time. But he had learned to use the new order to his advantage, sending raiding parties to the cities and bringing back slaves to serve him—and supply his food.

Just as he began scheming to widen his circle of influence, his adepts told him that virgin territory existed for the taking—in a world parallel to this one. A world where the old rules still held sway, and the people who lived there would be helpless to fight a powerful being who could dig his mental claws into their minds and bend them to his will.

But he hadn't lived for close to a thousand years by leaping unprepared into the unknown.

As he flew over his territory, he thought of the tasks that must be accomplished before the invasion. He had already started his preparations for the assault by sending spies to the other universe, men who had stayed for a few days and come back to give him a sense of the place. Now he must send someone else who would give him a more detailed report.

Who should it be?

Someone with psychic powers that would give him an advantage over the people in that other universe.

But not a man.

The spy should be an attractive woman because she would seem weak and vulnerable, yet her pretty face and sexy figure would disarm the men who ruled the place. As he thought of who it should be, the perfect candidate came to his mind.

But before he called her to him, he would feed.

Circling back, he landed in the ceremonial site fifty yards from the mouth of his cave. Lifting his head to the skies, he roared out four notes. Two long and two short. A signal to the people who did his bidding.

While he waited for them, he pictured his three hundred slaves instantly dropping what they were doing and hurrying to answer his call.

One by one and in groups, they stepped outside the cave, blinking in the morning sunshine.

He watched their stiff posture, their wary eyes as they stood in their color-coded tunics. White for adepts. Gray for house servants. Brown for those who did the dirtiest jobs like washing the floors and mucking out the toilets.

They knew what was coming, and they cringed, even as they came toward him with hesitant steps.

Standing before them, he began to change his form, his wings folding into his body. His claws retracting. The shape of his torso shrinking and transmuting to the incarnation he used when he walked among his minions.

He was vulnerable when he changed, but they didn't know that, and they trembled as he transformed from a silver-scaled monster to a tall, dark-haired man. He stood before them naked for several moments, letting them take in his well-muscled body with its impressive male equipment.

Satisfied that they had had enough time to contemplate his magnificence, he snapped his fingers. Two blond-haired women clad in white tunics came forward and walked to the carved wooden chest where he kept a set of clothing. From its depths, one of them removed a long black tunic of fine linen edged with gold braid. As he held out his arms, one of them slipped the garment over his head and the other knelt and strapped a pair of supple leather sandals onto his feet.

When he was dressed, they stepped back into the crowd. He turned and smiled at the waiting throng, feeling the waves of tension rolling toward him.

They knew he would feed now. On one of them. He could have done that in his dragon form, of course. But this was so much more intimate, and it impressed upon them that even when he looked like a man, he was as far above them as an eagle was above an ant.

Long moments passed as he let them sweat, let them wonder which of them he would select. And why.

A man or a woman?

They didn't know he had made that decision. In his mind, he kept a running assessment of his slaves' deeds— of the times they pleased him and of their transgressions. One man above all the others had earned the privilege of starring in this ceremony.

Finally, he raised his voice. "Bendel, come forward."

The man gasped. Everyone else breathed out a sigh of relief.

For long moments, nothing happened. Then Bendel broke and ran.

Vandar was ready for the man's futile bid for freedom. His tongue flicked out, lengthening like a whip, catching the man and pulling him back.

The man's face had turned white. His eyes were wide and pleading.

"Were you foolish enough to think you could outrun me?" Vandar murmured, his voice silky. "And foolish enough to steal food from the larder?"

The man's jaw worked, but no words came out of his mouth.

Vandar spread his lips, baring his teeth as he sent out his fangs. His gaze never leaving the man's terrified eyes, he grabbed Bendel's hair and arched his neck before sinking fangs into pale flesh.

The first draft of blood sent a burst of warmth through Vandar. He felt the life-giving liquid flow into his mouth, down his throat, and into his stomach.

The nourishment brought him a satisfying glow of energy. In his childhood, he had subsisted on a human diet, and he could still eat small amounts of food and drink. He had tried wine made from grapes and other fruit, and to his taste buds, the wine had a tang that was similar to blood.

He could have spared the man's life. He didn't need to drain any one individual to quench his thirst. He didn't even need to drink human blood. An animal would do. But an animal could not fear him with the intellect of a man, and that was part of the pleasure for him. He loved feeling a victim's terror swelling as his life force slipped away.

When he had drained the last drop of sweet-tasting nectar, he cast the husk of the body onto the ground and wiped his mouth on his sleeve before raising his head to stare at the other slaves.

Searching their faces, he let the moment stretch, prolonging the little ceremony and impressing the gravity of the occasion on the group of terrified watchers. Then he selected two men to take out the garbage.

FEELING an unaccustomed restlessness, Talon Marshall exited the former hunting lodge where he lived in the woods of rural Pennsylvania and walked to a stand of pines that he'd planted years ago. In maturity, they formed a tight circle, shielding him from view. After pushing through the branches, he pulled off his clothes, stowed them in the wooden box he kept in the clearing and stood naked among the pines, enjoying the feel of the humid air on his well-muscled body.

Then, in a clear voice, he began to say the ancient words that had turned the men of the Marshall family into werewolves since the dawn of time.

"*Taranis, Epona, Cerridwen,*" he chanted, repeating the phrase and going on to another.

"*Ga. Feart. Cleas. Duais. Aithriocht. Go gcumhdai is dtreorai na deithe thu.*"

The human part of his mind screamed in protest as bones crunched, muscles jerked, and cells transformed from one shape to another.

No matter how many times he changed form, it was never easy to feel his jaw elongate, his teeth sharpen, his body contort as muscles and limbs transformed themselves.

The first time, he'd been terrified that the pain would kill him—the way it had killed his older brother.

But he'd willed himself to steadiness. And once he'd understood what to expect, he'd learned to ride above the terrifying physical sensations.

Thick gray hair formed along his flanks, covering his body in a silver-tipped pelt. The color—the very structure—of his eyes changed as he dropped to all fours.

A magnificent beast of the forest.

With animal awareness, he lifted his head and dragged in the familiar smells of the forest—leafy vegetation, rotting leaves, and the creatures that made their homes here.

Racing past a stand of oaks, he caught the scent of a fox and automatically corrected his course to follow the trail. The animal gave him a good chase, taking him to a patch of wilderness that he hadn't visited in months.

As he stopped for a moment, breathing hard, a scent came to him. Not one of the familiar odors of the forest. Something that didn't belong in this wilderness environment.

Slowly, he walked around the area, sniffing, until he came to a place where the forest floor had been disturbed. As he pawed the earth, he found it was soft, with leaves brushed back into place over an area of fresh dirt.

The wolf dug down several inches, sure there was something buried here that didn't belong in the woods. A body?

He dragged in more of the scent and decided it wasn't anything living. But that was as far as he could go in wolf form. He needed hands to get to the bottom of this mystery.

Raising his head, he looked around at the silent forest. He considered himself the guardian of this natural area, and he knew someone had been here—invading this place. The visit had been long enough ago for the man's scent to fade, but he had left something behind him.

Turning, Talon raced back the way he'd come, to the circle of pine trees where he pushed through the change. As soon as he had transmuted from wolf to man, he pulled on his clothing, then strode to the five-door garage where he kept his outdoor equipment—some of it for his business, leading wilderness expeditions, and some of it for maintaining the property around the lodge.

Selecting a short-handled shovel, he slung it easily over his shoulder and strode back through the forest toward the place where he'd stopped in wolf form. After looking around again, he began to dig, scooping out the dirt and piling it to the right of the hole so he could easily refill it when he was finished.

When the shovel scraped against something hard, he dug around the object. Using the shovel as a lever, he pried up a metal box, which he hauled out and set on the ground beside the hole.

Obviously, the box was private property. But it was buried on public land. With the shovel blade, he whacked at the padlock securing the top of the box until the hasp broke. Then he knelt and lifted the lid.

What he saw inside made his breath catch.

CONN AP LLYR had not had sex with a mortal woman
in three hundred years.

And the girl grubbing in the dirt, surrounded by pump-
kins and broken stalks of corn, was hardly a reward for his
years of discipline and sacrifice.

Even kneeling, she was as tall as many men, long boned
and rangy. Although maybe that was an illusion created by
her clothes, jeans and a lumpy gray jacket. Conn thought
there might be curves under the jacket. Big breasts, little
breasts . . . He hardly cared. She was the one. Her hair fell
thick and pale around her downturned face. Her long, pale
fingers patted and pressed the earth. She had a streak of
dirt beside her thumb.

Not a beauty, he thought again.

He knew her name now. Lucy Hunter. He had known
her mother, the sea witch, Atargatis. This human girl had
clearly inherited none of her mother's allure or her gifts.
Living proof—if Conn had required any—that the children of the sea should not breed with humankind.

But a starving dog could not sneer at a bone.

His hands curled into fists at his sides. In recent weeks,

the girl's vision had haunted him from half a world away, reflected in the water, impressed upon his brain, burning like a candle against his retinas at night.

He might not want her, but his magic insisted he needed her. His gift was as fickle as a beautiful woman. And like a woman, his power would abandon him entirely if he ignored its favors. He could not risk that.

He watched the girl drag her hand along the swollen side of a pumpkin. Brushing off dirt? Testing it for ripeness? He had only the vaguest idea what she might be doing here among the tiny plots of staked vines and fading flowers. The children of the sea did not work the earth for their sustenance.

Frustration welled in him.

What has she to do with me? he demanded silently. *What am I to do with her?*

The magic did not reply.

Which led him, again, to the obvious answer. But he had ruled too long to trust the obvious.

He did not expect resistance. He could make her willing, make her want him. It was, he thought bitterly, the remaining power of his kind, when other gifts had been abandoned or forgotten.

No, she would not resist. She had family, however, who might interfere. Brothers. Conn had no doubt the human, Caleb, would do what he could to shield his sister from either sex or magic.

Dylan, on the other hand, was selkie, like their mother. He had lived among the children of the sea since he was thirteen years old. Conn had always counted on Dylan's loyalty. He did not think Dylan would have much interest in or control over his sister's life. But Dylan was involved with a human woman now. Who knew where his loyalties lay?

Conn frowned. He could not afford a misstep. The survival of his kind depended on him.

And if, as his visions insisted, their fate involved this human girl as well . . .

He regarded her head, bent like one of her heavy gold

sunflowers over the dirt of the garden, and felt a twinge of pity. Of regret.

That was unfortunate for both of them.

LUCY patted the pumpkin affectionately like a dog. Her second graders' garden plots would be ready for harvest soon. Plants and students were rewarding like that. Put in a little time, a little effort, and you could actually see results.

Too bad the rest of her life didn't work that way.

Not that she was complaining, she told herself firmly. She had a job she enjoyed and people who needed her. If at times she felt so frustrated and restless she could scream, well, that was her own fault for moving back home after college. Back to the cold, cramped house she grew up in, to the empty rooms haunted by her father's shell and her mother's ghost. Back to the island, where everyone assumed they knew everything about her.

Back to the sea she dreaded and could not live without.

She wiped her hands on her jeans. She had tried to leave once, when she was fourteen and finally figured out her adored brother Cal wasn't ever coming back to rescue her. She'd run away as fast and as far as she could go.

Which, it turned out, wasn't very far at all.

Lucy looked over the dried stalks and hillocks of the garden, remembering. She had hitchhiked to Richmond, twenty miles from the coast, before collapsing on the stinking tile floor of a gas station restroom. Her stomach lurched at the memory. Caleb had found her, shivering and puking her guts into the toilet, and brought her back to the echoing house and the sound of the sea whispering under her window.

She had recovered before the ferry left the dock.

Flu, concluded the island doctor.

Stress, said the physician's assistant at Dartmouth when Lucy was taken ill on her tour of the college.

Panic attack, insisted her ex-boyfriend, when their

planned weekend getaway left her wheezing and heaving by the side of the road.

Whatever the reasons, Lucy had learned her limits. She got her teaching certificate at Machias, within walking distance of the bay. And she never again traveled more than twenty miles from the sea.

She climbed to her feet. Anyway, she was . . . maybe not happy, but content with her life on World's End. Both her brothers lived on the island now, and she had a new sister-in-law. Soon, when Dylan married Regina, she'd have two. Then there would be nieces and nephews coming along.

And if her brothers' happiness sometimes made her chafe and fidget . . .

Lucy took a deep breath, still staring at the garden, and forced herself to think about plants until the feeling went away.

Garlic, she told herself. Next week her class could plant garlic. The bulbs could winter in the soil, and next season her seven-year-old students could sell their crop to Regina's restaurant. Her future sister-in-law was always complaining she wanted fresh herbs.

Steadied by the thought, Lucy turned from the untidy rows.

Someone was watching from the edge of the field. Her heart thumped. A man, improbably dressed in a dark, tight-fitting suit. A stranger, here on World's End, where she knew everybody outside of tourist season. And the last tourist had left on Labor Day.

She rubbed sweaty palms on the thighs of her jeans. He must have come on the ferry, she reasoned. Or by boat. She was uncomfortably aware how quiet the school was now that all the children had gone home.

When he saw her notice him, he stepped from the shadow of the trees. She had to press her knees together so she wouldn't run away.

Yeah, because freezing like a frightened rabbit was a much better option.

He was big, taller than Dylan, broader than Caleb, and a little younger. Or older. She squinted. It was hard to tell. Despite his impressive stillness and well-cut black hair, there was a wildness to him that charged the air like a storm. Strong, wide forehead, long, bold nose, firm, unsmiling mouth, oh, my. His eyes were the color of rain.

Something stirred in Lucy, something that had been closed off and quiet for years. Something that should *stay* quiet. Her throat tightened. The blood drummed in her ears like the sea.

Maybe she should have run after all.

Too late.

He strode across the field, crunching through the dry furrows, somehow avoiding the stakes and strings that tripped up most adults. Her heart beat in her throat.

She cleared it. "Can I help you?"

Her voice sounded husky, sexy, almost unrecognizable to her own ears.

The man's cool, light gaze washed over her. She felt it ripple along her nerves and stir something deep in her belly.

"That remains to be seen," he said.

Lucy bit her tongue. She would not take offense. She wasn't going to take anything he offered.

"The inn's along there. First road to the right." She pointed. "The harbor's back that way."

Go away, she thought at him. *Leave me alone.*

The man's strong black brows climbed. "And why should I care where this inn is, or the harbor?"

His voice was deep and oddly inflected, too deliberate for a local, too precise to be called an accent.

"Because you're obviously not from around here. I thought you might be lost. Or looking for somebody. Something." She felt heat crawl in her cheeks again. Why didn't he go?

"I am," he said, still regarding her down his long, aquiline nose.

Like he was used to women who blushed and babbled in

his presence. Probably they did. He was definitely a hunk. A well-dressed hunk with chilly eyes.

Lucy hunched her shoulders, doing her best turtle impression to avoid notice. Not easy when you were six feet tall and the daughter of the town drunk, but she had practice.

"You are what?" she asked reluctantly.

He took a step closer. "Looking for someone."

Oh. Oh, boy.

Another slow step brought him within arm's reach. Her gaze jerked up to meet his eyes. Amazing eyes, like molten silver. Not cold at all. His heated gaze poured over her, filling her, warming her, melting her . . .

Oh, God.

Air clogged her lungs. She broke eye contact, focusing instead on the hard line of his mouth, the stubble lurking beneath his close shave, the column of his throat rising from his tight white collar.

Even with her gaze averted, she could feel his eyes on her, disturbing her shallow composure like a stick poked into a tide pool, stirring up sand. Her head was clouded. Her senses swam.

He was too near. Too big. Even his clothes seemed made for a smaller man. Fabric clung to the rounded muscle of his upper arms and smoothed over his wide shoulders like a lover's hand. She imagined sliding her palms through his open jacket, slipping her fingers between the straining buttons of his shirt to touch rough hair and hot skin.

Wrong, insisted a small, clear corner of her brain. *Wrong clothes, wrong man, wrong reaction.* This was the island, where the working man's uniform was flannel plaid over a white T-shirt. He was a stranger. He didn't belong here.

And she could never belong anywhere else.

She dragged in air, holding her breath the way she had taught herself when she was a child, forcing everything inside her back into its proper place. She could *smell* him, hot male, cool cotton, and something deeper, wilder, like the briny notes of the sea. When had he come so close? She never let anyone so close.

His gaze probed her like the rays of the sun, heavy and warm, seeking out all the shadowed places, all the secret corners of her soul. She felt naked. Exposed. If she met those eyes, she was lost.

She gulped and fixed her gaze on his shirt front. Her blood thrummed. *Do not look up, do not . . .*

She focused on his tie, silver gray with a thin blue stripe and the luster of silk.

Lucy frowned. *Just like . . .*

She peered more closely. *Exactly like . . .*

Her head cleared. She took a step back. "That's Dylan's tie."

Dylan's suit. She recognized it from Caleb's wedding.

"Presumably," the stranger admitted coolly. "Since I took it from his closet."

Lucy blinked. Dylan had left the island with their mother when she was just a baby. Four months ago, he'd returned for their brother Caleb's wedding and stayed when he fell in love with single mom Regina Barone. But of course in his years away Dylan must have made connections, friends, a life beyond World's End.

Lucky bastard.

"Dylan's my brother," she said.

"I know."

His assurance got under her skin. "You know him well enough to help yourself to his clothes?"

A corner of that wide, firm mouth quirked. "Why not ask him?"

"Um . . ." She got lost again in his eyes. What? Crap. No. No way was she dragging this stranger home to meet her family. She pictured their faces in her mind, steady, patient Caleb, edgy, elegant Dylan, Maggie's knowing smile, Regina's scowl. She blinked, building the images brick by brick like a wall to hide behind. "That's okay. You have a nice . . ."

Life?
"Visit," she concluded and backed away.

CONN was affronted. Astonished.

She was leaving him.

She was leaving. Him. Sidling away like a crab spooked by the rush of the water. As if his magic had no power over her. As if he would pounce if she turned her back.

His lips pulled back from his teeth. Perhaps he would.

He had not exerted the full force of his allure, the potent sexual magic of his kind. Why should he? He had felt her yield, smelled her arousal. Her eyes, the soft gray-green of the sea under a cloudy sky, had grown wide and dark. For a moment, as he held her gaze, Conn had felt a twist in his belly, a click of connection like a barely audible snap in his skull.